"IT'S ONLY PHYSICAL ATTRACTION?"

Nick's voice was incredulous. "Then why haven't I ever felt this way before?"

Laurel ran the tip of her tongue over her sensitized lips and said with a false calm. "Let's not overanalyze a kiss."

"That was some kiss. Another minute and you would have created a new earthquake fault right here on Malibu Beach." When she looked at him oddly, he added. "You said you liked a man with a sense of humor."

Laurel picked up the purse she dropped in the sand, took a few steps past him and glanced back over her shoulder. "They say a word to the wise is sufficient. We'll just have to be more careful in the future, won't we?"

At least she knew *she* would have to be....

ABOUT THE AUTHOR

No doubt due to years of experience in the
television industry, Florida-based author Kelly
Walsh has a special knack for action-packed,
dramatic stories. *A Private Affair* is no exception.
This prolific author's hobbies include maintaining
an aviary—which houses such rare birds as
turquoisine parakeets and black-masked
lovebirds—and a greenhouse full to bursting with
all manner of exotic flora. There could be a book
in this....

Books by Kelly Walsh

HARLEQUIN SUPERROMANCE
248—CHERISHED HARBOR
286—OF TIME AND TENDERNESS
336—A PLACE FOR US

Don't miss any of our special offers. Write to us at the
following address for information on our newest releases.

Harlequin Reader Service
901 Fuhrmann Blvd., P.O. Box 1397, Buffalo, NY 14240
Canadian address: P.O. Box 603,
Fort Erie, Ont. L2A 5X3

Kelly Walsh

A PRIVATE AFFAIR

Harlequin Books

TORONTO • NEW YORK • LONDON
AMSTERDAM • PARIS • SYDNEY • HAMBURG
STOCKHOLM • ATHENS • TOKYO • MILAN

Published June 1989

First printing April 1989

ISBN 0-373-70360-0

CHAPTER ONE

FOR TENSE MOMENTS Laurel stared at the sign on the office door: Malone & Malone, Private Investigations. When her nervous fingers touched the cool knob, she began having second thoughts and drew her hand back, but after taking a long deep breath to calm herself, she entered.

Inside she scanned the attractively furnished reception area. No one was at the desk. Three doors led to what she assumed were other offices. The door to her right was partially opened, and she heard a baritonal humming coming from within. Hesitantly she moved to it, detecting an odor of paint as she glanced inside the room. There, standing high up on a ladder, she saw a man dressed in white denims and a sleeveless gray sweatshirt. He was painting the trim that edged the ceiling.

"Robert Malone?" she asked.

"Nick," he corrected her and half turned.

His full lips parted in a friendly smile, and his hazel eyes took on a lively sparkle as he appraised the elegant lady standing in the doorway. Her shining auburn hair hung in soft waves to the shoulders of her immaculate white linen suit. The June sunlight streaming through the undraped window was reflected in her blue-green eyes, but as lovely as they were, he detected a distinct wariness in them.

The moment he had turned toward her, Laurel had begun her own assessment of the tall, broad-shouldered man on the ladder. In spite of his loose-fitting San Diego State sweatshirt, she could see that he was athletically trim. His wavy dark brown hair was attractively sun-streaked and his tanned complexion could not be marred by the several specks of white paint that had found their way onto his face. There was a faint dark stubble along his strong jawline.

Aware of his attentive gaze, she explained, "I was looking for Robert Malone, the private investigator."

"He's out on a case." Nick twisted his body around and rested an arm on the top of the ladder, oblivious to the fact that paint was dripping from his brush onto his not-too-white sneakers. "Is there something I can do for you?" He saw the question in her eyes. "I'm Nick Malone, the other half of Malone and Malone. Bob is my father."

"I was hoping to speak with Robert Malone. Do you expect him back soon?"

"Not really." He positioned the brush on the edge of the paint can and started down the ladder. "He has a meeting with a client in La Jolla this afternoon."

Just as he stepped off the bottom rung, he shifted his weight suddenly, and Laurel saw him slap his left leg.

Embarrassed, his mouth curved into a grin. "A trick knee. A woman I was investigating hit it with a baseball bat." Reaching for a towel, he began to wipe his hands. "Sorry for the mess. We've been redecorating around here. Would you like some coffee or a cola?"

"A cold drink would be nice."

"Good. We can have it in my office."

He draped the towel across one of the ladder steps, took her arm gently and motioned toward the reception area.

Just then, the hallway door opened and a redheaded, bespectacled middle-aged woman came in. She hurried to the reception desk and dropped her purse on it. "Sorry I took so long, Nick, but the courthouse was jammed."

"No problem, Betty. This is..." He turned to his visitor.

"Laurel Davis," Laurel completed for him.

He noted the single pearl on her ring finger and said, "Miss Davis is here to see Bob, but we'll be talking in my office. Hold any calls that aren't emergencies."

Betty smiled at Laurel, then told Nick, "Randy said the Peters hearing is on the docket for 9:00 a.m. next Monday. He'll need you there, and he asked if you'd come by in the morning. He wants to go over your deposition with you again."

"Mental note made," Nick said, wondering what Randy Broderick's problem was with the straightforward deposition he had given the defence attorney on behalf of a former client. Jon Peters was no saint, he realized, but the man certainly wasn't guilty of embezzling money from the import company he worked for.

Returning his attention to Laurel, Nick smiled and led her to his office. After closing the door, he gestured toward a leather-backed chair in front of his desk. "Please, have a seat." At the wall unit along the far side of the room he opened a carved wooden panel and withdrew two cans of cola from a small refrigerator. As he poured her drink into a Styrofoam cup, he asked, "Do you live here in San Diego, Miss Davis?"

"No, in Santa Barbara." Crossing her legs, she adjusted her skirt and thanked him for the drink and paper napkin he handed her.

Laurel's eyes lingered on Nick as he walked around his desk and sat down. She judged him to be in his mid-thirties, though an unruly tuft of hair at his crown, along with the paint on his face, gave him an endearing boyish look.

Nick sipped his cola and took time to study his prospective client. In his business he saw a lot of troubled people, and Laurel Davis, he decided, was one troubled lady.

"Were you referred to us?" he asked casually.

"No, I came across your ad in the yellow pages. I was impressed with your claim of thirty years' experience. You'd have to be good to even stay in business that long."

For all of her attempted composure, Nick sensed that inside she was as tight as a coiled spring. He leaned back in his chair, wondering what it would take to put her at ease. "Miss Davis," he said, offering her a sincere smile, "I want you to know that whatever we discuss here will be strictly confidential, whether or not you decide to use our services for whatever problem you may be having. Would you like to tell me about it?"

"It's not exactly my problem."

"It's not?"

"No, it's my employer's. She's...being black-mailed." Just saying the word caused the nervous knot in her stomach to twist a little tighter.

Nick leaned forward and reached for a yellow pad on his desk.

Quickly, she asked, "Do you have to write this down?"

"No," he assured her and pushed the pad away. "Your employer is in Santa Barbara, I take it."

"Yes."

"Why hire a private investigator from an agency here in San Diego? Why not someone from Santa Barbara or Los Angeles?"

"I want an out-of-town investigator. Santa Barbara is a very small community, and the gossip mill in L.A. is alive and well."

"I see," Nick said reflectively. "Your employer must be someone of note."

A tiny muscle twitched at the corner of Laurel's mouth, and Nick saw the indecision that hovered in her eyes. He didn't quite know why, but he really wanted to help her, wanted to ease the tension that obviously had her in its grip. But he couldn't unless she was willing to open up to him. In an even, quiet tone, he began to probe. "How is your employer taking this extortion business?"

Laurel regarded him with cautious eyes, willing away her anxiety before answering. "She doesn't know about it."

Nick's eyebrows rose in surprise. "She doesn't know she's being blackmailed?"

"I haven't told her. The last thing she needs right now is a problem like this one."

He rested his crossed arms on the top of his desk and studied Laurel, thinking of the contrast between her dulcet tones and the strange scenario she was suggesting. In her eyes he could see the fear that was causing her nervousness and making her answer his queries in as few words as possible. But at the same time he caught an intriguing glimpse of the warmth that would undoubtedly be in her lovely eyes under the right circumstances.

"Let me get this straight. Your employer is being blackmailed, you haven't told her and you want us to find out who's doing it."

"Exactly."

"Uh-huh," he murmured, scrutinizing her stolid expression. "Just who is your employer?"

Laurel placed her cup down on the edge of his desk and met his inquisitive gaze. "Will you take the case?"

His eyes narrowed slightly, and he wondered how long he'd have to play this guessing game with her. From the determined look on her face, he was afraid it would be a while. "Before I can answer your question, I'd have to know more about the case . . . your employer's name, to begin with." He watched her as she lowered her eyes to her slender, well-manicured fingers that toyed with the straps of her white leather purse. "Remember," he reassured her, "our conversation is confidential."

Laurel's long lashes flicked up, and she studied him as though she were making an extremely difficult decision. In little more than a whisper she said, "Diana Baxter."

"*The* Diana Baxter, the film star?"

"Yes."

Nick had been a youngster the first time he had seen Diana Baxter in a movie. She was appearing in one of the biblical epics that had been so popular then, and he'd never forgotten the impression she had made on him. He couldn't recall if she'd been Delilah or Bathsheba, but he could still picture her long auburn tresses cascading over a diaphanous blue costume as she slithered down the marble steps toward the camera, her limpid blue eyes promising paradise to every male in the audience over nine years of age. But early in the eighties, although still beautiful, she'd vanished from the silver screen.

"Diana Baxter," Nick repeated, more to himself than to his visitor. "I can see why you'd want to handle this as quietly as possible. Miss Baxter is something of a national treasure. Why is she being blackmailed?"

Laurel reached for her cup, but when she took hold of it she realized her hand was trembling, and she placed it back down on the desk. For two weeks now she had lived with the fact of the blackmail. But she hadn't heard another living soul say the word out loud, other than from the man sitting across from her. In some strange way, hearing him say it made the nightmare even more of a reality. She had thought about it daily, dreamed about it nightly, and the terror of it had become like a second skin that threatened to squeeze the life out of her.

"Well," Nick asked again, "why is your employer being blackmailed?"

"I can't tell you that," she said, averting her eyes.

Nick searched her features and began to tap the desk with his finger, a habit he had when he was deep in thought. After several silent moments, he said, "You know, Miss Davis, I'm having a problem with this."

"A problem?"

His dubious eyes remained fixed on hers. "You want me to track down the extortionist without knowing *why* he's blackmailing Diana Baxter, who doesn't even *know* she's being blackmailed?"

Laurel fingered the gold chain at her throat and said calmly, "That's exactly what I'd like you to do."

He couldn't tell from her expression if she was getting his message, so he decided to be blunt. "No private investigator in his right mind would take on an extortion case without knowing the reason for the extortion."

"Perhaps it would help if I explained."

"Indeed it would."

Laurel took a deep breath and chose her words with extreme care. "Miss Baxter has contracted to star in a TV movie. Filming begins in two weeks, and she has a great deal on her mind."

"Just how do you fit into the picture?" He grinned sheepishly. "No pun intended."

Too tense to appreciate his attempt at humor, she said, "I'm Miss Baxter's personal manager. I coordinate the activities of her agent, publicist and financial manager, as well as her personal staff."

"That must make for a busy day."

"It does, Mr. Malone." Laurel rose, took a few steps toward the wall unit, then turned to face him squarely. "Miss Baxter's peace of mind is of the utmost importance right now."

"You certainly are devoted to her."

"I am, and adverse publicity right now would be . . . a problem."

"You're loyal, too. An admirable quality."

Laurel moved to the front of his desk and rested her fingertips on the edge of it. Softly and earnestly she informed him, "I would expect the same loyalty from you, Mr. Malone."

Nick caught a whiff of the pleasant fragrance she wore. It was light, clean-smelling and as tantalizingly mysterious as she was. He inhaled deeply and felt a pleasant sensation travel through his nostrils and down into his chest.

Laurel examined his pensive eyes, trying to read what she saw in them. Unable to, she straightened and returned to the chair opposite him. "Will you take the case?" she asked hopefully.

Nick had just finished with a draining embezzlement case—all but the court appearances—and he'd wanted to take a few days hiatus before taking on another. But he had to admit that he was fascinated by Laurel Davis. Still, he wasn't sure he could or wanted to operate on the terms she would impose. No, he decided, he wasn't ready to commit himself. Instead of answering her question, he asked, "How much does the blackmailer want?"

"I've already paid twenty thousand dollars, but—" she lowered her eyes and her voice weakened "—I'm afraid that might not be the end of it."

Nick heard the distress in her tone and saw her lovely features tense. He got up and walked around to the front of his desk. His first impulse was to tell her that everything would be all right, but he knew he couldn't promise that, not with the way she would be tying his hands if he were to try to help her. Leaning back against the desk, he crossed his arms. "You know, of course, that you should be telling the police all this."

She looked up at him with frightened eyes and shook her head. "I can't."

You mean you won't, he said mentally. "How was the blackmail demand made?"

"By letter. I was instructed to go to the Mission Santa Barbara on Laguna Street at 9:00 p.m. It closes at five. I was told I'd find a blue car with an Arizona license plate parked there."

"Do you remember what make it was?"

"No, but it wasn't a new car. In fact, it was in pretty bad shape. I was to place the packaged money inside, lock the car door, then leave and drive away immediately. The letter said I would be watched."

"And you did drive away."

"Yes, after I had memorized the license number."

Nick nodded. "You had it checked out and found that the plate had been reported lost or stolen."

"Yes, it was stolen, but how did you know?"

"Yours isn't the first case of blackmail that's come through this office, Miss Davis."

"Oh . . . of course."

"The police could have staked out the place if you had told them."

"That's exactly what I wanted to avoid," she said quickly.

"Then why have me track down the extortionist?"

"I need to know who I'm dealing with."

"And take matters into your own hands?"

"If necessary."

"Not smart. Someone could get hurt." When she said nothing, Nick shook his head. "Sorry, but I'm not a mind reader, and that's what it would take to get a hold on this thing. I'd have to know why your employer is being blackmailed to even begin to find someone with a motive."

"Isn't it obvious that money is the motive?"

He started back to the chair behind his desk. "That doesn't really narrow down the list of possible suspects. Is there anyone who couldn't use twenty thousand dollars?"

Sadly she asked, "Then neither you nor your father will help me?"

"I don't see how we can."

Laurel was about to get up to leave, but the buzzing of the intercom on Nick's desk stopped her.

Still standing, he pressed down the button. "Yes, Betty?"

"Your father's on line three."

"Thanks." He picked up the receiver. "Hi. How's it going in La Jolla?"

Laurel saw Nick's expression turn serious and his alert eyes glint with interest as he listened for several moments.

"All the earmarks of insurance fraud," he said as he rested against the edge of his desk. "I'm guessing the insurer was having credit problems and so on. Uh-huh. Well, the insurance company will have to file a civil suit since they've already paid the claim."

Nick's gaze drifted to Laurel; he noted the fidgety movements of her finger on her purse. When she looked up and her eyes met his, that feeling of wanting to help her took hold of him again, and he told his father, "We have a prospective client in my office."

At the word "prospective," Laurel experienced a surge of hope. Just moments earlier she had visualized going through similar interviews with other detectives who would probably be as leery as Nick Malone was. But her nerves were jarred again at Nick's next words.

"It's extortion, but somewhat complicated. The victim isn't aware of it." As he listened to his father's earthy comments, Nick tried to control the smile that tugged at the corners of his lips. "Right. I said it was complicated." Nick straightened, turned toward the window and gave his father a brief rundown of what Laurel Davis had told him so far.

Thinking about it, Laurel had to admit that from his point of view her case did indeed sound somewhat complicated. She had been as forthright as she could be with him, and she could understand his hesitancy, but she was at her wits' end. She needed someone she could trust, someone to lean on, if only temporarily.

Nick faced her again and admired her aura of quiet elegance. He wondered if she were aware of it. In the next instant, though, an inner voice reminded him of another attractive client he'd had not too long ago: Louise Hamilton. What a debacle that had been.

Although Louise had looked nothing like Laurel, she had been as lovely and as well-bred. She'd been the subject of an investigation by an insurance firm that had retained Malone & Malone. A greedy woman, she had sold the jewelry she claimed had been stolen from her San Diego home. Only Nick's innate skepticism had saved him from filing a report in her favor. Louise Hamilton was now doing a two- to five-year stint as a guest of the state of California.

Willing the memory away, Nick returned his full attention to his phone conversation. "Are you staying in La Jolla tonight?" Hearing his father's affirmative response, Nick grinned broadly. "I take it Janet is cooking for you. Uh-huh. Well, I'll see you in the morning." As he replaced the receiver, he saw Laurel rise and extend her hand.

"Thank you for your time, Mr. Malone. I can understand your reluctance to handle my problem."

In that instant, all of Nick's attention centered on the feel of the woman's slender hand in his; it was soft and warm, and he didn't want to release it. There was also something pleading in her distraught eyes, but it was her strained smile that really got to him. It made him feel like a first-class heel for showing the door to a lady with her kind of trouble.

As he held her hand, Laurel sensed that perhaps he was wavering in his decision. Hoping so, she asked, "Is there anything I could say that would make you reconsider?"

Nick hesitated, feeling his ability to reason begin to take flight. He glanced down and saw that he was still holding her hand. "I'm thinking about it," he admitted quietly.

The opening of the door drew their attention, and their hands separated when Betty stuck her head inside the office. "I'm leaving for my dental appointment, Nick. Frank checked in and said that he'd talk with you in the morning about the Dolan case. He thinks he'll have it wrapped up by next week. I told the answering service to take the calls so you won't be disturbed."

"Thanks, Betty. Have fun."

"Fun," she repeated dryly and sent her boss an insinuating grin. "You, too," she said, and closed the door.

"Frank is one of the two other investigators who work here," Nick explained and checked his watch. "I don't know about you, Miss Davis, but I skipped lunch and I'm starving. Are you heading right back to Santa Barbara?"

"No, I checked into the Airport TraveLodge when I arrived. I thought I might have to be in San Diego another day."

"Good. If you'd like, we could finish our discussion over dinner."

Since he was sounding more positive about taking her on as a client, Laurel quickly returned his easy smile and accepted his invitation.

As she watched him lock the file cabinets in his office, she decided that Nick Malone wasn't at all what she had expected a real-life private investigator to be like. Maybe she'd seen too many scripted stereotypes: the cold, iron-hearted macho man who drank his whiskey straight and had difficulty sensing another's pain.

Something instinctively told her that Nick Malone wasn't at all like that.

On the contrary, he impressed her as being quite sympathetic, a man with an open nature who said what he honestly thought, a man who was confident but not cocky. While he made a quick call to his answering service, Laurel found herself wishing that she had met him under more pleasant circumstances. He was good-looking enough to rate a screen test, and her fingers still tingled from the warmth of his and the gentle squeeze he had given her hand—a gesture of comfort, she had decided, not a calculated overture.

On the way to the parking lot, Nick asked, "Mind if we stop at my place so I can clean up?" He tugged at his gray sweatshirt. "If I don't we'll have to settle for an outdoor spot, unless you enjoy the odor of mineral spirits."

Laurel smiled and shook her head. Glancing at the appliqué on his sweatshirt, she asked, "Alma mater?"

"Good ol' San Diego State," he said, and opened the car door on the passenger side of his sleek blue Mercury Sable. Moments later, while fastening his seat belt, he asked, "Did you go to school in California?"

"No, the University of Arizona."

"Is Arizona your home?"

"Yes, or it was."

Nick recalled the instructions she had received to place the money in a car with an Arizona license plate, then he checked the rearview mirror and backed out of his parking space. After joining the stream of traffic, he headed east on Ash Street. "What brought you from Arizona to the Golden State?"

"A job."

"With Diana Baxter?"

Laurel nodded.

Nick mulled that over. With all the experienced talent in and around Los Angeles, he wondered why someone as famous as Diana Baxter would have to import a personal manager from out of state. Yes, there were several things that bothered him about Laurel Davis. For one, why would she fork over twenty thousand dollars to pay off a blackmailer if her boss didn't even know about it? Loyalty and dedication were one thing, but big bucks and secrets like that were a little outside of any job description. He also had to admit that he was curious as to what the extortionist had on the erstwhile star of the silver screen. And, like it or not, he was more than a little intrigued by Laurel Davis herself.

CHAPTER TWO

AFTER TURNING OFF Sixth Avenue, Nick headed down a quiet street in the Hillcrest area and pulled into a driveway next to a two-story house with a stuccoed exterior and a blue slate roof. "Home, sweet home," he announced, and led Laurel through a side archway, past a private patio and into the house.

Laurel glanced around, deciding that she liked the place, with its wide living room and uncluttered, airy feeling. The white walls were of smooth plaster, and a colorful, nubby Indian rug covered part of the polished wood floor. Warm earth tones and natural fabrics dominated in the decor. But she saw no signs of a woman's touch. The fact that Nick didn't wear a wedding band proved nothing, she realized.

"Have a seat, Laurel," he suggested, drifting easily into a first-name relationship. "I won't be long. Would you like something to drink?"

"No, thanks." She sat down on the beige sofa and rested back against the cushions, feeling her nervousness subside a little.

"The kitchen's in there—" he nodded to the room beyond a small archway "—if you change your mind." He switched on the stereo and exited under another archway, whistling as he bounded up the stairway.

The music coming from the stereo was country; a female vocalist sang about not letting the stars get in your eyes or letting the moon break your heart. Laurel smiled wistfully to herself, recalling the two times she had done just that.

Her mind's eye flashed her an image of Keith Dunbar, the young man she had fallen in love with in college. His father had held one of the top positions with Shell Oil. Keith was to have been groomed for a managerial assignment in Venezuela, and he'd wanted her to go with him as his wife. But Laurel had decided she had obligations elsewhere.

Much the same thing had happened with Brian Cannady, the architect that Laurel had met at the country club soon after arriving in Santa Barbara. Unable to understand her dedication to her job, he had presented her with an ultimatum, but again Laurel had remained firm in what she considered was her duty to Diana Baxter.

Forcing away the painful memories, Laurel looked around the room, taking in the hanging wicker baskets with their fountains of ferns, the large oil paintings depicting the California coastline and the greenery outside the tall windows draped in gold and brown. But as she tried to preoccupy herself with her surroundings, thoughts of the man upstairs intruded.

Was she doing the right thing? she asked herself. Perhaps there would be no more blackmail demands, but if there were, she knew she wouldn't be able to keep them a secret from Diana for long. If Nick Malone could find out who was behind it, she would try to reason with the individual. Both she and Diana had gone through too much and come too far to let an extortionist beat them down now. But if reasoning didn't work, she would have to find some other way to silence him—or her.

Why now of all times? she wondered. Just when
Diana's life was about to turn around, just when it
seemed as if all their problems were going to disappear.
Problems, she mused. She'd certainly had enough of
them since she had arrived in California. In fact, in her
thirty-two years, there had been one problem after another to cope with.

"That didn't take long, did it?"

Her reflections interrupted, Laurel looked up to see
Nick coming toward her. He was extraordinarily handsome in his brown suit, white shirt and tie, and she felt
a pleasant but unsettling sensation ripple through her
when he stood there silently, smiling down at her in an
intimate way that would have been more appropriate had
they known each other longer. She was relieved when he
suggested they leave.

Once again they drove off in his car, this time to the
Reuben E. Lee restaurant on Harbor Island.

At the restaurant, a replica of a paddle-wheel riverboat, they dined by candlelight on fresh seafood and
white wine. While they ate, Laurel learned that Nick had
originally planned to enter the field of forensic science
and that during college he had worked part-time with his
father at the agency.

"It was really a family business," Nick said, smiling,
liking the way Laurel was listening so intently. "Stella,
my mother, was the receptionist and just about ran the
office." His features turned solemn. "She died ten years
ago." But almost immediately his voice brightened. "It
was working at the agency that made me realize I'd be
happier dealing directly with people and helping them
solve their problems than I would being confined in a
police lab."

Laurel was surprised that talking with Nick was so easy, and she was glad he was comfortable opening up to her. Smiling softly, she remarked, "It's nice that you and your father are so close."

"Close?" Nick thought about that. "I wouldn't say that we're close. We just happen to work well together. Bob's every bit as independent as I am. During high school we lost the closeness we had when I was younger. You know how teenagers are. I was busy doing my thing, and he was busy building up the agency. After I finished high school, he was determined that I'd go on to college. I wasn't, and for a year I annoyed the hell out of him by taking jobs like unloading fishing boats, painting roofs and working as a lifeguard at Ocean Beach."

After a sip of wine he continued. "I didn't know what I wanted to do with my life then. My father chalked it up to my having a devil-may-care attitude about everything. He wasn't far from hitting the nail on the head, either. But that one year was something I had to get out my system. The next, I went on to college."

"I'm surprised you don't live together."

The statement threw Nick for a minute. Did any grown man live with his parents in this day and age? He chuckled. "No way. He has a condo in the Old Town. My father has his life, and I have mine. He's a head-strong man. He sure doesn't need me looking out for him."

Nick wasn't a man who wore his private hurts on his sleeve, so he didn't elaborate. He had never told any-one—not even Cheryl, his ex-wife—about the pain he'd felt when, at seventeen, he had discovered that his fa-ther was having an affair with a woman who lived on the same block that they did. Without his mother's saying so, Nick had felt certain that she knew. To this day, he could still remember the fight he and his father had had about his infidelity, and even now Nick regretted having hit him in anger. Time had healed almost all the wounds, but, no, he and his father weren't really close.

"Do you have any brothers or sisters?" Laurel asked, breaking the silence that had settled between them.

"No. How about you?"

"An only child, also. I wish I hadn't been," she said with regret in her voice. "Welden, Arizona, wasn't exactly a buzzing metropolis."

"Are your parents still in Arizona?"

Her lips tensed slightly, and she shook her head. "I was raised by an aunt and uncle. He was a mining engineer, and business took him away quite a bit, so it was usually my aunt, me and the chickens."

Her gentle laughter sounded like a ripple of music to Nick, and he found himself thinking of her as more than a possible client. But when he tried to continue their conversation and learn more about Laurel, he discovered that she didn't enjoy talking about herself. She was definitely more comfortable talking about her employer.

"Someday," she told him after their coffee had been served, "someone will make a movie of Diana's life. When she was seventeen she won a beauty contest in Texas that her parents didn't know she had entered. Her father, a minister, disowned her, and she left home and headed for Hollywood, where she first lived in a one-room studio apartment with a pullman kitchen and a shared bath. Glen Driscoll, who's still her agent, saw her when she had her first modeling job in L.A. He ran her through the publicity mill, had her name associated with prominent clients and arranged for her screen test. With natural talent, sex appeal and a good agent, she soon became MGM's golden girl. The rest is history."

"Tell me, is Diana Baxter just like us ordinary mortals? Does she do the dishes, go to the dry cleaners and shop at the local supermarket?"

Laurel smiled at the idea of Diana doing anything domestic. "No, her life has been extraordinarily complex. With the money she's made over the years, she's more like a corporation. Even if she had the time, she couldn't deal with negotiating contracts, planning, investing and everything else that comes with the kind of success she's had. No one person could. At first she had a personal secretary who tried to cope with a constellation of advisers, consultants, employees and a highly specialized support staff, but it eventually became too much for her. And that's where I came in ten years ago."

Nick leaned back in his chair, captivated by the enthusiasm with which Laurel spoke as she talked about Diana Baxter, but it was that same enthusiasm he missed when she talked about herself, and that troubled him.

"My job," Laurel continued, "is to make sure that eight people don't want Diana in eight places at the same time. All of the demands on her are funneled through me. I'm her coordinator and her communicator. I know Diana very well, and I'm aware of her interests and what makes her happy. With that in mind I take an active part in the long-range plotting of her career."

"Sounds glamorous," Nick commented.

"Glamorous," Laurel repeated and chuckled softly. "It's a great deal of work when you consider that I also see to her everyday needs, her transportation here and abroad, her on-the-road accommodations and general ego maintenance."

"Diana Baxter has an ego?" Nick teased.

"She's a star, and that's a job not based on talent alone. It takes an unbelievable amount of energy to get under the skin of as many different and diverse characters as she's portrayed, and that energy is fed by ego as well as belief in her talent."

"Doesn't seem like that would give you a great deal of time for a personal life of your own."

Laurel looked down at her coffee cup, and after a lingering silence she admitted quietly, "It doesn't, not really."

Nick almost said, "That's sad," but he caught the words in time. When Laurel lifted her eyes, he saw the way the glow from the candlelight reflected in them, and an intense yearning swept over him, a feeling that was almost an ache. It had been quite a while since he felt as interested in a woman as he did in Laurel, and the strength of his interest took him by surprise.

He wanted to tell her that she didn't just walk, she floated, and that her lovely features exuded a dignity and gentleness he'd never noticed in another woman's face. He wanted to slip his fingers through the silky auburn hair that waved so naturally, and he wanted to touch her lips to see if they were as soft as they appeared. He wanted to, but he didn't. He knew the kind of man he was; he never did anything halfway, and already he found her too attractive for comfort.

Nick forced away his disturbing thoughts when the waiter arrived. He took care of the check, and they left the restaurant.

Outside, the evening air was balmy; a breeze rustled in the trees on the shore. The summer sun had disappeared over the Pacific horizon, and the lights around the three decks of the riverboat shone in San Diego Bay as Laurel and Nick sauntered along the covered wooden walkway from the restaurant to the island.

At the foot of the staircase, he gently took hold of her arm. The city's night lights formed a scintillating screen as they walked slowly along the pier. "Diana Baxter never married, did she?" he asked.

Laurel glanced at him sideways and shook her head. "She always claimed that she'd seen too many of her colleagues go through the Hollywood mental-cruelty divorce scenario. Besides, she was too dedicated to her profession."

"As you are," Nick suggested.

His comment surprised her. "Is there something wrong with being dedicated to one's job?"

"No, no. Mine's rarely a nine-to-five one, but it's a matter of degree, though."

"And you think I go too far, I take it."

"Don't you?"

"I'm afraid you wouldn't understand."

"Maybe I would. Try me."

Laurel wasn't quite sure just what it was about Nick Malone that bothered her. Perhaps, she decided, it was the way he had of saying exactly what was on his mind. She had enjoyed their dinner conversation and had even begun to let down her guard a little, but now she realized she had been wrong in doing so. To change the subject, she said, "I thought we were going to discuss Diana's problem. Is there something you'd like me to explain that I already haven't?"

"Well, how about telling me where you came up with twenty thousand dollars to pay the extortionist?"

Laurel came to an abrupt halt and faced him, bristling inside at his question, but after judicious consideration she reminded herself that he was an investigator and that he was investigating. "From my savings," she said, her voice low and controlled. "As a personal manager, I receive fifteen percent of my client's income."

"I wouldn't have thought there would be all that much income during Diana's retirement from films."

"That only lasted four years. Two years ago she appeared on the stage in London, and last year she did theater work here in California. Besides, Tony Koop, her financial manager, has kept her money working for her."

"Well enough for her to live off the interest, or has she had to dip into capital?"

Laurel thought quickly and decided to tell him only as much as he needed to know in order to do his job. That didn't include making him privy to the current financial strain she was dealing with. As casually as she could, she said, "Diana's retirement years were costly, considering having to maintain the estate and—" she paused and looked out at the lights on the pleasure boats in the bay "—and other expenditures."

Nick wondered just what "other expenditures" included, but her response told him she wasn't yet ready to completely unburden herself to him. He'd be patient, he decided, and let her open up to him at her own pace. As they started toward the parking area, he asked, "This Tony Koop, how long has he been Diana's financial manager?"

"He took over the account seven years ago. Before that Wayne, his father, handled it."

"Tony Koop has other clients, I take it."

"Yes. His office is in L.A., but he lives in Santa Barbara. A number of people who work in Hollywood have homes there and in Montecito. It gives them a chance to escape the smog and Tinseltown gossip." She looked over at Nick. "Do you think one of Diana's support people could be the extortionist?"

"We can't rule out anyone. All we can do is to narrow it down to who has motive, method and opportunity. I'll need a rundown on all the people who work closely with her."

Laurel's voice became animated, and a light shone in her eyes. "Then you will take the case?"

Nick saw that she was looking at him as though he'd just told her he'd already solved all her problems, and he decided he very much liked the smile on her face. So much so that he couldn't help but smile himself. "At two-fifty a day plus expenses, but I want you to know that I don't have a crystal ball. It could take some time to ferret out your extortionist."

"When can you start?"

"I already have."

"I mean when can you come to Santa Barbara?"

"I need to be at the courthouse in the morning, then we can drive up together and you can fill me in on the staff." He glanced at his watch. "How about a nightcap before I take you to your hotel?"

"I'm not much for noisy lounges, Nick."

"The place I have in mind is quiet and very relaxing."

As he opened the car door for her, Laurel inquired uneasily, "Nick, you don't . . . carry a gun, do you?"

"No, but Sam Spade never did, either. The most dangerous thing I do in my work is drive on the freeway."

When Nick pulled up in front of his house instead of a lounge, Laurel was momentarily surprised, but, she told herself, he seemed to be a perfect gentleman. Smiling, she repeated his words. "Quiet and very relaxing."

"As well as extremely reasonable," he added, and opened the car door for her.

Once inside, Laurel asked if she could use the phone to call L.A. After letting the number ring longer than necessary, she set the receiver down and sat back in the chair.

Nick saw the look of concern on her face. "No luck?"

She shook her head, checked her watch, then murmured to herself, "I should have gone with her."

Although Laurel's voice had been but a whisper, Nick heard her troubled tone. "With Diana?" he asked.

"Yes. She's spending the night in her apartment in L.A. She was scheduled for fittings for the movie."

Nick took care to shade his words with lightness when he remarked, "Your employer's a big girl now. Surely she can handle a fitting all by herself."

Laurel stood, clasped her hands and began to rub them together. "It's my job to make sure everything goes smoothly for her."

He wanted to say he thought she worried too much about her employer, but the look on Laurel's face gave him second thoughts. Instead he asked, "Does Diana know you're here in San Diego?"

"Yes. There were two break-ins last month in Santa Barbara, and I suggested it would be wise to hire a security consultant to check out the estate."

"That's me, I take it."

Laurel nodded. "That way you can conduct your investigation quietly."

"Won't she wonder why you didn't have a local firm check the security?"

"No. Diana never questions my judgment."

"I see," he said reflectively, then asked, "How about a white crème de menthe and soda? It's refreshing."

Managing a smile, she said, "That would be nice." She glanced at the phone again. "May I make another call?"

"Sure." He half turned to head toward the kitchen, but looked back at her. "Do you always worry about her like this?" Before Laurel could answer, he reminded himself of what she had said and raised a hand, palm forward. "Right . . . it's your job."

Laurel watched him stride through the living room, then she lifted the receiver and tried the L.A. number again. Still no answer. Quickly she placed a call to the estate in Santa Barbara and talked to Ron Zowalski, Diana's fitness consultant, who lived in the apartment over the garage. She learned that he had been trying to reach Diana, also.

"I wanted to go with her," Ron said, "but you know Diana once she gets an idea in her head. Damn it, what's she trying to prove?"

The concern in his voice troubled Laurel, and she tightened her grip on the phone cord. "I'm sure she's all right. Maybe she's at Glen's house." Laurel didn't really believe that, but she hoped it was true. "What kind of mood was she in when she left?"

"A little hyper, I thought."

"Wonderful." Laurel moaned. "Well, there's not much we can do."

"Should I call Glen?"

"No!" Laurel said quickly. "If she even thinks we're checking up on her, it could destroy the self-confidence we've worked so hard to instill in her. I should be back around noon tomorrow. Try not to worry, Ron . . . promise?"

The tormented low laugh she heard in the receiver didn't help to allay the fears Laurel had, but after he said he would try not to, they ended their conversation.

"Diana," she murmured, and looked up when she heard Nick speak.

"Any luck this time?"

She saw him standing under the archway at the far side of the living room and shook her head. Seeing that he was holding a white tray with two glasses and napkins on it, she joined him, asking, "Can I help?"

"You can get the door for me," he said, and started toward the opposite side of the long kitchen.

Laurel opened the sliding glass door and saw that a cedar deck overlooked a private garden. The dark wicker lounge furniture with its thick tan cushions looked inviting. Numerous potted plants seemed to bring the garden right up onto the deck that was sheltered by a sloping cedar overhang.

"Lovely," she commented. "Are you a carpenter as well as a painter?"

"I like to work with my hands. It relaxes me and gives my suspicious mind a rest. Have a seat," he suggested, gesturing to one of the chaise longues. As he set the tray down on the circular wicker table between the two reclining chairs, he noted how her hair glistened in the soft yellow light of the nearby lantern and how long her eyelashes were. After handing her her drink, he lowered himself onto the lounge chair next to hers and raised his glass. "To a successful business association."

Laurel smiled softly and sipped her crème de menthe and soda. "Umm, you're right, it is refreshing." Her gaze drifted to the opposite end of the deck, to a sunken hot tub and a curved planter laden with orange bego-

nias and deep green ivy. "Are you also into horticul-
ture?"

"I like plants—not that I'm the world's most successful gardener, mind you. Any hobbies of your own?"

Laurel couldn't help but notice the way the soft light
bathed his attractive face in an amber hue and further
highlighted his sunstreaked brown hair. In that moment, she clearly felt the contrast between the hectic life
she usually led and the tranquility she felt here with
Nick. That minute of clarity brought with it a feeling
that life was somehow cheating her, but then she became concerned about Diana again.

"No hobbies?" Nick said, interrupting her thoughts.

"I paint a little when I can find the time." Recalling
seeing him on the ladder when they first met, she added,
"On canvas, though." Her thoughts returned to Diana.
If she isn't at the apartment in L.A., where is she?

"Water colors?"

"Oils, usually. I like the heavier consistency." *Maybe
I should phone Glen to see if she is there.*

"I bet you're good at it."

Laurel disciplined her straying thoughts and asked,
"Why do you say that?"

"I imagine you'd be good at whatever you chose to
do."

She acknowledged his remark with a smile, then raised
herself up and rested her arm on a cushion. For a moment she looked down at the ice cubes in the glass she
was holding and let the coolness penetrate her fingers.
Whatever you chose to do, reverberated in her inner ear.

It had been a long time since she had chosen to do
anything for herself, and at the moment she was feeling
exhausted and worried about Diana—and the damn
blackmail business. She knew that in one moment

Diana's life could be ruined and that her own would be affected, as well. Again she felt as though she had the weight of the world on her shoulders, and the pressure of it pushed at her chest and grabbed at her throat.

Seeing that she had become pensive again, Nick asked, "What are you thinking about so hard?"

She glanced at his pleasant expression and felt her facial muscles relax. Looking out over the moonlit garden beyond the deck, she listened to the soothing drone of the cicadas. "I was just thinking how peaceful it is here."

For the moment, Santa Barbara and Hollywood seemed a world away, and if she could have had one wish, Laurel knew it would be to never have to return to either place. All she wanted to do right now was to run far away and hide somewhere, someplace where she wouldn't have to think about careers, schedules or extortionists.

She faced Nick and said quietly, "There are things you should know before you meet Diana. Six years ago—" her voice became tentative and low "—she had a nervous breakdown. Before I became her personal manager, she was overworked, had gone through several unsuccessful romances and had tried to handle the complications of a huge house and the necessary employees with only a personal secretary to help her. Diana never could say no to anyone. When I first began working for her, I didn't realize she'd been relying on alcohol and prescription drugs, and when I did discover how dependent she was on them, it was already too late. I tried to persuade her to slow down and to get professional help, but she wouldn't listen. She was like a top spinning faster and faster."

Laurel had Nick's complete attention now. He sat up, rested his feet on the deck and listened intently.

"She was hospitalized and diagnosed as having a depressive neurosis. Her psychiatrist told me her problem had its roots in her early childhood, probably due to the conflicts that arose out of strict parental authority. At the time he wasn't certain just how long she would have to remain in the hospital, so I disbanded the support staff and most of the household employees."

Laurel's eyes shifted from Nick's, and she gazed blankly toward the garden. "After six months in a sanitarium, she came home to Santa Barbara, but her recuperation was slow and difficult, with several setbacks."

She looked at him again, and her voice became emotional. "It was awful, Nick. Diana was trapped deep down in a pit of depression, and it was a long, hard climb up for her. Two years later, with her doctor's approval, I set a plan in motion to get her back to a more active life." Laurel bit down on her lower lip and sighed as though she were reliving the experience. "She would just sit around the house. She wouldn't go out, nor would she have visitors. I had to do something!"

"It sounds like you had already done quite a bit," he said sincerely, remembering the strain his mother's brief illness had put on his father and him.

"Thank God for Ron, Ron Zowalski. He was working for an exercise center in Santa Barbara, and I had him come to the house twice a week. At first Diana would have none of it, but Ron cajoled and threatened, and after a touchy beginning he took a firm hand and did wonders with her."

"Ron must be quite a guy."

"He is. He helped Diana physically, mentally and emotionally. In fact, without his help I'm sure she'd still be wasting away at home. When I coaxed Glen into getting her a short-run job at the Haymarket Theatre in London, she wouldn't go unless Ron came along. And he had to be in the wings when she appeared on stage at the Theatre Center in L.A. last year."

"Was it Driscoll who suggested Diana for the role in the TV movie?"

Laurel's features stiffened, and she set her glass down on the wicker table. "Not exactly. I'd read the script, and it was perfect for her, but Glen was afraid she wouldn't be able to see it through to completion. I couldn't really blame him. He's co-producer of the film, and we both knew he'd be taking a chance with Diana." Laurel looked up and met Nick's sympathetic gaze. "A TV movie can cost millions to produce, and they're done at a furious pace—sometimes in just a few weeks, not like the theatrical films that Diana is used to. Pictures made for theater showings can take months or a year to complete."

"So Driscoll was hesitant," Nick said, making a mental note of the fact. "I suppose that twenty thousand dollars wouldn't mean all that much to him."

"To Glen? No. More important, I can't believe he'd try to hurt Diana that way."

Nick wasn't so sure of that. In his business he'd seen family members, let alone friends, do some pretty mean things when money was involved. But he saw that Laurel was upset right now, and he didn't want to add to her troubles, so he kept his suspicions to himself. Softly he said, "I hope Diana Baxter appreciates just what kind of an employee you are."

The jerking pulsation deep in Laurel's chest came first and was followed by a burning sensation in her eyelids. Just talking briefly about the past few years had brought back all the despair, the heartache and the disappointments that she had suffered through with Diana. Not wanting Nick to see that she was on the verge of tears, she rose and walked slowly to one of the cedar posts at the side of the steps that led down into the moonlit garden. Leaning against the post, she furtively brushed away the moisture that glistened under her eye and lowered her hand quickly as Nick approached.

In a gentle voice he asked, "Is something wrong?"

Facing him she did her best to smile. She shook her head, but her voice broke when she spoke. "I'm just frightened. It's this extortion business. If I thought it was really done with, maybe I could put it behind me and get on with my job."

"Get on with your life, you mean." He watched her expression change and saw the confusion in her eyes.

"Job...life," she repeated as if she were trying to sort out the difference. "They're the same, aren't they?"

In that instant Nick realized just how frightened and vulnerable Laurel Davis really was, and once more he had a strong urge to hold her and promise that everything would be all right, but again he knew he couldn't. All he could do was be supportive. "You aren't alone in this anymore. Together we'll work things out."

The feeling of being the one comforted was so unique for Laurel that suddenly all was warmth and solace, and she felt as though a great burden had been lifted off her. Nick's reassuring words echoed in her ears, but she wondered if everything could ever really be worked out.

CHAPTER THREE

THE BRIGHT MORNING sun glistened on San Diego's high rises as Nick left the courthouse and hurried to pick Laurel up at her hotel.

His stomach growled as he drove through the downtown traffic. Usually he took time to put away a healthy breakfast, but this morning he had rushed to the office to meet with Frank and Isaac. Before taking off for Santa Barbara, Nick had wanted to check up on the progress the two investigators had made on their respective cases. Satisfied, he had told Betty where he could be reached and had headed to the courthouse to meet with Randy about the Peters deposition.

It was midmorning when Nick and Laurel pulled onto the San Diego Freeway. As he questioned her about Diana's staff and support people, he learned that Francine Gregory, Diana's publicist, and Guy Swan, who took care of Diana's hair and makeup, had been hired two years ago. Sylvia Perlman had designed the star's personal wardrobe since 1970, but now her daughter, Reva, had taken over.

"Ron is the only one who works for Diana full-time," Laurel explained. "He has an apartment over the garage. You'll like him."

"I assume the rest have other clients."

"They do."

As Nick left the freeway to take the beach route to Santa Barbara, he decided to chance it again. "You know, I'd get a big head start on this case if you'd tell me why Diana Baxter was being blackmailed."

Laurel's throat tightened, and she felt a gnawing sensation grab at her stomach. She realized she was being unfair to Nick, but she knew that Diana's secret had to remain just that. "I'm sorry, but I can only say that it concerns something Diana was involved in when she was a young starlet in Hollywood."

He glanced over at Laurel, then returned his attention to the road ahead. "That should narrow the field of suspects down. The extortionist would have to be someone who's known her for quite a while. What about this Sylvia woman?"

"Sylvia Perlman. She owns a dress boutique on South Rodeo Drive in Hollywood, but Reva runs the one in Santa Barbara."

"Could either one of them need twenty thousand dollars?"

Laurel smiled at the suggestion. "Sylvia can't even tell a white lie without getting red in the face, and Reva's a good friend of mine."

"What about Glen Driscoll, her agent? You said he's been close to Diana ever since she came to Hollywood. He would have known quite a bit about her private life back then."

"You're really barking up the wrong tree. Glen has always been there when Diana needed him. Of course, he did very well financially with her as a client, well enough to start his own agency and to begin financing pictures in a co-production deal with Astro Films."

"And he's still an agent?"

"For only a few clients—really big ones."

Laurel gazed through the windshield, observing the dazzling silver-yellow sunshine that splashed over the surf and sand to the left of the highway. She tried to fill her thoughts with the clear blue sky, the white beach and foamy breakers, but the closer they came to Santa Barbara, the more anxious she felt.

As they passed through Montecito, she told Nick that Diana's home was midway between it and Santa Barbara, and minutes later she directed him to turn off the highway and onto a blacktop driveway that meandered between cypress and eucalyptus trees. Up ahead, in the foreground of the Santa Ynez mountain range, he saw a massive Spanish-style red-tile roof looming above the palm trees. When he neared the double gate of wrought iron hung between stone gateposts, a blue-shirted guard started toward the car, but when he spotted Laurel he gave a friendly wave and returned to the gatehouse. The gates parted mechanically, and Nick drove in.

Diana Baxter's home—a twenty-room mansion built in the thirties—was an imposing two-story edifice with thick coral-toned adobe walls with deeply recessed windows, graceful balconies and plant-studded loggias. It was situated just beyond an extensive man-made pond rimmed with palm trees and rose and camellia bushes.

Nick followed the driveway that curved around the pond and pulled into a parking area on the south side of the estate. As he walked around the car to open the door for Laurel, he glanced toward the rear of the house and noted two tennis courts adjacent to a swimming pool, where a svelte woman in a white bathing suit stood poised on the diving board. She took three quick steps and bounced off; her body hung jackknifed in the air, straightened gracefully and cut the water with hardly a splash.

Laurel led Nick along a terrazzo walkway, up the stone steps of a terrace and around to the pool area. The early-afternoon sun was strong and sprinkled the blue water in the pool with dazzling silver-white sparkles. He watched the woman's slender arms cleave the water cleanly and effortlessly as she swam toward them from the opposite side of the pool.

"Diana?" Nick asked.

"Yes," Laurel answered quietly.

Nick's senses sharpened as Diana Baxter tilted her head back in the water, then smoothed her shoulder-length auburn hair with her palms. Even though she wore no makeup, her oval face had the youthful, healthy complexion of a woman much younger than the fifty-some years he knew she had to be. It was when she opened her eyes and smiled that he found himself grinning back like a gawking fan: the eyes behind her long, dark lashes were a too-beautiful-to-believe blue.

"Laurel, darling," she said in a musical voice, taking hold of a stainless-steel railing and leaning back, "everyone was asking about you last night." She started up the tiled steps, each movement a vision of unstudied, natural grace.

As Diana reached for the oversize, orchid-colored towel lying on the umbrellaed table near her, Laurel asked, "Did everything go all right at the fittings?"

"Like a dream." She fixed her eyes on Nick and extended her hand. "Speaking of dreams."

"Diana, this is Nick Malone, the man I've hired to check out our security."

"Miss Baxter," Nick said, awed at meeting the woman he'd admired ever since reaching puberty. Now that she was closer, he could see the telltale lines at the outer corners of her eyes. Still, she was one of the most attractive women he'd ever seen. "I've always enjoyed your films and your performances, but you're even more beautiful in person."

Diana's lovely features formed a sincere smile. "How sweet of you to say so." She released Nick's hand and began to pat the water droplets from her face and arms. "At my age, though, I'm usually referred to as a handsome woman."

"You *are* beautiful," Laurel insisted.

Disregarding the comment, Diana returned her attention to Nick, "As for my performances, early in the game I learned that the most important thing in acting is honesty—" she gave Laurel an impish grin "—and once I learned to fake that, they started to call me a star."

"Really," Laurel chastised the other woman as she held open a white terry cloth robe, "someday you're going to be quoted saying that."

"Just because a woman makes a lot of money doing what I do, that doesn't make her a star. I was dreadful in the first movie I made...in 1951, would you believe? Now, Bette Davis and Greer Garson, they were stars."

"Just as you are," Laurel said decisively.

"Humph!" Diana tilted her chin up. "Today everyone's some kind of a star, particularly in television." While stepping into a pair of sandals, she glanced at Nick. "Have you noticed the billing? It's either starring, also starring, guest star or special guest star." Changing the subject abruptly, she asked, "Have you two had lunch?"

When Laurel said they hadn't, Diana insisted they join her on the enclosed patio just off the terrace. At one end a miniature waterfall provided a rhythmic splashing sound that punctuated soft music that seemed to come from nowhere. Dwarf palms, Chinese evergreens and orange-blue-yellow bird-of-paradise plants surrounded the pool.

On the opposite side of the patio, a display of blooming orchids, multicolored and vibrant, hung on a white floor-to-ceiling lattice screen. Diana unobtrusively pressed a button on the side of the rose-hued marble-topped table, and a uniformed, Spanish-speaking woman emerged from the house bearing plates of food.

Diana was effusive with compliments as she told Nick that the woman and her family just about ran the estate. Elena Aguilar cooked and served meals and her husband, Carlos, acted as butler. Felipe, their son, took care of the grounds and greenhouse, while his two sisters, Alicia and Dolores, saw to the housekeeping duties and served as maids. Alicia's husband had been killed in Nicaragua; she had a daughter, Rosa, who was five.

Nick's estimation of Laurel increased twofold as Diana related the plight of the Aguilars and Laurel's part in helping them. Illegal aliens, they had arrived from Nicaragua four years ago and were earning a paltry living as migrant farm workers. Felipe, the twenty-six-year-old son, had been the first to break away from the back-breaking labor, obtaining work as a gardener at the country club by using false papers. When he interviewed for the job at the estate with Laurel, she learned that his family was spread out over California. Since she was in the process of again hiring staff for the estate, she told Felipe she was willing to see if his family would work out. They did, and Laurel fought hard and long to have them awarded permanent resident status under the Refugee Act of 1980.

"I hope you like salads, Nick," Diana said, looking down at her plate. With little enthusiasm she rattled off,

"Fresh spinach and avocados seasoned with scallions, lemon juice and Tabasco sauce." Spearing a piece of avocado with her fork, she smiled wistfully. "Right now I'd give both my Oscars for a two-inch porterhouse and a baked potato with everything in the refrigerator on it, but Ron would have a fit."

"Where is he?" Laurel asked.

"In the gym. He's having some sort of weight-lifting paraphernalia installed. The man's a sadist, believes in no pain, no gain, that kind of thing." Her sparkling eyes examined Nick's broad shoulders and the shapely contours of his tan dress shirt. "Do you lift weights, Nick?"

He chuckled and confessed, "Only furniture when I have to."

"I would have thought you did." After a sip of mineral water, she said, "I wasn't sure why Laurel thought we needed added security, but with you here, I feel safer already."

"You know very well why. I told you about the recent break-ins in Santa Barbara."

"But they were in the Hope Ranch community."

"Laurel has a point, Miss Baxter. Better safe than sorry."

Diana dabbed at her lips with a linen napkin. "Please, Nick, make it Diana, and consider yourself a guest while you're here."

He nodded his thanks and heard Laurel say casually, "I tried to phone you in L.A. last night."

"I was celebrating," Diana announced with a mischievous twinkle in her eyes.

Nick smiled at the woman's obvious glee, but when he looked at Laurel, he saw that she wasn't amused.

"All quite harmless," Diana assured her as she cut into a mango wedge with her fork. "Everyone at the fitting was so complimentary about my being the same size as I was for my last picture, I invited them all for drinks at the Café Rodeo." She aimed a sideways glance at Laurel and lowered her voice. "I had a wine cooler."

Nick saw Diana look toward the French doors that led into the house. Turning slightly, he saw a statuesque woman, carrying a brown leather case, come out onto the patio. She wore a silky, copper-colored dress that was almost the same shade as her hair, which was drawn back rather severely. Her crisp eyes and body movements said *I'm here now. Look how important I am. My time is money.*

As she neared the table, her cool green eyes, hooded with shadow and liner, raked over Nick. "Afternoon, all," she said in a husky contralto voice.

Laurel made the introductions, and Nick learned the woman was Diana's publicist, Francine Gregory.

"God," she emoted, scanning the table, "that looks disgustingly healthy."

"Have some," Laurel suggested.

"Don't be funny. I'm a meat-and-potatoes woman. I've brought along the news release we talked about on the phone. If you approve it, I'll send it out."

Laurel took the copy from her and began reading.

Impatiently Fran tapped a fingernail on the table, then said, "I also need to know when those five movies of Diana's will be released on videocassette."

Laurel rested an elbow on the table and placed her fingers at the side of her neck. "No definite date. It seems there's a problem. Glen has filed a suit in the L.A. County Superior Court regarding the video rights. When he acquired the copyrights to the pictures from the original producers, it was for the TV market, but now the producers are saying that doesn't include the home video market. It's something the courts will have to decide on."

"That's a damn shame," Fran commented curtly. "That would really have made a nice story in advance of *Winner Takes All*."

Nick learned that that was the title of the movie Diana would be doing for television, and he listened as the two women discussed the star as though she were a commodity and not even present. He hadn't for a moment judged Laurel to be unfeeling, so he tried to chalk up her attitude as one of being businesslike. He wondered if Diana were really as unconcerned with being left out of the decision-making process as she appeared to be.

Fran set her cup down sharply, and there was a definite coolness in her tone when she asked Laurel, "Have you reconsidered my suggestion to contemporize Diana's image in the media?"

In a low voice with a calm that made its point, Laurel said, "We've been all through that."

After sighing exasperatedly, Fran retorted, "Moviegoers today are considerably younger than they used to be. How can they identify with Diana if her public persona smacks of yesteryear? Just give me a chance, and I'll show you what I could do to change that."

"You're doing a fabulous job now, and there's no way I'll let Diana be photographed dancing in discos at midnight or parading around in misshapen, mismatched clothes that look like rejects from Goodwill. Besides, ratings prove that men and women thirty-five and older prefer made-for-TV films over series. Those are the people who will be watching *Winner Takes All*. They know who Diana is and respect her for her talent and her elegance, not her public persona."

Nick had to admire the way Laurel protected her employer, but considering the extent to which she did, he also had to wonder if a fifteen-percent-of-earnings cut was the only reason she had for doing so.

Seemingly unaffected by Laurel's blunt remarks, Fran said, "So be it. When can Diana and I get together to do some more work on her biography?"

Laurel flicked through several pages of her appointment book again. "How about Friday?"

"No good. I have plans."

"Monday morning around nine?"

"That makes for an early drive, and I have an evening meeting in L.A., but okay."

Knowing that Nick wanted a chance to talk privately with each of Diana's staff, Laurel rose from the table. "Fran, be a doll and keep Nick company while Diana and I check her wardrobe. She's presenting an award at the Film Advisory Board ceremony next Thursday."

When the two women started toward the French doors, Nick got up and took the chair next to Fran. "How's the public relations business?" he asked casually.

"As hectic as ever." She removed her stylish glasses and returned them to a case. "Each day it gets more difficult to come up with something fresh to catch an editor's eye. In Hollywood everything imaginable has been done, so not much makes startling news, unless it's man bites dog or mayhem."

"Or blackmail, I guess," he added, watching for her reaction.

Fran observed Nick curiously before placing her glass case in her purse and taking out a nasal inhaler. After sniffing it, her eyes met his with a new interest. "An ex-

tortionist is particularly despised in Glitter City, Nick.
Just about everyone there has something to hide.''

"Don't we all," he said and leaned back in his chair.

Her lips formed a wide smile as she gave him the once-
over. In a voice laden with curiosity, she asked, "Just
what is it you're hiding?"

He grinned charmingly. "If I told you, it wouldn't be
a secret anymore."

"A man of mystery. How delightful." She leaned
back, too, and crossed her legs. "So, Nick, you're a security consultant."

"Right," he said, his eyes lowering to her feet, which
she was tapping steadily—nervously?

"And you're from San Diego. I saw the license plate
on the car I parked next to."

"You *are* good."

"If Laurel hired you, you must be, too. What is it that
needs to be made more secure around here?"

"Just checking for access and entry potential . . . the
alarms, that sort of thing."

Fran reached into her purse, withdrew a leather case
and slipped a cigarette out before handing Nick her gold
lighter. He flicked the wheel, observing the small ruby
stone on the side of the lighter. After inhaling deeply, she
blew a stream of blue-gray smoke off to the side. "Why
does Diana need additional security all of a sudden?"

"Something to do with an increase in robberies in the
area."

"Oh." She hooked a finger over a small crystal ashtray and pulled it nearer. After flicking her cigarette
twice, she took another puff.

Nick caught a whiff of her smoke and inhaled deeply,
wishing to hell he were a man of weaker willpower. But
it had been three months now since he'd had a ciga-

rette—three long months. Leaning sideways, he rested an elbow on the table. "Between you and me, this place looks fairly secure. I thought that my being hired might be part of some kind of a publicity stunt. You know, big star gets wild threats, needs more protection."

Fran's laugh was guttural, and her voice was fairly gravelly when she informed him flatly, "Diana doesn't need that kind of publicity."

"Why is that? I thought publicity of any kind was good."

"Not in her case." She glanced over her shoulder toward the entrance into the house, then lowered her voice. "Diana doesn't have the most stable history." She tapped a finger against her temple. "Giving the impression in print that she's paranoid now could be disastrous."

"Sounds like you know her quite well."

"I know how to do my homework on my clients. I used to be an investigative reporter. One of the less productive periods of my life, however, but I did learn how to do detailed research."

"I imagine you come across a lot of strange goings-on . . . in your research, I mean."

"Hollywood isn't exactly filled with Sunday-school teachers, Nick." She flicked her cigarette again and, without looking at him, asked, "Tell me, why did Laurel really hire you?"

"I take it you're not buying the recent-robberies bit."

She shrugged.

"Well, if I'm wrong about the publicity angle, maybe she thinks Diana may have an enemy here or there. Does she?"

"When you've been around Hollywood as long as she has, you're bound to gather a few enemies along the way. Considering how Laurel drives everyone, for Diana's sake, of course, well, that doesn't help create tried-and-true friendships.''

"Yes," Nick said, watching her snuff out her cigarette vigorously. "I've noticed that. Why do you suppose she does it?"

Fran's eyes roamed around the elegant patio. "I wouldn't go so far as to say Laurel exploits Diana, but it's possible that she's gotten used to living the high life here and doesn't want to lose it."

"I can see what you mean...servants, tennis courts, a pool, trips abroad." He saw the woman's lips purse slightly.

"Laurel Davis has never known what it is to live in poverty. She didn't have to work her way through college the way I did, nor did she have to struggle up the corporate ladder. She waltzed right out of the University of Arizona into this plush job."

At the sound of steps at the entrance from the terrace, Fran turned. "Hi, Ron. Diana's upstairs with Laurel."

Nick's eyes followed hers. Coming toward them was a male-model handsome dark-haired man, a year or two older than Nick's thirty-six. Taking note of Ron's trim, classically shaped body, and the white shorts that accentuated his tan, Nick decided that when he got back to San Diego, he was going to start jogging again.

"Well," Fran said as she gathered her things, "it's back to L.A. for me." Standing, she smiled at Nick. "Let's do lunch sometime. Or better yet, let's make that a drink. I'm in the book." Her high heels clicked rapidly as she crossed the tile floor and went into the house.

Nick stood and offered the man his hand. "Nick Malone, security consultant."

"Ron Zowalski," he returned, examining Nick with less-than-friendly sable-brown eyes.

Feeling the crunch of Ron's hand around his, Nick figured Diana's fitness consultant was strong enough to open bottles with his fingernails. He welcomed the feel of blood rushing back into his hand when the man released it. Smiling broadly, he said, "I understand that you're Diana's fitness consultant."

"Miss Baxter's."

Polite guy, Nick thought. When Ron did an abrupt about-face and started back toward the terrace, Nick called, "Hey, Ron!"

Over his shoulder, Ron aimed humorless dark eyes at Nick. "Didn't anyone ever tell you hay was for horses?"

Nick fell into step alongside him. "Touché. Got a minute?"

"For what?"

"I'd like to talk to you about security."

"What about it?"

"Laurel told me you live here on the property. Are all the adjoining estates occupied?" Ron said nothing. "Ever had anyone come over the walls?" Nick asked.

Maintaining his gait and looking straight ahead, Ron asked, "Are you expecting me to do your job for you?"

Nick had just about had it with the man's attitude, so he took hold of Ron's muscled shoulder and spun him around. "Look, we both work for Miss Baxter, and I assume we're both interested in her well-being. I can assume that, can't I?"

Ron glared down at the hand on his shoulder, then his threatening eyes bored into Nick's. *A word to the wise,* Nick decided and removed his hand. When Ron started toward the pond, Nick followed, taking off his jacket as he did. The other man stopped at a palm tree and braced a hand against it.

Joining him, Nick scanned the pond and the surrounding landscaping. It looked as if the gardener had been given carte blanche with someone's checkbook. "Nice, isn't it," he said, observing tautness in Ron's jaw.

"What kind of trouble is she in?"

"Trouble?" Nick said, feigning surprise. "Who said anything about trouble?"

Ron leaned back against the trunk of the palm tree and crossed his well-shaped arms. "Mister, you're talking to a college graduate."

"Which one?"

"UCLA."

"San Diego State, here . . . karate team, 1974," Nick lied, trying to keep a straight face. "Now what makes you believe that Diana's having trouble?"

"Why else would Laurel think she needed more security? There's a man at the gate around the clock, and this entire area is well patrolled."

Nick reminded himself that this was the man who had helped Diana work her way out of depression and into the tip-top shape she was now in. But he thought his attitude stunk, and until he knew more, everyone connected with Diana was a potential blackmailer. Nick hooked his finger under the collar of his jacket and draped it over his shoulder. "Maybe Laurel's just being cautious," he suggested.

Ron's eyes narrowed. "Has anyone been bothering Diana, threatening her or anything like that?"

"Like who, for instance?"

"Ask Laurel."

"I'm asking you."

"Why?" Ron asked curtly.

"Because I was told you had Diana Baxter's interest at heart. Was I misinformed?"

Nick could tell from Ron's expression that he was working through some inner struggle, and it became even more apparent to him when the man raised his hand and raked spread fingers through his curly black hair.

"Lyla Sayer, for one," Ron said, his voice somewhat more reasonable.

The name meant something to Nick, but for the life of him he couldn't place it.

"The actress," Ron clarified. "She has a house here in Santa Barbara."

Nick's memory clicked in. "Ah, yes, Lyla Sayer. Why would she be trouble for Diana?"

Ron leaned a shoulder against the trunk of the palm tree and looked out across the water. "Lyla and Diana both have the same agent."

"Glen Driscoll," Nick supplied.

"Lyla thought she had the lead role in *Winner Takes All*. She was furious when Driscoll gave the part to Diana after Laurel had the big fight with him."

Big fight. That wasn't exactly how Laurel had explained it to him, Nick reflected, and he was annoyed that she hadn't told him about Lyla Sayer. "Do you think that Lyla Sayer might make trouble for Diana somehow?"

"Isn't that what you're being paid to find out?"

"Nick!"

He turned toward the house and saw Laurel standing on the terrace. Facing Ron, he said, "I was told you were a pretty decent guy. Why all this hostility?"

"It ticks me off that Laurel brought in outside help. If Diana has a problem, Laurel should have told me about it first."

"Well, don't let it bug you, okay?"

"I'll try not to," Ron said, and started briskly toward the garage at the opposite end of the property. Nick followed him with narrowed eyes for a moment, then shrugged and began walking toward Laurel.

CHAPTER FOUR

SHE WAS HALFWAY down the steps when Nick reached the house. "Well," she asked, "any luck?"

He took hold of her arm, led her back up the stairs and through the first door he saw. Glancing around the spacious salon, he checked to make sure that they were alone. Brusquely he asked, "Why didn't you tell me that Lyla Sayer hates your employer's guts and that she also just happens to be one of Glen Driscoll's clients?"

That wasn't exactly new information to Laurel, but in her own mind she saw no connection between Lyla Sayer and Diana's blackmailer. She also knew she couldn't tell Nick why. She took a few steps toward a highly polished mahogany table, looked down at an arrangement of golden poppies, then turned. "All right, so it's true that Lyla's upset, but blackmailing Diana wouldn't get her the role, and as for Glen doing it, that's ridiculous. Neither one of them needs money that badly."

"Laurel, we can't overlook the fact that money might not be the motive for the blackmail."

"What do you mean?"

"How do you think Diana would react if she did know someone was threatening to bring up something from her past, a threat that you've gone to great lengths to keep from her?"

The possibility that money might not be the motive hadn't occurred to Laurel. Feeling chilled suddenly, she crossed her arms and said pensively, "It could send Diana over the edge again."

"Exactly. Lyla would probably get the role she wants, and Glen would rest easier, knowing his investment in his television production was safe."

When Laurel faced him, Nick saw the same desperate look in her eyes that had troubled him the previous night on the deck at his house. He had to wonder what the hell Diana Baxter could have done to turn the completely-in-control woman he'd seen functioning at lunchtime into one frightened lady. He hated to see her hurting the way she obviously was.

"Look," he said softly, "I'm only guessing about the motive, but it's my job to check things from all angles." Fear still lurked in her features, though, so he did his best to reassure her. "There's also the possibility that you'll never hear from the extortionist again."

Laurel's worried eyes met his. "Do you really think so, Nick?"

"Until we know otherwise, let's assume it to be true, okay?" Before she could say a word, he asked, "How's your schedule? Got time to have dinner with a stranger in town?" He watched a smile creep onto her face, though not without some effort on her part, but even her slightest smile pleased him more than he wanted to admit.

"Not tonight," she said softly.

"Tomorrow?"

"Can I have a rain check? I've got an NCOPM meeting in Hollywood tomorrow night." She saw the query in his eyes. "The National Conference of Personal Managers. I'm on the planning committee for a meeting we're having with the Casting Society of America and the Screen Actors Guild in September."

"Mind if I come along for the ride? I'd like to think you'd enjoy the company."

"Nick, I really would, but the meeting is a closed one, and I'm giving Reva a lift. Her car's in the shop, and she wants to spend the weekend with her mother in L.A. Sylvia's been under the weather."

"I could find something to do to keep myself busy. On the way back maybe we could stop somewhere for one of those drinks with seven kinds of fruit in them...if you feel like it. You could use a little relaxation."

"There you are!"

Both Laurel and Nick turned toward the terrace door where a grinning young man in a mauve shirt stood.

"Oh," Laurel said as she gathered her thoughts, "is it four o'clock already? Nick, this is Guy Swan. He does Diana's hair and makeup."

Nick smiled and met the young man halfway. Extending his hand, he said, "Nick Malone, security consultant."

Guy's grin widened into a broad smile as he pumped Nick's hand. Glancing over at Laurel, he arched the sun-bleached eyebrows that matched his blond mustache. "Security consultant? My, my, are you expecting a visit from royalty?"

"That's all I'd need," Laurel quipped. "I was concerned about the recent break-ins in town."

Guy glanced around the elegant furnishing in the salon. "A burglar would have a field day in here, wouldn't he?"

Nick studied the coveting expression on the man's face as his eyes moved from one expensive piece to another. "You're right," he said. "This place could be turned into a museum with very little touched."

"It is lovely, isn't it?" Guy said as he sauntered toward the marble fireplace. His lively gray eyes fixed on the painting over the mantel. "That Cézanne landscape alone would solve all my financial problems, let me tell you." He looked back at Nick and smiled. "In fact I could create a few more."

Nick asked, "Are you into painting, Guy?"

"Me? Ha! Laurel's the artist. Have you seen her studio upstairs?"

Nick turned toward her. "No, I haven't."

"The hobby I told you about," she said.

"Hobby!" Guy sang out. "Laurel, dear, you should be in Paris in the spring and in the south of France in the winter doing your 'hobby.'"

Nick moved closer to Guy and smiled. "Maybe you should take up painting. It might help solve your financial problems."

"I didn't know you were having money trouble," Laurel said. "Didn't you just buy a second mobile unit for your business?"

"Yeah, but now I've got a chance to buy into a partnership with a guy in Montecito. Lots of bucks in that little burg, but I'd need a third unit to work both places." He turned to Nick. "Sheila, my beautician, uses a mobile unit, too."

"Mobile unit," Nick repeated. "Is that like a van?"

One side of Guy's mustache lifted as his lips spread into a wry smile. "'A van,' the man says. My mobile units are moving laboratories on wheels. I need lots of supplies, what with the rainbow of colors people want their hair nowadays."

"That must have cost a pretty penny—the new mobile unit, I mean."

"More than twenty thousand bucks."

Hearing the exact figure of the blackmail money she had paid, Laurel lifted a meaningful eyebrow at Nick, then faced Guy. "Wait here, would you, Guy? I'll see if Diana's ready for you."

"Sure, Laurel."

After she left the salon, Nick asked, "How's the beauty business?"

Guy studied Nick's face and hair. "It'd be lousy if all my customers were in as good a shape as you are." He sauntered close to him and ran his fingers through Nick's thick, dark hair. "You could use a little conditioner, though."

Nick edged away from him. "I understand that a lot of Hollywood types live around here. That must keep you busy."

"Yeah, it does. When actors are on the set in L.A., studios use their own stylists and makeup people, but actors call me in when they're doing publicity shots at home or have magazine interviews. Some, though, like Diana, have regularly scheduled appointments. Been doing her for almost two years now."

"Bet you get an earful of gossip in your line of work."

Guy sat down on an easy chair, brought an ankle over his knee and clasped his hands around the back of his neck. "Buddy, you get a woman under a hair dryer and you wouldn't *believe* what she'll talk about." His eyes rolled heavenward. "And they say there's nothing new under the sun."

Nick eased onto the adjacent chair and leaned forward. "Any gossip about Diana?"

"For a security consultant you ask a lot of questions."

"Part of the job. I need to know who or what she might need protection from."

"Protection?" Guy lowered his leg and leaned forward. "Is someone giving Diana a hard time?"

"You'd want to help her if someone was, wouldn't you?"

"Damn right," Guy said, rising and going to the marble bust of the star that rested on a pedestal. He placed his fingers under the stone chin and said, "She's one great lady, not like some of the bitches in the *theaytuh*."

"Hear about anyone putting her down?"

"Only the usual jealous crap."

"Such as?"

"That she's a has-been, box-office poison." He turned. "I near to hell shaved one lady's head when she started in about Diana and Ron."

"Ron Zowalski?"

"You don't know about them?"

"Uh-uh."

After glancing toward the door, Guy sat down next to Nick again. In a secretive tone, he said, "The man's been living here for...what?...about three years now. Before that he was making twice-a-week trips out here like I do. Let me tell you, he and Diana were a real item. Whenever you saw her, you saw him...at the Arlington Theatre, at the symphony, sailing off West Beach. Hell, it's no skin off my nose that she's old enough to be his mother."

"And it's still going on?"

"Naw. Rumor is that about six months ago she got tired of him."

"Is that what you believe?"

"The only thing I know is that lately you take your life in your hands if you say hello to the bastard." He shrugged and grimaced. "Go figure. Maybe he was planning to live off of her Social Security while he was still in his prime."

"You don't like Ron, do you?"

"Hell, I used to! But how can you respect a guy who hangs on after he's been given the heave-ho?"

Nick let that sink in. "I guess that could rankle a fellow, couldn't it? It might make him want to get even."

"Tell me about it, man." Guy moaned and crossed his arms over his chest. "Spurned love has been the story of my life. I'm heavily into celibacy now."

Smiling, Nick said, "That's rather drastic, isn't it?"

"I have been *hurt* for the last time. From here on in, I will accept nothing but unconditional love."

"Sounds reasonable," Nick said. After pausing a moment, he asked, "Do you ever do Lyla Sayer's hair?"

"Puuuleeze. I'm not into working with shellac. Did you catch her on TV last week? God! If she could find a man who'd be willing to run his fingers through her hair, he'd break every bone in his hand."

Nick cocked his head and grinned. "Is that a fact?"

"You heard it from these very lips, didn't you?" Guy pushed himself up from the chair and shoved his hands into his pants pockets. "I shouldn't put Lyla down like that, though. She's talented, but not in Diana's class, of course."

"They both have the same agent, don't they?"

"Yeah. Glen Driscoll."

"What's the word on him? I heard there was some kind of rivalry between Diana and Lyla for the film he's co-producing."

Guy's gray eyes narrowed. "Are you really a security consultant?"

"What else?" Quickly Nick asked, "Is it true that Driscoll wanted Lyla for the starring role?"

"Well, from what I've heard while making my rounds, he could lose a helluva lot of money if the critics blast Diana in his TV movie."

"How? He sells it to a network before reviews come out."

"The home video market. Sixty percent of American homes have one or more VCRs now. Driscoll's trying to get the rights to some of Diana's top pictures and plans to make cassettes from them. He'd be the sole distributor here and abroad. If she flops in his film, how many of those cassettes do you think he'll sell?"

"If she's a success, how many could he sell?"

"A friend of mine operates a chain rental store in L.A. He told me that Stallone's *Rocky* has already made more than fifty-six million dollars in home-video revenues. If Diana's combined films do one-tenth as well, we're talking five million dollars plus."

Nick's brow furrowed as he absorbed that bit of information. Almost to himself he commented, "So, Driscoll and Lyla Sayer may not be the best friends Diana has."

"I doubt if either one of them is planning to throw a grenade over the seven-foot brick wall, if that's what you're worried about."

"No, I'm just trying to cover all possibilities."

"You really take your job seriously, don't you?"

"That way I sleep at night."

"Pity," Guy commented, and checked his watch. "Where did Laurel go to look for Diana...San Diego?"

"Are you familiar with San Diego?"

Guy's eyes twinkled, and he smiled, exposing beautiful white teeth. "I've hit a few bars down there and in Tijuana, too. Hell, I've covered most of the bars on California's coast at one time or another. Ever been to

San Francisco? Man, they've got a few places there that could put a smile on Rasputin's face.''

In a serious tone Nick said, ''Guy, I know you think a lot of Diana. Confidentially, is there anyone else who could be trouble for her, someone who's having money problems, maybe?''

''You might want to check out Tony Koop, Diana's financial manager.''

''Why would he make trouble?''

''Because at heart he's a bastard. Gossip has it that he's had a bad year in the stock market. He likes the ladies, too...a lot. He might as well have a turnstile at his bedroom door.'' Guy grinned. ''The man's got style, though. He has a habit of giving each lady a gold cigarette lighter when he's about to kiss her off.''

Nick was about to say something, when Laurel opened the door to the salon.

''Diana's ready for you, Guy.''

He raised his arms and wiggled his fingers. ''Magic hands, do your thing.'' Glancing back at Nick, he said, ''Nice meeting you. Hang loose.''

Closing the door after him, Laurel asked, ''What do you think?''

Nick rested a hand on the door behind her. ''Suspects are coming out of the woodwork. Just about everyone I've met so far seems to have a motive for blackmailing Diana.'' With a glimmer in his eyes he asked, ''By the way, you didn't happen to need twenty thousand dollars, did you?''

With her chin lifted, she said, ''It was my money, remember?''

''That's what you told me.''

Laurel's lips became a grim line, and she started to move past him, but Nick took hold of her arm. ''Look,'' he asked, exasperated, "how do you expect me to do my job if you're going to keep pertinent information from me?"

"Like what, exactly?" she asked, pulling her arm from his grasp.

"Like Diana and Ron had been lovers, like her agent could lose a bundle in videocassette sales if she bombs in his TV flick, and like her financial manager just might have a reason to join the ranks of the homeless pretty soon. How's that for starters?"

Laurel's breathing became almost painful, and each and every nerve ending in her body tingled. She regarded Nick silently, regretting ever having brought him into the mess she now found herself in. But she really hadn't had a choice. She'd been at her wits' end, not knowing which way to turn. Ever since the extortion demand had been made and paid, she'd felt herself sinking deeper and deeper in a hateful situation that had been none of her doing. When she'd met Nick, she thought she had been reaching out to someone who would be understanding and kind. Instead he was hurling accusations at her, even insinuating that she could possibly be the culprit.

"Well," he asked, "what else will I have to find out on my own?"

She flattened her palms against the door in back of her and looked up at his stern expression. After swallowing, she managed a weak smile and said, "You know, it's a good thing you didn't decide to become a doctor. You would have had a lousy bedside manner with your patients."

Slipping by him, she walked quickly to the rosewood grand piano near the windows and placed her hands on its edge. Nick followed and sat down sideways on the bench. Resting an arm on the keyboard cover, he looked up at her. "I'm sorry if I sounded a bit touchy. It's just that I don't like surprises when they're unnecessary."

Rubbing the back of her neck to relieve the tension she felt there, Laurel said quietly, "We don't always get what we like in life, do we?"

"No, we don't, but that doesn't mean we give up trying."

"Trying for what?"

Nick's lips settled into a half smile, and a sparkle brightened his eyes. "For one thing . . . a better bedside manner."

His lightened mood was catching, and Laurel returned his smile. "You have a ways to go, but I think there's hope for you." After a silent moment, she became serious. "I'm not purposely keeping things from you—about the people you mentioned, I mean. It's just that I can't believe any of them would blackmail Diana."

"That's exactly why you hired a professional who can look at things objectively." He rose and stood next to her. "No one wants to believe that someone they know and may even like could be an extortionist. But believe me, situations can arise that make nice people do desperate things, even though they hate what they're doing."

In Nick's eyes Laurel saw the understanding and kindness she had so anxiously wanted to find there earlier. And, she had to admit, he was exactly right. She was desperate, and she hated what she was involved in, but she had no choice. She had to protect Diana and herself. Softly she said, "I'll tell you anything I can, Nick."

"What do you know about Tony Koop's bad streak in the market?"

As Laurel moved slowly to a nearby chair and sat down, she said, "His specialty is investing clients' monies in the stock market. Six months ago he was questioned by lawyers from the Securities and Exchange Commission in connection with a stock scam involving Enterdyne, a company that sells pay-per-view movies via hotel room TVs. Tony came out of it with his reputation intact, but rumor had it that the venture cost him quite a bit of money. But I personally check Diana's financial statements, and she hasn't been affected by it. Besides, I like Tony." Watching Nick's face, Laurel could tell he was mulling over what she had just told him.

"Why," he asked, "do I have this feeling we're talking trouble with a capital *K* as in Koop? He could be doing a juggling act with his books that would take a computer to figure out." With his hands in his pants pockets he began to pace slowly. "But, then, there's Guy and his new mobile unit, and he was pretty quick to chat about Glen Driscoll and Lyla Sayer." Nick stopped pacing and looked over at Laurel. "And there's Ron Zowalski. Nursing a broken heart can make a person do some pretty mean things. I've seen it happen time and time again."

Laurel rose quickly. "Not Ron. I've told you how good he's been for Diana. What they had together just wasn't meant to last, that's all."

Nick noted that Laurel became extremely nervous when the conversation centered on Diana and Ron. He could see it in the way her facial muscles tensed and in the way her fingers moved. "Why couldn't it last?" he asked.

"There are many reasons why a relationship ends."

"Relationship? It wasn't love?"

"Diana has only one love...her work."

The absolute certainty with which Laurel said that made Nick think of what Francine Gregory had suggested earlier: that Laurel had gotten used to living the high life and didn't want to lose it. He hated to put any credence to that supposition, but as he had stated, he had to be the objective one.

Questions, Nick mused. *Always so many questions.* Like where, exactly, would Laurel fit in if Diana did marry? After giving her employer ten years of her life, would she fit in at all? But why would she defend Ron so? For the same reason she might have hired a private investigator—to throw everyone off the track if there was a full-fledged extortion investigation? Laurel had told him that she had Diana's power of attorney, and if it hadn't been her own money she'd paid the blackmailer, somewhere along the line her employer would eventually miss twenty thousand dollars. He hated even thinking that, but his new client was making it awfully difficult for him to totally trust her. "Laurel," he asked, "who, other than you and Tony Koop, has access to Diana's financial records?"

"No one. Why?"

"Just a routine question, but doesn't that give him quite a bit of control over her money?"

"I have an independent auditor check the books every two years."

"Oh, that's wise."

"Nick," she said, touching his arm, "you have every right to be suspicious of anyone who knows Diana, but you're wrong to even consider Ron. He's a good friend, and she's become quite dependent on him."

"Yes, she seems to be good at becoming dependent on people, particularly you."

Laurel pulled her hand back and lifted her chin in defiance. "That's exactly what I'm paid for." Turning on her heel, she went to the wall near the fireplace and pressed a button. "I had Carlos take your luggage to your room. He'll show you the way." Her steps past Nick were sure and firm. At the door she glanced back at him. "We have dinner at seven."

CHAPTER FIVE

PROMPTLY AT SEVEN, Nick descended the staircase and headed for the dining room. In the softly lit room, he saw Laurel and Diana sitting at the far end of the long table, which was covered with a teal-blue cloth that matched the cushions on the ornately carved high-backed chairs. He wondered if Ron took his meals alone in his garage apartment.

As soon as Carlos saw Nick enter, he pulled back a chair directly across from Laurel. Diana was to her right at the head of the table. Nick's eyes scanned the highly polished silver and sparkling crystal on the table. Over the long mahogany sideboard hung dual embroidered tapestries depicting the coats of arms of Aragon and Castile.

"Right on time, Nick," Diana said, smiling at him as he sat down. "Laurel runs this household with the precision of a Swiss watch. I'd be lost without her."

"Efficiency is an admirable trait," he said, looking directly at Laurel, who appeared uncomfortable, despite looking gorgeous. The silky aquamarine dress she wore made her eyes look even lovelier, and the soft glow from the chandelier highlighted her faultless complexion. Taking note of Diana's stylish silver-beaded white dress, he complimented himself for having had the sense to wear a jacket and tie—he, a man who was used to eating a microwaved dinner while watching the evening news on television.

Picking up on Nick's comment, Diana said, "Efficiency is Laurel's specialty, but it's her companionship and devotion that I treasure more." She reached over and patted Laurel's hand. "I was sincere when I said I'd be lost without you." Her eyes flashed back to Nick. "But I do wish she would take some time for herself."

"I have all the time I need," Laurel insisted, glancing at Nick for an instant before she turned her attention to the fruit cup Carlos had placed before her.

"Really, darling, when was the last time you took a vacation? One trip to Paris two years ago doesn't count. Honestly, Nick, she spent more time on the phone talking business with my agent than she did with Ron and me."

"You're exaggerating, and I'm sure Nick isn't the least bit interested in how I spend my time."

"But I am," he said, his smile more friendly than curious. "I'm a firm believer that all work and no play—"

"Will get a lot more accomplished," Laurel stated resolutely.

Diana warned, "Not when we get to Hawaii."

"Hawaii?" Nick repeated.

"The movie I'm doing. Much of it will be filmed at Universal Studios in L.A., but the outdoor sequences will be shot on location in Hawaii. Have you ever been there?"

"No, but I'd like to visit the islands someday."

Diana smiled at Carlos as he served the Chicken Divan, then she said, "I did a film in Hawaii early on in my career, a remake of Maugham's *Rain*. A wonderful experience, and it was quite successful at the box office.

Afterward, the studio wanted me to don a long black wig and wear a sarong. Ha!''

"You didn't?'' Nick asked lightly.

"Certainly not. The leading man they'd picked was prettier than I was. Now, if I had had Laurel's face and figure, I might have chanced it.''

"Yes,'' Nick agreed, his eyes lingering on Laurel. "I imagine she would look good in a sarong.''

Laurel's eyes met his over the rim of the glass of white wine she was sipping. As she lowered it slowly, she tried to force her gaze from his, but she couldn't. Why was he looking at her so intently and so intimately? she wondered. And why had the rhythm of her heartbeat gone from andante to allegro?

"Laurel,'' Diana asked, breaking into her reverie, "are you purposefully dripping wine over your dinner?''

Laurel looked down and saw that her wineglass was nearly empty and that the broccoli tips were swimming in white wine. Embarrassed, she apologized. "How careless of me.''

Carlos moved from the sideboard where he was standing and reached for the dinner plate. Quietly he said, "Elena will fix you another right away.''

"Thank you, Carlos, but I'm not really hungry tonight. Just take the plate, please.''

He did, and after placing it on the sideboard, he refilled Laurel's wineglass.

"You must not have a very big appetite,'' Nick commented. "You barely touched your dinner last night, either.''

"Oh,'' Diana remarked, surprised. "Where did you dine?''

"On a riverboat in San Diego Bay," Nick said, remembering how much he had enjoyed Laurel's company.

"How delightful—and romantic!" She looked over at Laurel. "Darling, you're not coming down with anything, are you? Your face is flushed."

Laurel's hand was halfway to her cheek before she pulled it back down. "Diana, why don't you tell Nick about *Winner Takes All*?" She lowered her eyes and toyed with the stem of her wineglass.

"Is it a love story?" Nick asked, his gaze still riveted on Laurel.

Diana took a sip of wine, the strongest alcoholic drink she'd had since Ron had taken her in hand, and that usually only at dinner. "It's a romantic comedy. I play a middle-aged woman who wins a lottery and goes to Hawaii, where she falls in love with and reforms a compulsive gambler. She learns that he supports his habit by stealing jewels from women of a certain age, as the French nicely put it. A forgettable film, but considering what they're cranking out today, it should be enjoyable."

She saw Nick glance at the fourth place setting at the table. "Ron said he would be back in time for dinner. I wonder what's keeping him in town."

Just then Elena brought in the coffee, and Carlos served. Diana asked, "What security changes do you have in mind for us, Nick?"

"I won't know until I see what you're living with now. I'll check out your alarm system, for one thing, and I assume you have a wall safe here."

"Oh, yes. Laurel can give you a complete rundown. We do have a guard at the gate day and night."

"That's good, but it doesn't make the house impenetrable."

Diana feigned a shiver of fear. "I've never thought of it in those terms. On the contrary, I've always felt safer here in Santa Barbara than in my apartment in Bel Air. Laurel, you did remember to tell Elena that she'll be going with us to L.A. when filming starts, didn't you?"

"Yes, she knows."

"Foolish of me to ask. You're so on top of everything." After a sip of coffee, she dabbed her lips with a napkin and said, "I guess I really should go over the script. Glen will be checking up on me. Of that you can be sure." Rising, she kissed Laurel's cheek. "Good night, darling, sleep well. You, too, Nick. If there's anything you need, just ring and Carlos will take care of it."

Nick watched in awe as Diana all but floated across the room, turned at the doorway and sent him and Laurel a sample of the smile that had charmed millions of moviegoers over the years.

"Quite an exit," he remarked.

"She's quite a lady."

"And seems to be very fond of you."

"The feeling is mutual. After all, I've been with her for most of my adult life." Standing, she asked, "Would you like some fresh air?"

"Sounds good. Dinner was delicious, but I think I overdid it."

"Not for a growing boy."

"Is that a comment on my maturity, or are you flirting with me?" he joked as they left the dining room.

Flustered, she said, "Not at all. I don't know why I said that."

When they reached the terrace, Laurel went to the stone railing, rested her hands on it and gazed out across the quiet gardens. The balmy breeze felt good on her cheeks, and she concentrated on watching the twilight hues color the swaying palm fronds.

Nick came up behind her and was tempted to smooth his fingers over her silky hair and to run his hand over the curve of her shoulder. Instead, he moved next to her and rested against the railing. As his eyes drifted over her, he noticed how the breeze caressed the silky dress she wore, accentuating her graceful curves. An instant excitement tugged deep within his chest and spiraled downward.

He turned, forced his attention to the garden below and explained away the almost overpowering desire he had to take hold of Laurel, to wrap his arms around her and feel the softness of her lips on his. The explanation: she was a lovely woman and he was a normal red-blooded male. The problem: he didn't know if he could trust her. Of one thing he was certain. She wasn't telling him the whole truth about the extortion business. She protested too much whenever he suspected one of Diana's staff people; yet, she was completely willing, even helpful, when he wanted to feel someone out in conversation. Why? he wondered. To appear innocent herself? That was a distinct possibility. Wasn't that exactly what Louise Hamilton had done?

Nick looked over at Laurel again, and the tugging inside resumed, even stronger now. *Hell,* he thought, *maybe she's right. Maybe I do have some growing up to do.* To get his mind off of it, he said, "It's relaxing out here, isn't it?"

Laurel glanced at him, and he could have sworn that on her face there was something more than a faint mimicry of the smile that Diana had given them when she'd left the salon. It appeared innocent, yet at the same time, it was intimate, even tantalizing.

"Yes," she said in a wisp of voice. "In the evening when it's quiet like this, it is relaxing." She looked back at the house. Her smile evaporated; her tone darkened. "When things get to be too much for me, I come out here at night to think."

"I wouldn't have thought that anything could ever be too much for Laurel Davis to handle."

Her fingers strayed over her bare arms as she said sadly, "Yes, Laurel Davis is a tower of strength. Nothing can ever hurt her. She has no feelings, no fears."

When she turned to start toward the house, Nick took hold of her hand. "I didn't mean that to sound the way it did," he said apologetically.

"What did you mean, Nick?"

"Only that you strike me as being extremely competent. I can only guess what it takes for you to accomplish all the things that you do. In managing Diana's career, you deal with diverse people and have to wear many hats. You even go to bat for her when some creep is blackmailing her, and as she said, you run this entire household. What I don't understand is what you get out of all this, why you're so willing to sacrifice your own life for—"

"For an aging movie star's?"

His eyes told her he wasn't thinking of disputing her assumption. She eased her hand free and walked slowly down the terrace, running her fingers along the stone railing as she did.

Nick followed, and his voice was gentle when he said, "You have to admit that you do come off as being dedicated to a fault."

Without looking at him, she remarked, "You gathered all that in two days. Do you always come to such quick conclusions about people, and are you always right?"

"I haven't got a perfect score, but in my line of work you develop a sixth sense about people."

At the end of the terrace she stopped and faced him. "What does your sixth sense tell you about me?"

"That you're a complicated lady. At times you're strong, and at times you seem quite vulnerable. You're lovely and sensitive, but scared as hell of something."

Laurel flushed at his description. "A moment ago you told me I could handle anything. You ought to be more consistent, Nick."

She watched him move closer until he was standing directly in front of her, the moonlight washing over his tanned face like a soft spotlight. From the moment she had first seen Nick Malone, she had felt an unusual stirring, a feeling so intense that she'd unconsciously denied it. Now, with him standing so near, long dormant emotions became so powerful that they threatened to blot out all thoughts of anything but the desire she had for him to take her in his arms and hold her.

But when she felt his fingertips glide slowly over her arms and saw his head lean toward hers, she summoned every ounce of emotional strength she had. She placed her hands against his chest and whispered, "Don't . . . please don't."

Turning away, she drew in a long breath of evening air. After moistening her lower lip, she turned back and saw the strained look on his face. Softly she said, "California evenings can certainly do funny things to people, can't they?"

Nick swallowed hard and slipped his fingers through his hair as he tried to control the jarring sensations that rioted throughout his body. "It's not just the California evening," he confessed. "You're a beautiful woman, Laurel. I'd be fooling myself if I said I wasn't attracted to you, and I'd be lying if I said I didn't care how you felt about me."

"Maybe this isn't the best time for honesty for you or for me, Nick. Under other circumstances I'd like to get to know you better."

"And now you don't want to?"

"No," she admitted candidly, "because it would be very easy for me to become too attracted to you, if I let myself."

Confused, he asked, "Why do you feel you have to fight it?"

"It's a matter of priorities, and right now my employer is at the top of the list. I have to remember that, no matter how much I might like to forget it temporarily."

He ran the back of his fingers over the smooth line of her chin. "I've always thought that honesty was the best policy, and we've both reached the age of consent."

"Yes, but I went from that directly to the age of reason, and reason tells me you'd only be trouble for me."

"Never intentionally, and I don't see how a kiss would—"

"Mr. Malone!" They both turned and saw Carlos standing at the open French door. "You have a phone call from San Diego."

"Who knows you're here, Nick?"

"Only Betty and my father. I'll be right back."

Laurel watched him cross the terrace and enter the house. Left alone, she struggled to get her emotions in check. Her heart was pounding, and her legs still felt unsteady. An inner voice warned her that Nick was not a man to be taken lightly; he was too virile, too desirable and, for her, too dangerous. Instinctively she knew that he could upset all of the plans she had worked at so long and so hard. No, she couldn't afford to risk letting him do that.

But just for those few moments when she had almost let him kiss her, she had been ready to forget the obligations she felt to Diana. Placing a hand over her thudding heart, she ordered herself to think clearly. Where would an involvement with Nick lead? Only to heartbreak, just as it had with Keith in college and with Brian just before Diana had her breakdown. Yet, perhaps Nick would be different. Perhaps he wouldn't be as demanding.

What are you thinking of? she questioned. *You have your hands full as it is. Where would you find time for a fleeting romance? And that's all it could be.*

Yet, as Laurel stood at the railing, looking up at the night sky, she permitted herself the momentary luxury of pretending that hers was an ordinary job. Surely she, like so many other people, could juggle her job with a relationship—even if there were extenuating circumstances. The simple touch of Nick's fingers had been enough to send shivers of excitement rushing along her skin—and his lips were so soft-looking and inviting. She was attracted to him, she had to admit. Not just because he was handsome, but because he was sensitive to her situation and honestly seemed to want to help. Perhaps it wouldn't hurt if she were to—

"It was my father," Nick said as he came back out onto the terrace.

Laurel forced away her ponderings and met him halfway. "Is everything all right?"

"I'm not sure. A man who said his name was Walter Amhearst phoned the office this afternoon and asked if I was there. When my father said I wasn't and offered to take a message, the man wanted to know where I could be reached. When he wasn't told, he hung up."

"What's so strange about that?"

"I don't know any Walter Amhearst. It could be that someone is checking up on me, wanting to know if I'm here."

"Here?" His implication caused an icy fear to twist around her heart. Hopefully she asked, "Couldn't he be involved in one of your other cases?"

"The only other case I'm involved in now is the Jon Peters embezzlement scam, and that's all but wrapped up. I doubt that Walter Amhearst is the man's real name."

"Nick," Laurel asked tentatively, "do you think he could be the extortionist?"

"Possibly, but if there is a connection, that doesn't rule out a woman being behind it. It would be smart of her to have a man make the call."

Laurel walked slowly to the wide steps leading down into the garden area surrounding the large pool. As she descended, oblivious of the large terra-cotta pots of geraniums and bougainvilleas, her thoughts raced through the possible problems that lay ahead. Perhaps, she wondered, she was wrong in trying to find out who the extortionist was. Maybe the one payment was the end of it. No, that would be too good to be true. So far, life hadn't handed her anything that simple.

The odor of chlorine became stronger as she walked toward the pool, and she became aware of Nick at her side.

"My sixth sense tells me that things are about to start happening."

Laurel stopped and looked over at him, a wave of apprehension sweeping through her. "Why do you say that?"

He leaned against the brick wall that curved alongside the pebblestone pathway, and crossed his arms. "If the extortionist thinks you brought in a private investigator, it's going to make him a little nervous. We can't be sure how he'll react, but you can bet there will be a reaction."

"You don't think it might frighten him off?"

"If you just made a quick twenty thousand dollars, would you be frightened off that easily?"

"Nick, you're scaring me."

"I want you to be scared, scared enough to tell me the truth about why Diana was blackmailed. If you don't, you'll have to think about hiring someone else."

That was exactly what Laurel was afraid Nick was going to say eventually, and having thought it over time and time again, she decided she still couldn't tell him the entire truth—not unless it became absolutely necessary.

Bracing herself, she leaned back against the wall next to him and gazed out over the pool into the semidarkness. "Years ago, when Diana was a starlet, she was involved with a lawyer who represented the syndicate in Las Vegas."

When she hesitated, Nick asked, "So?"

Laurel knew that she was misleading him, but she had convinced herself that he didn't have to know the real reason for the blackmail. Clasping her hands together tightly, she continued to shade the truth.

"It was at the time when the syndicate began to invest in Hollywood productions. If that relationship were to be made public, the gossip columnists would distort the facts and make it look like Diana got her start with dirty money. That kind of publicity just now could hurt the sales of her videocassettes when they're released." She tilted her worried face toward Nick. "What concerns me more, though, is that dredging up the past could drive Diana back into depression and maybe worse."

Nick pondered what Laurel had just told him. "Her agent would probably have known about the affair, wouldn't he?"

"Yes," she admitted with some reluctance. "Glen was aware of it, but why would he jeopardize the financial success of his videocassette project?"

Nick remembered that Guy had told him Driscoll had wanted Lyla Sayer for his TV movie. "Maybe something else is more important to the man than money." Seeing that Laurel was about to object again, he asked, "Who else could have known about the lawyer Diana was involved with?"

"No one," she stated quickly and turned away, knowing that she was getting in deeper and deeper with lies to protect Diana. Laurel also realized that Nick would probably never forgive her if he did find out the whole truth. That possibility upset her more than she wanted to admit.

CHAPTER SIX

FROM THE WINDOW of the library, which also served as her office, Laurel's gaze followed Nick. The early morning sun was bright and glistened on the golden highlights of his hair as he strode toward his car. He was going into Santa Barbara to check on Guy Swan's financial status.

She toyed with the slim gold chain at her throat pensively while studying Nick's broad shoulders. There was no doubt about it; he was a handsome man, and any woman in her right mind would be attracted to him.

Sighing, she wondered if she had been wrong when she had stopped him from kissing her the previous night. Would that one kiss have been so dangerous? *Yes,* she warned herself. She already felt vulnerable where he was concerned. Besides, his accusation still rankled.

What right did he have to accuse her of being dedicated to Diana to a fault? Of course, he had no way of knowing that her dedication was a duty. But was she overdoing it? Laurel pondered. No, she didn't think so. And why had it bothered her so much when Nick had suggested that she felt she had to fight her attraction to him?

Well, Laurel, she chided, *be honest. You're fighting it all the way, but you know the reason for it. You've got to keep your goal in mind and not let anything or anyone distract you from it.*

But what a wonderful distraction Nick would be, she admitted, watching his car head toward the front gate. Letting her thoughts stray again, she wondered how many women there were in his life at the present.

None of your business, she told herself firmly, and went back to work.

Her first project was to finish certifying the payroll list and bills that Tony had sent for her approval. It was a routine matter, but she kept a close watch on expenses. The last thing she wanted Diana to know right now was that they did have to be careful with money, even though the financial arrangement Laurel had worked out with Glen for his TV movie would go a long way into keeping them in the black—if Diana saw the project through to completion. And Laurel was practically sure she would. She'd been taking exceptionally good care of herself. At this very moment, Laurel knew, Diana was in the gym, going through her morning workout with Ron....

"COME ON, DIANA, let's put a little more effort into it. Hold the stretch and feel your muscles pull. Good, now the other leg."

Lying on her back with her arms at her sides, Diana drew her left leg up, pulled her knee toward her chest and held it until Ron said "Release" thirty seconds later.

After ten of the fanny-firming exercises, he said, "Up now for midriff stretches." He reached down, took hold of her hands and pulled her to a standing position on the exercise mat. "Feet together."

Breathing heavily, Diana set one hand on her hip and ran the back of the other across her damp forehead. "Dear God, Ron," she said facetiously, "I know this is exhausting you. Why don't you take a break?"

"You're funnier than the Sunday comics," he said dryly. "Let's get with it. You want your abdomen to be as firm as your fanny, don't you?"

"Why? There are no nude scenes in *Winner Takes All*."

He tossed a towel at her. "Ah, so if it's not for a film, why keep in good shape? Is that it?"

"Good shape! For my age, I'm in damn good condition."

After she wiped her face with the towel, Ron took it from her and ran it over her shoulders. "I take it you'd like to stay that way."

"All right already. I suppose that if I don't do ten midriff stretches, my next job will be replacing the fat lady at the carnival."

She stood erect with her feet together. Without bending her knees, she leaned over to pick up an imaginary heavy object from the floor, raised it over her head and leaned backward with it.

Ron, ever the taskmaster, scrutinized her every movement. "Keep your arms straight and concentrate on your midriff muscles. Feel them working with you." He took her through the exercise a fourth and a fifth time. "Don't jerk back. Think like a ballerina. That's good. Eight...nine...and ten. Now the bust and arm swing."

Diana leaned over and grabbed her knees for support. Tilting her face up she sent him a stony stare. "Now for a glass of orange juice, you mean. I've already lost a pound of perspiration." She snatched the towel that was draped over his shoulder and headed across the gym to the wet bar.

"I'll get it," he said, and hurried his strides to reach the refrigerator before she did.

Diana rested against the counter. Lifting her ponytail, tied with a lavender scarf that matched her leotard, she wiped the back of her neck with the towel.

"Your bedroom light was still on at one o'clock this morning," he said, handing her the glass of orange juice. "What time did you finally put the script down?"

She took a long gulp of the cool drink and offered him a flippant smile. "One minute after you last checked."

"Cute, but you need a full eight hours. I doubt if you got that when you were in L.A. earlier this week."

Diana judged that he had tried to phone her at the apartment, but she offered no explanation.

After studying her casual expression, he realized that none was coming. "Ready to get to work again?"

Diana groaned, propped her elbow on the counter and let her chin rest on her hand. "You may have a schedule where your heart should be, but I don't."

"What makes you think you have a heart?" he asked stiffly.

He saw the blood drain from her face and wished to hell he hadn't said what he just had. When she turned away from him, he made a fist and smacked it into his other palm. Climbing onto the Tunturi exercise bike near the counter, he began pedaling furiously.

Diana faced him with saddened eyes as he tried to work his anger away. His question echoed in her ears, and she knew he had every right to be upset with her. She placed the half-full glass of juice on the counter and walked slowly to him. Seeing that his knuckles were white from the hard grasp he had on the handlebars, she slipped a hand over one of his.

"Ron, we were good friends once. Why can't it be like that again?"

He stopped pedaling and smiled wryly. "From friends to lovers to friends again. It's that simple for you, huh? Just like a faucet . . . turn it on, turn it off."

Averting her gaze from his accusing eyes, she murmured, "Not quite."

As he tilted her face toward his, he said in a strained voice, "Don't be sad. I do miss the closeness we used to have, but I understand. You're a big name, and I'm a nobody who teaches famous people to pump iron."

"Don't put yourself down like that. You're more of a human being than any of the men I've known."

"Maybe that's the trouble. You've known too many."

Diana stepped back and turned away, feeling as if Ron had just slipped a knife into her heart, and it hurt like hell, but she knew he was right. What she didn't know was just when she had lost the ability to separate the screen image of Diana Baxter that the studio had created from the real-life woman she was. When she had left Texas at seventeen, almost immediately Hollywood had welcomed her with opened arms, taken her to its bosom and begun spinning a fairy-tale world that became her universe.

But Ron was wrong. She hadn't lost her heart. She had only misplaced it somewhere in the world of make-believe, where cameras and lights and ephemeral happiness reigned supreme. It was he who had helped her find it again, tattered as it was.

"Diana," he called quietly, and she looked back at him. "I don't think I should stay on here. I'm miserable, and I'm making you miserable."

She blanched and rushed to him. "I need you, Ron."

"As a friend, I know. But damn it, I don't want to be just a friend! If I could only understand why you stopped loving me. You did love me. I know you did."

He placed a hand alongside her face. "You're a great actress, but you couldn't have been faking it for so long."

Backing away from him, she said, "The kind of love you're talking about is for people younger than me. I'm fifty-six, for God's sake. You should have more sense than to want a woman who's been going through a mid-life crisis for more than a decade. You should be dating someone Laurel's age, thinking of a future, a family of your own and miniature Rons to bounce on your knee." She turned and covered her face with her hands.

Ron got off the bike, stood behind her and placed his arms around her. "I'm not exactly cradle material, and you could pass for forty easily."

When she felt him kiss the side of her neck, Diana pulled herself from his embrace. Her arms flew up in exasperation. "Please don't put me through this emotional wringer—not now. I've got to be able to do my job, to give my best in Glen's film. I need to be able to concentrate, and I'm scared. I don't know if I can still do it."

"Then why even try?"

"I can't disappoint Laurel!"

Ron grabbed the towel from off the counter, wadded it and tossed it on the floor. "Sometimes I believe you think more of Laurel than you ever did of me."

With her palms flattened against her thighs, Diana inhaled deeply and wet her lips before saying calmly, "Ron, I'm under a great deal of pressure right now. I don't expect you to understand, but going before the cameras again is so terrifying, it's making me physically sick."

"Cancel out, then! Haven't you had your fill of the limelight and the fantasy world you live in? Aren't thirty-three pictures enough?'' His hand made a wide arc in the air. ''Do you really need to live in this palace to be happy? Why not try coming down to earth and taking a good long look at us mere mortals? We might surprise you, Diana. You may even learn to like us.''

She took slow steps toward him and pressed her hands together, as though praying. ''Try to understand. I have to succeed...for Laurel's sake. You know how hard she's worked to get me back together in one piece again. You've both worked so hard that I've got to succeed, even if it kills me.''

''Even if it kills you,'' he repeated sarcastically. ''I guess you're a better actress than I thought. But if you're determined to kill yourself doing the damn picture, do it for yourself, not for Laurel! Why can't you live your own life and let Laurel live hers? As it is, you depend on her too much.''

''I know I do—'' her eyes focused on her fingers ''—and I'm only too happy to let her make all of my decisions for me. A psychiatrist would tell me it's unhealthy to do so.'' She raised her eyes to meet his. ''But sometimes I just want to scream. Laurel is the one holding me together. She has the emotional strength that I don't have right now.''

''Will you ever change, Diana?''

''I'll try to. I promise.''

Ron shook his head slowly and asked, ''Why can't I believe you'll try hard enough?''

Diana lifted her chin in much the same way he had seen Laurel do when she was angry, then she tore the lavender scarf from her hair and threw it aside as she stormed out of the gym.

Ron left by the other door and rushed through the library to get out of the house, not even acknowledging

Laurel or Nick, who was leaning against the edge of her desk.

"What's with him?" Nick asked.

Laurel shrugged her shoulders. "I don't know. Lately his mood has been pretty bleak."

"Anyway," Nick continued, "I found out that Guy paid cash for his new mobile unit."

"How did you learn that?"

Nick grinned. "Secrets of the trade. Let's just say I charmed the dealer who sold him the van." In a more serious tone, he asked, "Guy can't be more than what...twenty-six, twenty-seven? Is the hairdressing business that lucrative?"

"A lot of wealthy people live here in Santa Barbara, and for people in show business his services are tax deductible, just as Ron's are."

"Does Guy strike you as the kind of man who saves his pennies?"

"Really, Nick, what he does with his money is no concern of mine."

"Maybe twenty thousand of it was yours."

"Guy?" She eased back in her chair. "I find that hard to believe."

"I'm not ready yet to cross him off the list of suspects."

Laurel's voice softened. "Am I still on your list?"

He scanned her features, and in her eyes he thought he detected a sadness coupled with—what? Confusion? Fear? He wasn't sure. "Let me get back to you on that," he mumbled. He stood and glanced toward the door that Ron had slammed on his way out. "I think I'll drop in on Mr. Perfect Body and see what got his dander up. You'll be here when I get back, won't you?"

"Why? Do you plan to interrogate me, too?"

He smiled down at her. "Oh, I've got lots of questions to ask you. For one, what time are we leaving for that meeting of yours in L.A. tonight?"

"I'm surprised you still want to go."

"Wild horses, et cetera," he stated vaguely.

Laurel had to admit she was flattered by his interest in her. Letting her expression relax into a soft smile, she said, "I told Reva I'd pick her up around six o'clock."

"Well, back to business," he said, and headed for Ron's garage apartment.

As he climbed the outside stairs at the rear of the garage, Nick heard noises that sounded as if someone was tearing up the place. Finding the door ajar, he pushed it open and looked inside to see Ron ripping down a poster from one of Diana's movies. On the floor, in the center of the room, were several others along with a man's jewelry box and some clothes.

Ron spotted Nick at the doorway and asked gruffly, "Don't you have anything better to do than to go around spying on people?"

"Even a security consultant takes a coffee break," Nick said lightly.

"Security consultant, hell! You're a private detective with a half-page ad in the San Diego yellow pages."

Nick braced a shoulder against the door frame, guessing that Ron had been to either the telephone company or the library. "Mr. Amhearst, I presume."

"I borrowed the name from a roommate at college." Ron balled his fists. "Any objections?"

"Uh-uh. Phone books are in the public domain. Have you told Diana?"

He shook his head, looked down at the mess he'd made and kicked the jewelry box with his sneakered foot. "I was waiting for her to tell me why she'd hired a P.I."

"She didn't, Laurel did."

"Laurel?" Ron's eyes darkened, and he placed his knuckles on his hips. "Is she having you check up on Diana?"

"Nope."

"On who, then?"

"Listen, there's a draft in this doorway. Mind if I come in?"

"If you've got something to say worth listening to."

Nick entered, closed the door behind him and scanned the cozy apartment. "Nice place you have here. I see you've been redecorating."

Ron jerked a large plastic garbage bag from a box on the kitchen counter and began to stuff the scattered items in it, including several sets of gold and silver cuff links and an expensive-looking gold chain that had fallen out of the jewelry box.

"Donations to the Salvation Army?" Nick asked.

"I came here with little more than the clothes on my back, and that's the way I'm leaving."

"Leaving?"

"Your understanding of the English language is awesome," Ron spit out, and heaved the bag onto a chair by the door.

Nick leaned back against the small table near the refrigerator, wondering what had set the man off. "Someone got up on the wrong side of the bed this morning."

Ron smirked. "Are you a sleep therapist as well as a P.I.?" He went to the fridge, took out a can of beer and snapped it open.

"Thanks, I'd love one," Nick said, and held his hand out.

Begrudgingly Ron handed the beer to him and opened another for himself, moving the cold can over his forehead before taking a healthy swallow. Going to an easy chair across the room, he slumped onto it and extended his legs. "So who are you checking up on?"

"Laurel's my client. She'll have to tell you—if she wants to."

"She and I don't have secrets where Diana is concerned, and I'm guessing your being here has something to do with her."

"Could be," Nick allowed.

Ron plunked his beer can down on the table next to him, picked up the phone and punched three numerals. He aimed stony eyes at Nick as he spoke into the receiver. "Laurel, it's Ron. The private investigator you hired is here with me. He says he needs your okay to tell me what the hell's going on." He listened briefly, then held the receiver out to Nick.

"Laurel?" Nick asked, just to be sure, then he explained, "I was having a beer with Walter Amhearst here, when the topic came up." He glanced down at Ron while she said he might as well tell him the truth, but only as much as he had to. "Nothing says we have to tell him a thing," Nick advised, "but that's up to you." He handed the receiver back to Ron, who slammed it onto its cradle.

Sitting down on the easy chair on the other side of the little table, Nick smiled blandly. "Trust is a wonderful thing, isn't it?"

"Look, are you going to dance around this, or are you going to explain why Laurel hired you?"

"Her stipulation is that you don't tell Diana. Laurel doesn't want her to know—not yet, anyway."

Ron's jaw tensed, and he nodded.

"Diana's being blackmailed."

After picking up his beer, Ron leaned forward, a lethal calm in his expression. As he rolled the can between his large hands, he asked darkly, "Why is she being blackmailed?"

Nick had a good idea of what was going on in the man's mind. Most likely he was wondering if whatever it was that Diana had done that would warrant her being blackmailed had been done since he had met and fallen in love with her.

Softening his tone, Nick said, "I can't tell you why. I can only say that it's because of something that happened a long time ago—years before she met you."

"Is she in any kind of danger?"

"I don't think so, not now, but if you care for her, why don't you unpack that stuff—" he glanced toward the garbage bag "—and stick around for a while. She can use all the friends she has right now."

"Friends," Ron repeated and chuckled bitterly. He stood, drained the beer can and crushed it in his hand before tossing it in the garbage can under the sink. Resting his hands on the Formica counter, he stared out the window over to the house. With quiet emphasis, he said, "I developed a crush on Diana when I first saw her films during my college days at UCLA. I watched every one of her pictures at least five times. I even wrote to the studio and got an autographed picture of her."

A smile replaced his frown, and he looked back at Nick. "Sitting in a darkened theater and watching her on the big screen is an experience that can become quite intimate. When she's up there, larger than life, you don't even notice anyone else in the scene. That's star quality."

He turned toward the house again and fixed his eyes on Diana's bedroom window. "I taught physical education in high school for two years, then did a tour of duty in the air force, and her picture was with me wherever I went."

"Does she know that?"

Ron shifted his body around, crossed his arms over his chest and shook his head.

"Why not? I'm guessing it would mean a lot to her."

"No, she'd think I was some kind of weirdo with stardust in my eyes. When Laurel interviewed me about coming out here to work with Diana—" he emitted a quick, strangled laugh "—I couldn't believe it. I was actually going to meet Diana Baxter."

Ron moved to the chair by the kitchen table and grasped the back of it. "When I did, though, she was a mess, emotionally and physically. I guess Laurel told you Diana had been ill."

"Yes, and she also told me how much you helped Diana."

"She was stubborn at first, but as she regained her physical strength, I got to know the real woman and saw past the facade of the screen star. I realized that the only thing she had ever really wanted was to be loved, but she had never been able to see the difference between being loved and being used by a lot of people. The whole world adored her, but she didn't like herself. I'm not sure she does even now, and I can't understand that."

"You love her very much, don't you, Ron?"

He went to the plastic garbage bag, took out one of the crumpled posters and began to smooth it out with his fingers. "I wish I didn't." Gazing at it, he said decisively, "The best thing that Laurel could do for Diana would be to get her the hell out of show business. That's what I'd like to see happen."

Enough to ruin her career? Nick wondered.

CHAPTER SEVEN

LAUREL HAD JUST FINISHED rechecking the financial statement that Tony Koop had sent, when Carlos showed Glen Driscoll into the library. She closed the folder she'd been working on and took out the one that Glen had mailed to her the previous week.

"Hi," she said cheerfully from her desk.

He acknowledged her greeting with a quick nod as he took giant strides toward her, agile steps for a man in his early sixties. Though his silver-gray hair picked up the light streaming through the wide windows, Laurel saw that his gray-blue eyes lacked the luster that had been in them before his wife died two years ago.

"The drive from L.A. gets worse by the minute," he complained, setting his briefcase down on the credenza next to her desk. "How's Diana?"

Laurel knew he was asking if she thought the star would hold together long enough to get through filming. "She's fine. How are you?"

"Tired. Why I stay in this rat race, I'll never understand. Some kind of death wish, a shrink would probably tell me." Taking a file from his briefcase, he asked, "Have you gone over the schedule for Diana's promotional appearances?"

Laurel flashed him a bright smile. "I'm fine, too, Glen. Thank you for asking."

He looked up from the file he held in his hands and smiled in earnest. "Forgive me. I'm happy that you're fine—" his eyes assessed the paisley silk dress she wore "—and as always you look lovely. I have to be back at the studio for a late meeting, so let's get this over with as quickly as possible."

"Will you please relax! You'll give yourself a heart attack if you don't slow down. Would you like some coffee?"

"No, no, thanks."

As Laurel poured herself a cup from the coffee decanter on her desk, she reverted to her business tone. "The network interviews the week *Winner Takes All* is to be aired are fine, but to have Diana go traipsing around to local stations across the country is out."

Glen's jaw muscles tensed. "Competition for viewers is all-out war now. More and more people are watching cable TV and using their VCRs. If they learn that Diana will be on a network movie, the ratings will soar."

"I agree."

"Then you see that we need her face on TV as often as we can get it."

"Again, I agree." Laurel leaned forward and looked him square in the eye. "Don't be so damn cheap, Glen. Buy some thirty- or fifteen-second spots and use a clip from the movie showing Diana's face. You'll get your much-needed ratings."

A bleak, tight-lipped smile worked its way onto his weary face, and he sat down. "That's what I like about you. You soften with age." Leaning back in his chair, he shook his head and said, "And to think what a sweet, demure child you were."

Smiling, she said, "Everything I've learned about bargaining, I learned from you." Opening the folder on her desk, her expression turned serious. "We need to discuss Diana's contract for her next project."

"If there is a next project. We don't know how *Winner Takes All* will do." When he saw that Laurel was about to speak, he put his hand up and sighed. "I knew I'd regret your making me give her an option in the *WTA* contract. But if the movie bombs, are you going to hold me to it?"

"What do you think, Glen? I love you dearly, but I love Diana more." She flicked through several pages in the folder. "There are a few stipulations to be included in the next contract. Diana gets the absolute right to approve her director, and she may terminate filming if the director she approves is replaced. She gets $800,000 up front, plus ten percent of net profits."

"Laurel!"

"If the film is to be shot on location, she gets first-class transportation and a per diem that covers two persons. Her name will be billed on a separate frame above the title on all prints of the film and must be the same size as the title."

"Is that all?" he mumbled.

"Not quite." Her attention returned to the folder on her desk. "She'll have the right to keep her wardrobe, to a one-hour daily lunch period, a first-class trailer for her sole use and also an assistant, who is to be paid one thousand dollars a week." She looked up at Glen and smiled sweetly. "Sure you won't have some coffee?"

"Yes, I think I will, but why don't you just poison it and get it over with?"

As she poured him a cup, she said in silky tones, "Think about that palatial home of yours in Beverly Hills, your penthouse apartment in New York, your yacht and your twin-engine Cessna. Diana's hard work had a lot to do in helping you finance all of them.''

"Who's the personal assistant that's to be paid a thousand a week . . . Ron?''

"Who else? How's the suit regarding the video rights on Diana's films coming along?''

"My lawyers are trying to get an early hearing, but they don't foresee any real problems.''

Outside the library, Nick stopped when he heard a man's voice inside.

"That's good,'' Laurel said.

"Good, yes, but everything depends on Diana doing a first-class job in *WTA*. If she doesn't, I won't be able to give her old movies to university film departments.''

With a touch of sarcasm in her tone, Laurel asked, "Do you still think Lyla would be able to do a better job?''

Nick moved a little closer to the door, listening intently.

"Quality-wise, no, but I'd be sleeping a lot sounder.''

"Diana will be just fine. She's never looked lovelier, and she's never been more enthusiastic about a project.''

"Let's not fool ourselves. She could have another breakdown. We both know it's a risk.''

"Come down to earth, Glen. Who knows better than you that risk is the name of the game in Hollywood? If *WTA* doesn't get you another Emmy, don't lay it at Diana's doorstep. Just get better writers for her next film.''

Next film, Nick repeated mentally, realizing that Laurel was bargaining for long-term plans for her employer. He wondered if Ron knew that, too. Quietly he backed away from the library door and went upstairs to get ready for the trip into L.A.

AT THE FRONT DOOR, Laurel kissed Glen on the cheek, then went directly to Diana's sitting room. Murals—garden scenes with peacocks and scarlet-winged flamingos—covered the walls. The furniture, upholstered in white velvet, sat on a rose-and-blue Oriental carpet. Between the tall windows, draped in white chiffon, were glass-covered chests with memorabilia from the star's thirty-three films.

"Diana," Laurel called, and went into the spacious adjoining bedroom. At the far side, four slender posts supported a white silk canopy that draped down the back of the bed. The splash of pink roses in the silk bedspread and ruffled pillows was duplicated in the draperies that hung over the arched door to the balcony.

Laurel's steps across the room were muted by the soft white carpet. She saw Diana on the balcony, pensively gazing out over the grounds toward the garage. She was wearing the floor-length crimson silk robe they had picked out at Balmain's in Paris the year before last. "Diana," Laurel said softly when she was behind her.

She turned. "Was that Glen's car I saw go down the driveway?"

"Yes. He said to apologize for hurrying off, but he had to rush back to a meeting at Universal."

"Poor Glen, he hasn't been the same since Florence died. He's not a man who can be happy living alone. He should marry again."

Laurel laughed lightly. "I don't think he'd be able to stand still long enough to say 'I do.'"

"For the right woman, he would—" her lips twisted into a cynical smile "—not that Lyla could qualify as that."

"In L.A. they're saying that he and Lyla are having problems."

"That doesn't surprise me. Lyla's never met a man she didn't like . . . or sleep with."

"To each his own," Laurel commented casually. "But she does seem fairly content with her life."

Remembering Ron's words regarding her dependency on Laurel, Diana's tone became serious. "What about you? Are you content to watch your life go by as you take care of me?"

The question took Laurel by surprise. Moving to an umbrella-shaded table, she sat down on one of the cushioned white chairs, crossed her legs and clasped her fingers around her knee. "And what makes you think I'm watching my life go by?" She glanced out at the beautifully landscaped grounds. "How many women can live like this, get to travel and have a wonderful companion like you?"

Diana's chuckle was halfhearted as she approached Laurel. "You always say exactly what you think I want to hear."

"I always tell you the truth."

"Do you really?"

"My, but you're in an odd mood today. Did Ron put you through a particularly strenuous workout this morning?"

"I don't want to talk about Ron. I want to talk about you and about your future."

Laurel glanced down and toyed with the pearl ring on her finger, the one Diana had given to her on her last birthday. "My future is here with you. This is where I belong."

"Sometimes I can't help thinking that maybe your future should have been with Brian Cannady."

"Brian wasn't the right man for me."

"He adored you. He was intelligent and handsome and, as an architect, his future was brilliant."

With an odd lilt to her voice, Laurel asked, "Are you trying to get rid of me by marrying me off?"

"Of course not," Diana insisted, sitting across from her at the table. "You know I'd fall apart without you. But I also want you to be happy. I'd hate it if you ended up alone like me."

Laurel cupped Diana's hands in hers. "You are *not* alone. You have me, and you have Ron."

"I know I have you. Thank God for that." She stood and looked over at the garage. "I think Ron may leave us."

"What? He can't. Did he actually say that?"

"Just about. I don't know what to do. I really don't."

"Well, don't worry about it. I'll talk to him."

"Darling," Diana said hesitantly, "Ron thinks I should retire...for good. He also believes I'm much too dependent on you."

Laurel did her best to control the anger she felt. Standing, she said, "Yes, I'll definitely have a talk with him."

"If I did retire, I'd want you to stay on, of course. But as it is, I feel so guilty that my career takes up so much of your time."

Becoming more agitated by the minute, Laurel rubbed her hands together and said quietly, "If things were different, you'd have to settle for a nine-to-five employee, but we've come a long way together, and nothing is going to stop us now. We've both worked too hard to get your life back on track."

"And what about your life?"

Laurel checked her watch. "My life can wait for the time being. I've got to change for the personal managers' meeting in L.A. Nick and I have to pick Reva up. Her car's in the shop."

"Nick is going with you?"

"Yes, he wanted to."

Diana experienced a momentary feeling of panic, and the promise she made to Ron in the gym was forgotten. Nervously she said, "Nick is quite an attractive man, isn't he? You will be careful, won't you?"

Wondering at the word of caution, Laurel reassured her. "I'm a defensive driver, remember?"

"I mean...about Nick. I've noticed the way he looks at you. It's just that I—I don't think I could bear it if you were to leave me."

Laurel took one of Diana's hands in hers and asked quietly, "Do you think I really could, even if I wanted to?"

AFTER PARKING the blue Mercedes in downtown Santa Barbara, Laurel told Nick she wouldn't be long and started toward the entrance to the La Arcada shopping plaza. He followed her with his eyes down the brick walkway until she turned off at the fountain. Moving from the passenger seat in the front to one in the back, he scanned the red-tiled roofs of the plaza's Spanish architecture and the colorful flags over the tall, arched doors of the shops.

Minutes later he saw Laurel and a willowy blonde heading toward the car, busily chatting away. With a sense of pride, he decided that Laurel looked much bet-

ter in her tailored rust-colored suit than Reva did in a
garishly colored dress that looked as if it could have been
painted by Picasso.

Nick leaned over the front seat and opened the car
door for Reva, who did a double take when she saw him.
Her magenta-colored lips spread into a wide smile, and
her lively brown eyes raked over him. "Thank you," she
crooned, and glanced over at Laurel, who slid behind the
wheel and fastened her safety belt.

"Reva, this is Nick Malone. Nick, Reva Perlman, en-
trepreneur, fashion designer and a good friend."

Extending her hand over the seat to Nick, Reva's eyes
locked with his. "It's a good thing we are good friends,
Laurel. Where have you been hiding this man?"

Nick sought Laurel's eyes in the rearview mirror, and
when they met, he cocked his head and grinned to
punctuate Reva's comment. But when he felt Reva
squeeze his hand a little too intimately, his eyes shifted
back to her.

Retrieving his hand, he said, "Laurel's been telling me
about the new line of sportswear you're marketing."

"It's doing very well, both here and in the Rodeo
Drive store. I'm hoping to break into the East Coast
market next spring."

Laurel checked the sideview mirror and pulled into the
flow of traffic on State Street. "I've seen your TV spots.
The clothes are gorgeous. Was that Debbie Rogers
wearing the yellow jumpsuit, the one with the white
cummerbund? She's lovely."

"Yes," Reva acknowledged, "but she'd better stick to
modeling. As an actress, she's the pits. Did you see *Cu-
pid's Darling*? I mean, really. Debbie hasn't been an innocent for so long, how could she possibly act like one?

Would you believe she actually wore panty hose with lead-crystal rhinestones to Bob Chittendon's funeral!''

"She didn't!''

"God's truth. Did you know Bob's wife has been seeing Max Berger? She certainly didn't waste any time.''

Nick listened as the two women talked of goings-on in Hollywood, and he noted another difference between them. Laurel had an innate sense of fairness in her comments, while Reva went right for the jugular, and happily so. Maybe she hadn't always been so bitchy, he conjectured, remembering that Laurel had told him the woman had just gone through a messy divorce. A little of the bitterness could be showing, he decided.

"So,'' Reva said, eyeing Nick, "you're a security consultant. Interesting work, I'd imagine.''

"At times it is.''

She reached into her tote bag and pulled out a blue velvet case. After slipping a cigarette out, she lit it with a gold lighter with a small ruby stone embedded on one side, a lighter identical to the one Nick had seen Fran use. His radar began picking up a flurry of signals as he recalled Guy's telling him that Tony Koop had a habit of giving gold cigarette lighters to his lady friends just before kissing them goodbye.

"Cigarette, Nick?'' she asked, offering him the pack.

"No, I've taken the pledge.''

"Ugh! Another one. Pretty soon we smokers will be society's new pariahs.''

"This marketing for your sportswear,'' Nick probed, "it must be a pretty expensive undertaking.''

Reva's pencil-thin eyebrows shot up. "For what a thirty-second TV spot costs during prime time, the three of us could vacation on the Côte d'Azur. The models get scale for just standing there, and studio time costs more than having all your teeth capped."

"Hmmm. You're talking thousands, I guess." From the corner of his eye he saw Laurel glare at him in the rearview mirror.

"I think that's the reason my mother hasn't been feeling well lately." She turned to Laurel. "You know Sylvia—no spirit of adventure, and she constantly worries about money. What's it for, I say, if not to be spent?"

Conversation between the women in the front seat continued as Reva belittled Sam, her ex-husband, and cast aspersions on the femininity of several of her best customers. When they dropped her off in front of the Rodeo Drive boutique, Laurel told her to give Sylvia her best and to apologize for not stopping to see her.

After Nick hopped back into the front seat and Laurel pulled away from the curb, she said, "I hope that you don't for a minute believe Reva could be the extortionist."

"I'm interested in anyone who has a cash-flow problem."

"She's a competent businesswoman. I don't doubt for a minute that she has her finances completely under control."

"How about her love life? Is she on Tony Koop's list of playmates?"

Laurel hesitated before saying, "He's the reason Sam divorced her." She cast Nick an inquisitive glance. "How did you find out about Tony?"

"Guy is a world of information and a born gossip."

"Oh," she murmured.

"This Tony, he must be quite a man."

"If you like the type."

"What type?"

"Low-cut shirts, gold chains, tangerine margaritas."

"Doesn't sound much like your everyday financial advisor."

"He looks good in an Armani suit, too."

Nick turned a bit in his seat. "Not your type, I take it."

"Hardly. I'd have a hard time finding a man attractive who keeps a spare key hidden in a lantern over the back door of his beach house for the exclusive use of his lady friends."

"Oh?" Nick felt an uncomfortable stirring of the green-eyed monster. "How do *you* know about that?"

As she pulled into a parking space next to a tall building, Laurel offered him an arresting smile. "Does everyone always answer all of your questions?"

"I usually get my answers one way or the other. By the way, do you trust me with this Mercedes?"

"Sure, but if you dent it, you'll have to explain it to Diana. It's hers."

"Want to see my driver's license?"

"I'm not sure exactly why, but I trust you. Just be back in two hours to pick me up. It's a long walk to Santa Barbara."

"It's a date. One more thing."

With one foot out of the car, she faced him. "What?"

"I need Tony Koop's office address."

"He won't be there now."

"I'm banking on it."

"What are you thinking of doing?"

"I want to check his files and learn more about his supposed financial problems."

Laurel jerked her foot back in and closed the car door, realizing what he was planning. "You could get arrested for going through Tony's files."

"Do you think that if I asked nicely, he'd show them to me?"

"But if you get caught, the whole world would know that I hired you!"

"No, that's privileged information . . . like between doctor and patient, et cetera, et cetera."

She glanced toward the building, thinking quickly, then she faced him. "I'm going with you."

"Uh-uh. I work solo."

"You work for me," she reminded him, "and I'd know what to look for much better than you would."

"Like Diana, I'm a quick study."

"Do you know where he keeps his files?"

"What about your meeting?"

"Give me a half hour," she said and dropped the car keys into her purse.

"Laurel—"

"It's settled, Nick."

Against his better judgment, he nodded and watched her get out and walk to the side entrance of the building. Forcing his eyes from those gorgeous legs of hers, he glanced across the street and saw the blinking Schlitz beer sign in the window of a lounge. He got out of the car, locked the doors and maneuvered through the oncoming street traffic.

Inside the lounge, Nick edged his way through the Friday-night-after-work crowd. He perched on a stool at the bar and ordered a bourbon and water, wondering why the hell he had agreed to let Laurel go with him. He had never taken a client along with him when he was doing his job.

He put a five-dollar bill on the counter and took a swallow of his drink when the bartender brought it. *Why are you letting her tag along, then?* he asked himself. He needn't have; he knew why.

Without even trying, Laurel had gotten under his skin. He couldn't get her out of his thoughts. There was something about the way she walked, that light perfume she wore and the feel of her silk blouse on his fingers—not to mention those long, slender legs of hers.

But there were other things about her that made her special. He liked the fact that she was so damn competent and so completely in charge of her job. She certainly was dependable and loyal, although he thought she overdid it where her employer was concerned. After hearing the tail end of her conversation with Diana's agent in the library, it was obvious that Laurel was planning to be with her employer for the long haul. *Who knows?* he wondered. *Maybe she's as star-struck as Ron is.*

He took another sip of his drink and checked his watch. Immediately his thoughts returned to Laurel. Every instinct he had told him that she was unlike any woman he'd ever known, and he was having tantalizing, lewd ideas—like making wild, passionate love to her.

Nick chuckled to himself, wondering if he was losing his grip on reality. He'd fallen head over heels in love once before. In those days he had believed that when two people were really in love, getting married was the natural thing to do. Cheryl had agreed with him.

"Cheryl," he muttered and shook his head. Compromise had been alien to her nature. Like Laurel, she had been career oriented. He was, at first, proud of her being a fine administrative assistant on the rise in international banking. And like Laurel, Cheryl had been a paragon at her job. But Mrs. Nicolas Malone's ambition had clashed with her impatience, and she'd decided to rise in the ranks via selected banking officers' bedrooms.

For Nick, the hurt had passed, but he wasn't a man to forget history, lest it repeat itself. Something told him, however, that Laurel was different. Yes, she was wrapped up in her career; there was no doubt that she was also ambitious. And when he was with her, he had this strong possessive urge. He wanted her, that much he knew, but with a lady like her, he was fairly sure that permanency would have to be tacked on to getting her.

He took another swallow of his drink and smiled at himself, thinking how ludicrous it was to even assume that she would be interested in him, a private investigator who had a two-bedroom house with a mortgage on it.

So what's the big deal? he chided himself. *It's not as though you could fall in love with her.* He thought about that, then convinced himself that any man who could give up smoking had enough willpower not to fall in love if he didn't want to.

"Sure you do," he said to his image in the mirror behind the bar before he drained his glass and headed to the car to wait for Laurel.

CHAPTER EIGHT

AS THEY DROVE PAST Paramount Studios and turned left on Santa Monica Boulevard, Laurel found herself becoming panicky. She could visualize Nick and herself being fingerprinted by the LAPD.

With her fingers clenched on the steering wheel, she said, "There's an all-night guard on duty in the lobby. How do we get into Tony's office?"

"Isn't there a service entrance?"

"I don't know."

"Well, we'll find out. Park a block away."

After doing so, she pointed out the building and whispered that the office was on the fourth floor.

"Why are you whispering?"

"Aren't we supposed to?"

"Right," he said, feeling that this wasn't going to be one of his easier capers.

Quietly Laurel followed him around to the back of the building to the service entrance.

"Locked, naturally," Nick said, and glanced up at the smog that lay over the city like a gray blanket.

Laurel watched intently as he slipped a credit card between the door and the frame and worked it a bit before the knob turned. He pulled her inside and quietly closed the door.

Whispering again, she asked, "Why do they make locks that are so easy to open?"

"So they can sell you more locks if you want privacy." He glanced around the dimly lit area and led her toward a door with a sign over it that read Stairs. "C'mon," he said quietly.

When they reached the fourth floor, he peered out into the deserted corridor. "Which office is his?"

"The last three on the right." She pointed toward the end of the hallway.

"Wait here."

She grabbed the sleeve of his jacket and tugged hard. "I'm going with you."

"If I can get one of the doors open, you are, but there's no sense in both of us getting slapped with an illegal entry charge."

Nick took cautious steps down the corridor and stopped at the first door. When he slipped the credit card between the lock and the doorjamb, nothing happened. He reached into the inside pocket of his jacket, took out a small leather case and tried two picklocks before he heard the click. Glancing back at Laurel, he gestured for her to join him.

It was dark inside, but some light from the adjacent building filtered in through the venetian blinds. "This is his secretary's office," Laurel said softly.

"Where's Tony's?"

"Two rooms down," she said and followed Nick as he entered the next room.

He looked around at the three desks, each with a computer on it. "Who works in here?"

"Tony's assistants. His junior partners have offices across the hall."

Inside Tony's office he pulled the cord to open the draperies and took note of the elaborate crystal chandelier, the plush sofa and easy chairs near a curved bar.

It was backed by shelves of crystal glasses and decanters with silver labels of just about every kind of booze made by man. "Nice," he remarked. "Our boy must be doing something right ... with someone's money. Where does he keep the client files?"

Laurel went to a carved panel on the wall in back of the desk and fingered the side of it. The panel swung open, exposing two rows of file cabinets built into the wall. "He usually gets the key from his top left drawer."

"I bet it's locked, too," Nick mumbled. It was, and the picklocks came out again.

Fascinated by the deft movements of his fingers, she asked, "Is this what you usually do in your work?"

"Not exactly," he said and tried another picklock. "P.I. work is ninety percent checking out old newspapers, libraries and government offices when you're not bored to death on a stakeout. Patience is the name of the game."

"How come you're so good at what you're doing?"

"My father was a good teacher. He spent two years in a California state prison."

Laurel's eyes widened. "Your father did?"

He slid the drawer open, looked up at her and grinned. "He started out as a rehabilitation counselor and learned a lot from the inmates."

After Nick found the key and opened the two cabinets, Laurel said, "Diana's file is usually in this drawer." She indicated a middle one.

He eased it open and fingered through the beginning of the alphabetically placed folders. "Basch, Beckley ... no Baxter."

Laurel moved next to him and began going through the folders as Nick checked the other file drawers. "I know some of these people. They're also clients. Why isn't Diana's file here?"

"That's a good question." He took several of the folders to the desk. Using a pocket flashlight, he began going over the recent investments recorded for each client as Laurel peered over his shoulder. He told her to get several more folders and went through those, also. "Ever heard of Worldwide Securities?"

"Yes, it was one of the investments Tony made for Diana a few months ago. Why?"

He pointed to several of the documents he'd spread out on the desk. "It's the only company in which every one of these clients bought twenty thousand dollars in shares." He looked at Laurel. "How much did he invest for Diana?"

"Twenty thousand dollars."

"That number should ring a bell."

"But Diana made a fifteen-percent profit on that deal in less than two weeks. It was a case where he short sold the stock."

"I'm not into the market. What does that mean?"

"Tony would place a client's money in escrow and borrow shares from a stockbroker, with the promise to return the same number of shares in the future. Then he'd sell the stock on the open market, making a profit for his client and a commission for himself. When the price of the same stock dropped far enough, he'd buy back the shares on the open market and return them to the broker. He told me it was all very legal and said that large banking institutions and insurance companies did the same thing."

"I wish to hell Diana's file was here. It'd be interesting to see if it's twenty thousand dollars short."

"Nick, I rechecked her statement just today. It looked okay to me."

"You went over what Tony sent you," he said, carrying the folders back to the cabinet. "I'd like to see his office file."

When they had replaced all the folders, Nick locked the cabinets, returned the key to the desk drawer, and flicked through the Rolodex on Tony's desk. "Oh?" he muttered.

Laurel glanced down at the card. "Guy Swan," she read. "That's his home phone number."

"Is that the kind of company Tony keeps? You told me he was a ladies' man."

"Tony definitely has a Don Juan complex."

"Was he ever involved with Fran?"

Laurel stiffened. "Nick, I don't like talking about people's private lives."

"Do you like being blackmailed?"

"Not really," she said dryly, and decided to tell him what he wanted to know. "When Tony lived in Beverly Hills, he and Fran had an affair, but it supposedly ended when he sold his house and moved to Santa Barbara."

Nick tapped Guy's card on the Rolodex. "I wonder what that doodle means."

Laurel looked at the dollar sign with the *X* through it. "No money?" she guessed.

"Or no *more* money."

Their eyes shot toward the wooden door to Tony's office when they heard the knob being rattled. Nick clicked off his pocket flashlight, took hold of Laurel's arm and was about to hustle her behind the bar when he whacked his knee on the corner of the desk.

He muffled a curse and began limping as he rushed her behind the bar. "Get down," he whispered, and bit his lower lip as the pain shot through his leg.

Laurel crouched and helped Nick ease himself down onto the carpet. She knew something was wrong when she saw him leaning on one arm as he kept his left leg out straight.

The sound of the door opening caused the hairs at the back of her neck to stiffen. Nick put a finger to his lips, but he needn't have. Laurel almost stopped breathing as the beam of a flashlight swung over the top of the bar. She squeezed her eyes shut, wondering if women still had to work in steamy laundries in prison. Chancing it, she peered through her lashes, saw the ray of light pass over the bar again, then breathed a long sigh of relief when she heard the door being shut.

"That was close," Nick said in a jagged voice, and lay down on his back.

"Nick, this is no time for a siesta. Let's get out of here."

"In a minute. My trick knee is acting up."

"I can see the headline now," she moaned. "Private investigator's trick knee foils break-in. What would we have done if the guard had caught us?"

Nick smiled up at her. "I'd have gone to plan B."

"What was that?"

"I'd have thought of something."

"Wonderful." She sank down next to him on the carpet and rested her chin in the curve of her hand. "How long do we lie here like this?"

"As long as it takes," he said softly, his eyes holding hers.

In the semidarkness, Laurel studied Nick's strong features: the symmetrical eyebrows, the finely sculpted nose and mouth and the square chin with the cleft in it. "Does your knee hurt badly?" she asked as she guided her fingertips through the waves in his hair.

At her touch, his scalp tingled. He looked up at her quizzically and murmured her name.

She leaned closer. "Yes?"

He could feel her sweet breath waft against his lips, and his blood pressure went wild when she placed her hand on the side of his face. In the next moment he felt her lips brush over his.

Laurel could think of only one thing; she had been right. Nick's lips were warm and soft and tantalizing. She felt them move under hers ever so slightly—as though he were speaking silent words. A flash of heat rushed to her face, and a giddiness dulled her reasoning. Deepening her kiss, she eased her fingers across Nick's cheek and traced the outer curve of his ear. When she felt his arms close around her and pull her down over his prone body, she heard a sigh. Was it his or hers? She didn't know. Delight and carefree abandonment sent the tip of her tongue searching for his. But when he moaned and squeezed her so tightly that she could barely breathe, her eyes shot open and she pushed herself up quickly.

Resting her head back against a cabinet door, she stared straight ahead in their cramped quarters, wondering what on earth had possessed her. Trying to control her erratic breaths, she didn't dare look down at Nick.

He, too, was having a difficult time bringing some kind of order to his pounding pulse. After swallowing hard, he bent his left leg and straightened it a few times. "I...uh...think you fixed my trick knee," he muttered.

Laurel tugged at her suit jacket and drew upon all of her emotional resources in an effort to sound nonchalant. "I'm pleased," she managed to say in a strained voice. "Can we leave now?"

"I think we'd better."

After exiting the building the same way they had entered, they headed back to Santa Barbara. Laurel was more than happy when Nick offered to drive; she had some serious thinking to do.

What was she imagining? she demanded of herself as they pulled onto the Pacific Coast Highway. She had known Nick for only a few days, and here she was throwing herself at him on the floor in Tony's office! What must he think of her? What should she think of herself?

It was a purely physical attraction, she decided. Nothing more. Certainly one impulsive kiss wasn't cause for alarm. And a physical attraction didn't mean she was headed toward a physical relationship. She glanced over at Nick as they approached Malibu and noted how the lights over the highway cast a golden sheen over his attractive profile.

Immediately she forced her eyes back to the road ahead, wondering if the world would actually come to an end if she were to let her defenses down for just a while? It had been a long time since she had experienced the joy of being loved, wanted and needed by a man, and much too long since she had felt a man's loving arms around her and had heard whispered intimacies.

Chancing a furtive glance at Nick again, she wondered what it would be like to have him hold her in that way and to share those intimacies with him. No, she thought sadly, it would only be a repeat of the episodes with Keith and Brian. Eventually she would have to give Nick up, too.

Don't be idiotic, she chided herself silently. *You can't give up something you don't have. It was you who attacked the poor man when he could hardly move. What makes you think he's remotely interested in having any kind of a relationship with you in the first place?*

"Hungry?" Nick asked, and she jerked her head toward him.

"What?"

"We haven't had dinner."

The last thing Laurel felt like doing just now was eating, but she knew Nick always had a healthy appetite. "There's a beach restaurant just down the highway," she said, then chewed her lower lip.

Upon arriving at the restaurant, a smiling hostess greeted them, and Laurel requested a table on the outdoor patio that faced the ocean. The sky was clear now, a black velvet backdrop for myriad twinkling stars; the air was cool, laden with the zesty aroma of the Pacific.

They dined on steak for two and baked potatoes that, as Diana would have put it, had everything in the refrigerator on them. Attempting to put what had happened at Tony's office out of her mind, Laurel brought up the subject of Nick's posing as a security consultant.

"How long do you think we can keep up the masquerade? Ron already knows you're a private investigator. Are you conversant enough about home security to keep Diana from suspecting you're a fraud?"

"Nicely put," he joked, "but don't worry. Part of my investigative skill is to know if and how security is bypassed. I can usually tell if an alarm or an electronic system has been tampered with, if a company's safe has been violated or if your phone's been bugged. A good friend of mine in San Diego recently developed a new microprocessor burglar alarm system. I learned a lot about security from him. Speaking of San Diego, I've got to drive back down tomorrow. There are some things Bob and I have to go over before I appear in court Monday morning."

"Oh." Disappointment was more than obvious in her face and tone when she asked, "What time are you leaving?"

"Not until early evening. I thought I'd let the maniacs on the freeway do their thing before I start out."

Dispirited, Laurel rambled on. "We've never had to use the alarm system at the house. I mean it's never been activated by a prowler. I told Diana I'd take you on a tour in the morning, so she'll probably expect some kind of a report from you."

"I'll work up something." After a bite of steak, he said, "You seem to be shouldering all the burden of Diana's well-being alone. Doesn't she have any relatives?"

"Her parents are deceased, and she never maintained contact with her relatives in Texas."

"Too busy with her career?" he asked, then took a sip of red wine.

"Diana's career is her life."

"Does it have to be yours, too?" The question had just tumbled out, and Nick regretted having asked it so bluntly when he saw Laurel's face freeze.

She placed her fork down and wiped her lips with a napkin before saying matter-of-factly, "I take my job seriously, Nick. Not only because Diana pays me extremely well, but because I happen to think a great deal of her."

Might as well put both feet in your mouth, Nick decided. "Ron does, too."

"He doesn't understand Diana as well as I do. I know what makes her happy."

"He may know her in ways that you never could hope to," Nick said quietly. "He's in love with her and has been since his college days."

Remembering Keith, the young man she had fallen in love with at the University of Arizona, she said quietly, "College romances have a way of evaporating with time."

"Are you speaking from experience?"

When she looked up at him, she saw a sincere friendliness in his expression that made his personal question sound quite natural. "Yes," she admitted. "There was a young man I liked very much." Willing a smile, she asked, "And what about San Diego State? Did you leave any broken hearts in your wake?"

"Several, and one of them was mine. Some day I'll tell you about her."

At this point Laurel wasn't so sure she wanted to hear about the woman who had broken Nick's heart. She signaled their waiter, gave him her credit card and, a few moments later, signed the charge slip.

Nick suggested a walk on the beach, and as they sauntered alongside the water's edge, he wondered at the strength of the tie between Laurel and her employer. Casually he said, "I never realized just how involved the job of a personal manager could be. Did they teach you all that in college?"

"I have a degree in business administration. Everything else I had to learn the hard way, through experience, but Glen was a big help."

"Working for Diana is pretty glamorous, isn't it? I don't imagine you could ever settle for a house with a white picket fence, two children and a dog."

Surprised by his question, Laurel remarked, "You certainly say whatever comes to mind, don't you?"

"I'm a very straightforward person."

"Then tell me, where are your wife and your two children?"

Candidly he answered, "I was married for a few years, but there were no children. Cheryl was a lovely lady and a good cook, too, but not big on children or fidelity."

Laurel blinked a few times and whispered, "Oh." After an uneasy pause, she asked, "Are you bitter now?"

Nick stopped at a palm tree and leaned his shoulder against it. "Not at all. I'm just waiting for the right woman to come along. How about you?"

She tried to ignore the impact of conflicting emotions that assailed her. It was too late to pretend she wasn't deeply attracted to Nick, however. The strength of the attraction was setting off alarm bells, a warning she realized she had better heed. But since he was being honest and open with her, she decided she owed him as much. Quietly she replied, "I guess I've been waiting for the right man."

"How will you recognize him when he does come along?"

Perhaps it was the moonlight and the wine, perhaps it was because Nick seemed so easy to talk with, perhaps it was the need to express her deepest longings. Whatever the reason, Laurel rested back against the palm tree, her head close to Nick's. In a quiet, dreamy voice, she said, "He'll be kind and understanding... be intelligent and have a sense of humor, and it wouldn't hurt if he were also attractive.''

She tilted her head slightly toward his and had to admit that with the moonlight shining on his face, Nick looked even more handsome now than he had lying on the carpet in Tony's office. More important, though, she also recognized that she had just described him as the man of her dreams.

When Nick shifted his body until he was directly in front of her, Laurel realized that he could look at her a certain way—just as he was doing now—and make her feel that she was the most beautiful and the most desirable woman in the world.

He leaned closer, and she knew he was going to kiss her. She wanted him to, but she was afraid. She knew that things couldn't possibly work out between them; he'd always be complaining about her dedication to Diana. If only she could tell him the truth. But she couldn't. And why ask for a broken heart again? She knew how much Diana depended on her, and regardless of how she was beginning to feel about Nick, she just couldn't get sidetracked and neglect her duty.

For all of her self-warning, she shuddered when Nick's lips brushed her forehead and then left a feathery kiss on her cheek. Steeling herself, she murmured, ''Nick, about what happened in Tony's office—'' The rippling sensation along her skin became almost unbearable when she felt his fingers caress the side of her neck.

''Yes?'' he whispered.

In a thread of a voice, she said, ''I—I don't want you to get the wrong idea.''

''I won't,'' he promised, and placed his lips on hers, but there was little gentleness in his kiss.

His mouth, like that of a hungry man, rolled over hers, and he pressed her back against the palm tree, starving for more of her, needing more of her. His senses magnified the soft feel of her silky hair in his hands as he cupped her head. Her warm, firm breasts heated his chest, and when he felt her arms move around his waist to hold him, an agonizingly delightful pulsation began to throb in his groin. It worsened when she returned his kiss with an impetuousness that surprised him.

Finally he drew his head back, breathed deeply and saw that Laurel was doing the same. Her face was flushed, and her lips seemed slightly swollen. "Laurel," he whispered, "what are you doing to me?"

Her eyes opened slowly, and she placed unsteady fingers against his chest. She was shaking inside, and the realization that Nick's kiss could do that to her was a further warning signal. In a tremulous voice, she said, "We're attracted to one another, Nick. It's nothing more than that."

"If that's all it is," he asked, his voice raspy, "why haven't I ever felt this way before?"

Laurel ran the tip of her tongue over her sensitized lips and said with a false calm, "Let's not overanalyze what was just a kiss."

"That was some kiss. Another minute and you would have created a new earthquake fault right here on Malibu Beach." When she looked at him oddly, he added, "You said you liked a man with a sense of humor."

Laurel picked up the purse she had dropped in the sand, took a few steps past him and glanced back over her shoulder. "They say a word to the wise is sufficient. We'll just have to be more careful in the future, won't we?"

At least she knew she would have to be.

IT WAS A GLORIOUS California morning as Diana and Ron were finishing their tenth lap in the pool. Seeing Laurel and Nick coming toward them, Diana held on to the edge of the aqua-colored tile and asked, "Why don't you two come in? It's delightful."

"Business before pleasure," Laurel said, smiling. "Nick's just checked out your safe."

Nick sat down on the diving board and drew up one knee. "It's fairly adequate, but I'll get you a brochure on a heavy-gauge steel wall safe that you might want to consider. It's fire and explosion-resistant, has insulated walls, interlocking body and door jambs and a recessed electronic lock. Its stainless-steel numerical keyboard is virtually pickproof."

"What do you think, Ron?" Diana asked.

In one smooth motion, he lifted himself out of the water, spun around and landed on the edge of the pool near Diana. Looking up at Nick, he advised, "You have an expert here. I'd listen to him."

"Thanks for the vote of confidence," Nick returned, and looked back at Diana. "I'm afraid your alarm system wouldn't keep a draft out of the house. Laurel told me it was installed before you bought the estate."

Diana began treading water, holding on to Ron's leg with one hand as she did. "Then it must have been."

Laurel said, "Nick has a friend in San Diego who just developed a new burglar alarm."

"A microprocessor system," Nick explained. "It's expensive, but it's wireless and can reliably monitor all points of entry into a house. The beauty of it is that the alarm would go off here in the house and alert the police before an intruder could gain entry. Yet, the circuitry is designed to discriminate normal household activity."

Diana smiled and raised a hand to adjust her bathing cap. "Your friend must be an electronic genius."

"He is. In fact, he's now in charge of security for all of Senator Garrison Howard's campaign headquarters."

At the mention of the name, Diana's face paled. Without explanation, she swam to the ladder on the opposite side of the pool, quickly climbed up and rushed toward the house.

"Diana!" Ron called, but she didn't stop.

"Did I say something wrong?" Nick asked. He looked at Laurel and saw that her face had the same shocked expression on it that Diana's had had before she'd taken off as if a banshee was after her.

Laurel raised a hand and said casually. "Uh...no. I'll see what the problem is."

Pushing himself up quickly, Ron said, "I'll go with you."

"No, please. I'll handle it." She turned and hurried toward the house.

When she reached Diana's bedroom, Laurel saw her shrugging into a terry cloth robe. The wet bathing suit and cap lay in a heap on the white carpet.

Diana sent her a desperate look and cried, "I want him out of this house immediately!"

"Please, I realize you're upset, but Nick couldn't know that—"

"Do you think it's just a coincidence that he mentioned Garrison's name?"

"Yes. Just as I meet people from all over the country at meetings, Nick probably attends conferences and does the same."

"And he just happens to know Garrison?"

"Nick didn't say he did. He only said that a friend of his is working for him."

Diana covered her face with her hands, then let her slender fingers slip downward. She gazed over their tips at Laurel, her blue eyes a vacant stare.

"You just read too much in Nick's innocent comment," Laurel insisted.

"He suspects." Diana groaned and went to one of the slender posts at the bottom of the bed. She grasped it and rested her forehead against it. "I know he does, and pretty soon the whole world will know. Oh, God, why now?" She whirled around and rushed to the bathroom.

Laurel dashed after her, saw her slide back the glass door of the medicine cabinet and take out a small plastic pill container. When Diana snapped open the lid and let it drop in the sink, Laurel cried, "Please, Mother, don't!"

CHAPTER NINE

"DO YOU HAVE ANY IDEA what that was all about?" Nick asked as Ron dried himself off by the pool.

"Obviously she's not a Garrison Howard fan." He tugged the towel sideways across his back. "I would have thought she would be. He's a good man, one of the most popular, productive and dedicated members of the senate."

"Does Diana know him personally?"

"She's never mentioned him, and in the scrapbook I've kept over the years, I've never come across a newspaper or magazine picture of the two of them." He draped the towel over one of the chairs and stepped into his thongs. "How's your investigation coming along?"

"Like a puzzle with a lot of pieces still missing."

"Think you'll find them?"

"I'm going to give it my best shot."

"If I can help, let me know."

"I've got to get back to San Diego for a few days...other business. Do you think you could find out where Guy got the cash to buy his new mobile unit?"

"The bartender at the country club told me that Guy borrowed it from Tony Koop."

"Koop?" Nick thought of the doodle he'd seen on the man's Rolodex. "Why would he loan Guy twenty thousand dollars?"

"They do business together."

"What kind of business?"

Ron propped a foot up on a chair and rested a forearm on his knee. "In Guy's work he meets a lot of women."

"Hmm, that kind of business. Twenty thousand dollars is a great deal of money for entertainment, though. Do you think it was really a loan or blackmail?"

"Blackmail...Guy? You've got to be kidding. He just about faints after he files his income tax. If even the possibility of being questioned by the IRS terrifies him, how do you think he'd handle the threat of a real criminal investigation?"

"I don't know, but it's been my experience that greed can give a person a lot of courage." Nick's eyes drifted toward the house, and again he wondered what he had said to set Diana off.

LAUREL CHECKED the doctor's name on the prescription label before emptying the pill container in the commode and flushing it. Then she went into the sitting room and saw Diana wringing her hands as she paced.

"How long has Dr. Ryan been prescribing the Librium for you?" Laurel asked quietly.

Without looking at her daughter, Diana murmured, "I saw him when I was in L.A. for the fittings."

Laurel sighed and ran her fingers through her hair as she watched Diana continue her nervous meanderings. Calmly she said, "I thought that kind of behavior was behind us."

Turning, Diana made an imploring gesture with her hand. "It is, honestly. I just thought that...well, in case— Oh, I don't know what I thought, but please don't be angry with me. I couldn't stand that."

Slowly Laurel slumped down on the chair near the fireplace. Her head was buzzing, and she wanted to scream at her mother. She wanted to yell that there were things she couldn't stand, either. She was tired of playing nursemaid and terrified that her mother might fall apart again, as she had six years ago. No, Laurel knew she couldn't live through that nightmare again. Somehow, some way she had to hold herself and her mother together for just a while longer. She jolted when she felt Diana's hand rest on her shoulder.

"I've only taken two of the pills...honestly. I won't use them anymore."

Hearing the childlike apology, Laurel looked up at her mother's penitent expression. Immediately she felt trapped in the role that fate had handed her, the role of parenting her own mother. With great effort, she tried to force away her resentment and the recurring hurt of childhood years of neglect.

She had been eight and living with the Davises in Arizona when she had learned that her mother had hidden her away from the world, that the Davises weren't her aunt and uncle and that her father wasn't dead. At that tender age, she'd had to grow up quickly. She'd agreed to the pact of secrecy Diana had proposed, which would shape both their lives.

The Davises were kind people, but they were only caretakers, not family. And Laurel could not shake the belief that somehow she herself was to blame for having to live a life so different from those of the other children she knew. But she endured and almost saw a normal life ahead of her—until that Christmas holiday when she had made her first trip to visit her famous mother in Santa Barbara.

It had happened during Laurel's sophomore year at the University of Arizona, where she was enrolled as an art major. At nineteen she had been enthusiastic about her future, but when she arrived at the star's estate, Laurel entered a world totally foreign to the rural one in which she had been raised.

She had been shocked to find that Diana, in her own milieu, was a different woman. She was no longer the concerned, down-to-earth lady who had visited her daughter twice a year in Arizona. She seemed obsessed with filling each waking moment with frenzied excitement: flamboyant parties that lasted all night long, day trips to Las Vegas to gamble and spur-of-the-moment excursions to San Francisco on expensive shopping sprees for her daughter.

During the holiday season, Laurel tried to keep up with her mother, but soon she realized that the woman was driven by unhappiness and loneliness, in spite of the young men who fawned over her. They, more than the drinking and the other excesses, had bothered Laurel the most.

Diana had a knack for choosing handsome but shallow male companions who came and went almost as often as the tide. Laurel feared that her mother would not be able to last very long if she continued her way of life, but when she tried to discuss it with her, the conversation was cut short and another all-night party began. Laurel knew what she had to do.

She had a long talk with Glen, her mother's agent, who was just as worried about Diana as Laurel was. Upon her return to the university, she changed her major to business administration, her goal set on becoming her mother's personal manager after graduation.

It was heartbreaking for Laurel to set aside the plans she had made for her own life, and that included Keith, who had wanted to marry her and carry her off to Venezuela. But she told herself that Diana had not only given her life, she had seen to it—in the best way she knew how—that her daughter was given a stable upbringing. The decision for Laurel was simple: it was now her time to give. If she wasn't able to keep her mother from heading straight into disaster, at least she would be there when disaster hit.

It certainly had, and with a vengeance.

"You know, darling," Diana said, stroking Laurel's hair and drawing her from her painful memories, "sometimes I feel like I'm the daughter and you're the mother. I don't see how you put up with me."

Unnerved by the remark, Laurel rose from the chair and moved away.

Diana's gaze followed her daughter for silent moments, then she asked, "You do know that I love you, don't you?"

Without facing her, Laurel responded softly, "Yes, I know you do."

"With all of the problems we've had these past years, the last ten have been wonderful because you've been with me. You've been my one source of strength. Before you came here, I never felt I really had a daughter."

And I never felt I really had a mother, Laurel added silently. But years of self-discipline had taught her that recriminations were useless. Time would never change her mother or the choices she had made. And even though she could be self-centered and overly dependent, Laurel did honestly believe that her mother loved her.

Diana moved closer to her and studied her downcast expression. Quietly she said, "It's a wonder that you don't hate me. When I look back I can only imagine the resentment you must have felt toward me for leaving you in Arizona with Frieda and Jerome." She clasped her hands together so tightly that her knuckles whitened. "I made myself believe that because you were so young, you were better off there than living with me—" she chuckled painfully "—considering the way I lived then."

Laurel lifted her eyes and saw the grief in her mother's. "That's all in the past. Let's not dwell on it."

"I wish I could simply set the memories aside, but I can't. There are too many accusing voices that haunt me and criticize me daily, bring back all the guilt that I deserve."

"Mother, please stop it. Remember what Dr. Winston told you when you were ill. You're prone to look for ways to beat up on yourself. You've made mistakes, and I've made mistakes. Everyone has. The important thing is to learn from them and try not to repeat them. That's all any of us can do. For you, particularly, embarking on guilt trips can be dangerous."

"Yes," Diana agreed halfheartedly, "as always, you're right."

Managing a smile, Laurel asked, "Have you gone over the script changes that Glen sent?"

Diana picked up the screenplay of *Winner Takes All* and nodded.

"Good. Now try and forget what Nick said." With that advice, Laurel kissed Diana on the cheek and left the sitting room. She hoped her mother couldn't see just how worried she actually was.

WHEN NICK RETURNED to the house, Alicia told him
that Laurel was in her studio at the far end of the second floor. He hurried up the stairs and found her there,
standing in front of an easel, holding a palette in her left
hand, a brush in her right. Her expression was somber.

"Hi," he greeted her cheerfully. "Are you sensitive
about having someone watch you work?"

Laurel smiled unconvincingly and shook her head.

Quietly closing the door behind him, Nick walked
over to the wide window and studied the canvas. It was
a portrait of Diana. "You are good," he complimented
sincerely.

"It will be used in *Winner Takes All*," she said, adding highlights to the auburn hair in the portrait. "I find
that painting relaxes me."

With the brush poised in midair, she apologized. "I'm
sorry Diana and I rushed off so suddenly. She's extremely nervous. The filming begins in ten days...if
everything goes well," she added in dark tones. "I'm a
little uptight myself. It's been six years since Diana's
been before the camera. There will be nine workdays to
complete all studio scenes at Universal, and only eleven
days on location in Hawaii. It's bound to take longer
than that and go over budget. Everyone will be on
edge."

Nick realized she was keyed up and decided not to in-
quire about Senator Howard just now. He glanced
around the studio, taking in the large number of un-
completed paintings. The large majority were beach
scenes and landscapes that represented the natural
beauty of the Santa Barbara area. He wondered why
none of them had been finished.

On the opposite side of the window, in back of Laurel, he saw another easel with a covered canvas on it.

Lifting the cloth, he saw a copy of the Cézanne land-scape that hung downstairs in the salon. "Did you do this?" he asked.

Laurel turned, startled by his seeing the painting. She set her brush and palette down, hurried to the easel and drew the cloth back over it. "A hobby," she tossed off lightly, but when she saw the dubious glow in Nick's eyes, she walked slowly to the window and stared out over the grounds.

"No," she said in a strained voice, "that's not the truth." She faced him, her features mirroring her anxiety. "If the extortion continues, I plan to sell the original to a private collector."

Nick guessed the rest. "You'll hang this in its place, hoping Diana won't notice the difference." He took measured strides to the window and glanced at the beautifully kept gardens, the swimming pool and the tennis courts. His gaze strayed toward the garage, and he saw Felipe polishing the blue Mercedes. Facing Laurel he asked, "Is money that tight?"

"It will be if Diana doesn't do the movie."

"And the two of you live in this palatial house with servants?"

"Diana's illness was expensive, Nick. It made a big dent in what had been substantial savings, and except for the few plays she did and the income from investments that Tony made, there hasn't been that much money coming in for six years. Thank God for Glen's movie. Now, maybe, you can see why it's so important that Diana makes it through the filming."

"But you're treating her like a defenseless little girl who has to be protected from the real world. That's not healthy for her or for you."

Laurel's gaze roamed over the grounds. "This is Diana's real world. She's used to living this life-style and being adored by everyone. That's why I work so hard to keep her from worrying. I do it for her, so she can give her total energy to her acting. That's the only thing that truly makes her happy."

"You really are protective of her, aren't you? It's rather like an obsession, don't you think? You won't even allow yourself the time to finish a painting. Or are you afraid to finish one, afraid to see how good an artist you are?"

Laurel ignored his questions and glanced around at the half-completed canvases in the studio. "I've been painting ever since I was ten years old." She chuckled wryly. "I was going to be a world-famous artist."

Nick held up a painting of the Santa Ynez hills at dawn. "Why didn't you pursue it?" He looked over at the portrait of Diana. "You certainly have the talent."

"Other things were more pressing."

"Like Diana," he said flatly. When Laurel didn't deny it, he asked, "Why is it so apparent to me and so unclear to you that you're giving up your own interests in life for your employer's?"

There was a disconcerting remoteness in her eyes when she replied, "It's simply a matter of choice."

"Don't you have any inner turmoil or regret about that choice?"

Laurel took the painting from him and let her eyes drift over the splash of sunrise colors that washed over the lavender hills. *If only you knew, Nick,* she thought, well aware that she had given up a great deal more than a career in art.

"Yes," she said quietly to answer his question, "I have had some regrets about giving up a career in art."

To herself she added, *And Keith, then Brian...and now you.*

She set down the painting she had been holding, stepped slowly to the easel and began to clean her brushes. "But," she said quietly, "regrets are useless. Diana needs my help. She's extremely vulnerable right now."

"Vulnerability can be the other side of the coin of power," Nick commented in an accusing tone, frustrated by what he deemed Laurel's narrow point of view.

Laurel's head whipped toward him. "If you're suggesting that Diana is using me, you're dead wrong."

"It could be that you're using each other without even realizing it."

Her expression stilled, then grew hard. "I see that added to all of your other skills, you're an armchair psychiatrist."

"It doesn't take a psychiatrist to see that there's something ultratheatrical about your relationship with the woman."

Angered and hurt, she informed him coolly, "You're being presumptuous, Nick, and it's not very attractive."

She turned quickly to finish cleaning her brushes, the curt response she'd given him weighing heavily on her. What else could he possibly think, though? Her only comfort was that she was positive Nick would be more than understanding if he knew that Diana was her mother. But the pact of secrecy the two women had made years ago still demanded silence of both of them.

Laurel felt exhausted physically and emotionally, and her head began to throb. She pressed her fingertips against her brow, attempting to lessen the pain. She was worried about the extortionist, trying her best to be supportive of Diana, and filled with guilt for offering Nick only half truths.

When she felt his strong hands grasp her shoulders from behind, his comforting warmth shot down her arms and into her hands, hands that she wanted to place over his and had to fight to keep from doing so. If only she could follow the dictates of her heart, she thought. She knew she would turn, throw her arms around Nick's neck and offer herself to him. But years of self-denial had become a way of life for her, and she had existed too long as an unacclaimed martyr to change things now. As always, her first priority would have to be to her mother, regardless of her feelings for the concerned man holding her shoulders.

Nick's thoughts were also in turmoil. She was trembling, and he berated himself for having spoken so bluntly. Helplessly he wished he could recall those words, but it was too late for that. Why, he asked himself, did he become so damned upset every time Laurel exhibited the honest concern she had for Diana? If he didn't know better, he'd have to call it some kind of a perverse jealousy on his part. Of course, that was ridiculous. If his heart ached, it was because he knew that a woman like Laurel came along only once in a lifetime. But why the hell did she have to drag so many complications with her?

Moving his hands slowly over her arms, he said gently, "I'm sorry. I shouldn't have spoken the way that I did. Rather than wait until this evening, maybe it would be better if I left for San Diego now."

Laurel felt a stabbing pain in her heart. Nick was just talking about leaving, and already her sense of loss was beyond tears. She didn't face him, and her voice broke when she asked, "You will come back, won't you, Nick?"

"Yes, I'll be back after the Peters hearing on Monday."

She felt Nick's hands slip away, and she cupped her arms, attempting to capture the comforting warmth of his touch. Motionless, she listened to his steps fade away as he went to the door and softly closed it behind him.

FOR LAUREL, the weekend was long in spite of the many duties she had to take care of. What she didn't need was Ron's constant nagging about what it was in Diana's past that had to be so well hidden. Laurel was thankful, however, that the relationship between him and her mother seemed to have taken a turn for the better. That, she knew, was good for Diana—for the time being.

Monday morning, shortly after nine o'clock, Fran arrived to do further work on Diana's biography. Laurel had been at her desk in the library for more than an hour when Carlos showed her in.

"I wonder how difficult it would be to get a license to pilot a helicopter?" Fran asked as she lowered herself onto the side of Laurel's desk.

"Traffic that bad?"

"Only until I turned onto your driveway. Is Diana ready?"

"She's upstairs with Guy."

"Guy? I thought this was my time."

"I'm sorry, Fran. It's my fault. I forgot to enter him in the schedule."

"Well, well, so you're not perfect after all."

Laurel looked up and saw Fran smirking. "I can live with that. I told Guy he'd have to be through by ten o'clock."

"What do we do until then, dish the neighborhood lovelies who are sleeping around?"

Laurel was barely able to force a pleasant expression. She had never been able to accept Fran's cold and calculating personality, but the woman was extremely good at what she did—when controlled—and that was all that mattered.

After Fran declined a cup of coffee, Laurel asked, "Have you seen Tony lately? I've been trying to reach him all weekend, but I keep talking to his answering machine."

Fran's lips curved into a snide smile. "You mean Tony, the man who finds it impossible to relate to women while standing?"

"I wouldn't know about that," Laurel said with little emotion in her voice.

"Have you tried his office in L.A. this morning?"

"His secretary said he wouldn't be in today."

"My guess is that he's had a real swinging weekend and either can't move or doesn't want to. He's a sad specimen of American manhood. Not much of a lover, either, in spite of what he'd like everyone to think."

"Really, Fran."

"Don't look so shocked. The man's a weakling. Eventually some woman's husband is going to cut off his assets." Bitterly she suggested, "Why don't you ask Reva where he is?" Her voice hardened ruthlessly. "On second thought, having the IQ of a plant, Reva barely knows where she is."

Sorry that she brought it up, Laurel said, "I'll just keep trying to reach him."

Fran checked her watch and said, "Let's see if we can rush Guy along. I've got a million things to do in L.A. before the business-communicators' meeting this evening. You know how Guy is when he hears the sound of his own voice. He goes on and on.''

Reproaching herself for not handling Diana's schedule more carefully, Laurel agreed, and the two women went upstairs.

At the far left side of Diana's sitting room, the white louvered doors were open, exposing the sink, equipment and paraphernalia that Guy used when he gave Diana facials and did her hair. Diana was sitting in a low-backed chair, a blue cloth draped around her shoulders.

Noting the two women coming in, Guy said, ''Listen and learn, ladies.''

''When you say something intelligent,'' Fran quipped as she sat down and placed her attaché case on the floor beside her.

Straightening to his full five-foot-six height, Guy's nostrils flared. ''E equals MC squared.'' Immediately he shifted his attention back to Diana's slightly damp hair. ''Now we put a little more mousse onto a wide-toothed comb and run it through for that smooth look.'' He glanced over at Fran's disheveled hair. ''What did you do, dear, drive here with the top down?''

''Oh, the sting of your wit. How much longer will you be?''

''Patience is a virtue. You do know about virtue, don't you?''

Fran smiled smugly. ''In your case, it would mean a lack of opportunity.''

Guy's moist fingers pointed upward. ''A pithy saying this early in the morning. How refreshing, and from a woman who wears a snood and faux pearls to a premiere.''

Diana's eyes rolled heavenward. "Please, you two, I'm trying to meditate."

"Sorry, love. Close your beautiful eyes again. Now, a little sculpting gel at the roots to give your hair more volume, and we finger-style it." His hands danced rhythmically over her hair. "We lift and we scrunch to give the hair direction."

Fran turned to Laurel, who was sitting nearby. "One of my friends—"

"Her only friend," Guy whispered in Diana's ear.

Glaring his way, Fran advised him, "Guy, being in the same room with you is as much fun as flossing. Will you please hurry up?" Turning to Laurel again, she said, "One of my friends told me that Michael Douglas is scheduled to present an award at the Film Advisory Board's ceremony Thursday night. Do you think we could manage a picture of him with Diana?"

"How about with Kirk instead?"

"Better yet."

"I'll see if he's planning on attending and give you a call this evening."

"I'll be at the apartment until sevenish."

"Remember, love," Guy told Diana, "a diet rich in vitamins, protein and minerals feeds happy hair, and exercise brings circulation to your head and nourishes the follicles." His eyes swept to Fran. "Stress is the number one cause of lackluster hair and scalp conditions like dandruff."

His agile fingers worked Diana's waves a bit more. "There, lovely. I'll be by Wednesday to give you a facial."

"You're an artist," Diana complimented him as she examined her hair in the mirror over the sink. "This style softens these high cheekbones of mine."

"Be thankful. Those cheekbones keep your skin nice and firm." He sent Fran a sideways glance. "Some women are more fortunate than others." Looking back at Diana's reflection in the mirror, he said, "You'll look gorgeous at the awards ceremony. I can see you floating across that stage, the envy of every—"

"Goodbye, Guy," Laurel said in a good-natured tone. "Fran is next."

Once Fran and Diana began to discuss the book, Laurel returned to the library.

While Nick was in San Diego, her days had been filled with routine duties, but her nights had been spent going over what they had found in Tony's office—what they hadn't found, rather: Diana's file.

That twenty-thousand-dollar figure that Nick pointed up to her did sound too coincidental, and she was determined to confront Tony with it. She still found it hard to believe that he would have actually blackmailed Diana. What Laurel hadn't been able to answer, at first, was how he could have found out that she was Diana's daughter. But last night, as she had tossed and turned, it struck her: from his father's old records.

Wayne Koop had been Diana's financial advisor ever since she'd made her first dollar in Hollywood. Glen had stressed the importance of her having an advisor, given the often fleeting nature of stardom. It had been Wayne who had routed checks to the Davises for Laurel's upbringing in Arizona and for her education at the university. If Tony had, for whatever reason, gone over his father's files, he could have put two and two together.

And Laurel was going to find out.

Again she tried to phone him at his beach house; this time he answered.

"Tony, where have you been?" she asked, relieved at having gotten hold of him. "Never mind, I didn't mean to ask that. I need to talk to you. Can I come over now?" She listened briefly. "How about this evening? That's late, but all right, I'll see you then."

She hung up and forced her attention back to the work at hand. Soon she was flipping through the bills that had arrived in the morning mail. She gasped when she saw the total on the one from the garden supply company. Felipe was doing a marvelous job taking care of the grounds, but— "Seven hundred dollars for mulch and fertilizer?" she mumbled, then recalled having approved the purchase.

She dropped the bill onto the pile of others, longing for the day when Diana would be strong enough to be her own person and take charge of her life. She was tired of taking so much on her shoulders, tired of trying to be everything to everybody, tired of having to check every little thing and tired of having to always look ahead to foresee what could possibly go wrong. Would it ever end? she wondered.

Nick arrived at the estate a little after six that evening and found Laurel still at her desk in the library. He explained that the Peters hearing had been delayed until the afternoon and that the defense had requested a continuance until the following Monday, when he would have to reappear before the court again.

Laurel tried to sound interested in what he was saying, but all she could think of was that he was standing right in front of her. She wanted to jump up, throw her arms around his neck and hold him close. Ever since he'd left on Friday, she was forced to realize how much he already meant to her. His absence had left a void in her life that she couldn't ignore. Now that he was back, she felt a giddiness and a contentment that she didn't know how to handle.

Once more Laurel thought of the evening they had walked on the beach at Malibu, and she felt a warmth creep up over her cheeks. Still checking the excitement she felt at seeing him, she said, "You don't know how happy I am to see you again."

"Why? Did anything happen while I was in San Diego?"

She got up from behind her desk and walked slowly around the side of it. "No, it's just that everything is suddenly getting to me. There's just too much going on, and I have an awful feeling that I'm losing control. I'm starting to make mistakes in scheduling for Diana and forgetting purchases that I've approved. It's scary."

He took hold of her shoulders and smiled softly. "Listen, everyone's entitled to make a mistake now and then. It doesn't mean a person's losing control. It only means that you're human like the rest of us. What you need to do is get away from her for a while. How about the two of us going into Santa Barbara for dinner?"

"I'd like that, but I can't, Nick. Ron won't be here, and that would mean Diana would have to eat alone."

"Oh," he said, failing to hide his disappointment.

While driving from San Diego, he'd thought about the two of them having dinner at some quiet little restaurant with dim lights and soft music. Over the weekend, he'd missed Laurel more than he'd ever missed anyone in his entire life, and he'd had to face the fact that his feelings for her were growing stronger by the day. He was certain that she had been happy to see him again, but he was also miffed that he still had to compete with Diana for her attention.

During dinner, Nick's antenna began to pick up some strange signals. Diana's attitude toward him had changed dramatically. Gone was the carefree, friendly lady he'd known her to be. In her place was a guarded, overly polite woman who seemed to be obsessively interested in Nick's political beliefs. When she learned that he had made a business trip to Washington, D.C. the previous year, she left her dinner half finished and excused herself by saying she had to work on her script.

Laurel seemed just as nervous, and where was Ron? Nick wondered. Except for dinner the first night he had arrived at the estate, Ron had taken all his meals with them. Something was up, he decided, but he didn't have a clue as to what.

After dinner, as he and Laurel walked on the terrace, he asked, "Where's Ron?"

"He said he had some business to take care of in town."

"How are he and Diana getting along?"

"Fine," Laurel told him, her features softening.

"Good," he said, deciding that Diana's aloof attitude couldn't be blamed on Ron.

Laurel glanced at her watch. "I think I'll call it a day, Nick."

"So early?"

"I've got some work that has to be done, and tomorrow's going to be hectic."

"Sure, I understand," he lied.

She started to cross the terrace, but halfway to the French doors she turned and smiled warmly. "Thanks for coming back. I wasn't really sure you would."

Returning her smile, he said, "I'm a man of my word."

"Yes," she said softly and entered the house.

A little after 10:00 p.m., Laurel quietly made her way to the garage and drove off in the Mercedes. When she pulled onto the highway, she failed to see Ron driving home from the opposite direction. Seeing Diana's car speeding down the road, he followed it.

CHAPTER TEN

IT WAS AFTER EIGHT when Laurel awoke Tuesday morning—late for her, since she was usually up and about before seven and rarely set the radio alarm. But it had been a little past midnight when she'd arrived back at the house and long past one o'clock when she'd finally been able to sleep.

During the drive back from Tony's, she had vacillated about whether or not to tell Nick what she had learned. Finally she determined that there was no reason she had to, nor did she need the services of a private investigator any longer. She and Diana were home free!

Exhilarated, she tossed back the covers and greeted the new day with a smile, something she hadn't done in quite some time. She showered quickly, humming as the water pelted her body, and got ready for her 9:00 a.m. meeting with Reva.

Dolores and Alicia were carrying fresh linens up the stairs as Laurel started down. "Good morning," she said. "Has Mr. Malone had breakfast yet?"

Alicia giggled. "He told Miss Baxter that he wanted to look at the walls around the estate."

"Thank you," Laurel said cheerfully, and checked her watch, knowing that Diana and Ron would be in the gym now.

In the kitchen, while she had coffee and toast, Laurel discussed upcoming menus with Elena, promising the cook that she would have something more substantial to eat after her morning appointment.

Reva was on time as usual, but in the library, as she removed three gowns from their garment bags, Laurel thought her friend seemed exhausted.

"Diana would look lovely in this," Laurel said, examining the ivory satin dress with an off-the-shoulder white fox trim. She looked over at the gown Reva was holding up. "But I like the beaded bodice on that blue taffeta, too."

Reva ran her fingers over the tight-fitting white gown with the organza ruffles at the skirt that was draped across a chair. "I thought this might be nice for the awards ceremony. Diana has the figure for it."

"No," Laurel said, thinking out loud, "I like the white satin. It has a simple elegance that will look stunning on her . . . no necklace with it, just pearl earrings."

"When I designed it, I had Diana in mind."

"Leave this and the blue taffeta, would you?"

"Sure," Reva said listlessly as she replaced the dress with the Spanish flair into its garment bag. "Damn!" she spit out, and shook the finger she'd caught in the zipper.

"Are you all right?" Laurel asked. "You seem a little uptight this morning. Didn't you sleep well?"

"It's not that. I was at the store taking inventory until after one o'clock this morning."

"That certainly made for a long day." Laurel held up the satin gown. "What will this one run?"

"For you, six hundred and fifty dollars."

Laurel groaned and smiled weakly. At her desk, she made a note in a ledger book and looked over at Reva's drawn expression. Concerned about her, Laurel asked, "How are things between you and Tony?"

Reva turned away, and a lengthy silence passed before she asked blandly, "Tony who?"

"Oh? Trouble in paradise?"

"We're finito, kaput. I would rather you never mentioned his name again."

"Any chance of you and Sam getting back together?"

Reva chuckled bitterly and folded the garment bag over her arm. "He's not even speaking to me. I was an idiot, Laurel, but there's no use crying over spilled milk, is there? Let me know which gown you decide on, and I'll bring out an evening bag to go with it," she said and made a hasty exit.

At the window facing the parking area, Laurel watched her friend get into her car. She felt sorry for Reva and wondered how a man like Tony could sleep at night, considering the wake of misery his affairs left behind.

The ringing of the phone on her desk drew her attention. It was the guard at the gate. A detective from the police department wanted entry to speak with Diana Baxter. Laurel told the guard to pass him through, and she went to the front door. The car pulled up, and the driver waited while another man got out and headed for the house.

Standing at the door, Laurel scrutinized the middle-aged man's unsmiling eyes and pockmarked face. "Yes?"

"Diana Baxter?"

Laurel had to assume he hadn't been to a movie for the past quarter of a century since he was mistaking her for Diana. "I'm Laurel Davis, her personal manager. May I ask why you want to see her?"

He removed a piece of folded black leather from his jacket pocket and flashed an identification badge at her. "Police business. I'm Detective Rodriguez."

Laurel's stomach did a flip-flop, and an ominous foreboding clouded the sunny disposition with which she had arisen. "May I ask what it's in reference to?"

"I need to speak with Diana Baxter."

"Certainly. This way, please," she said, and led him to the salon.

Inside the room, she saw him glance around, and she wondered what possible business he could have with Diana. "I take care of all of Miss Baxter's affairs. Perhaps if you tell me why you're here, I could answer your questions."

When he again insisted on talking to Diana, Laurel asked him to wait and went to the gym. As the two women crossed the entry hall toward the salon, Nick came through the front door. Laurel explained that there was a detective waiting to speak with Diana.

In the salon, Nick went to the man and extended his hand. "I'm Nick Malone. I understand you want to talk to Miss Baxter. Is something wrong?"

Detective Rodriguez shook Nick's hand and looked directly at Diana. "Miss Baxter?"

"Yes," she said, removing the pink sweatband from her head and fluffing her hair.

"Where were you between 11:00 p.m. and midnight last night?"

"I was here at home, in bed. Why?"

"Can that be verified?"

Not liking the intensity of the detective's look, Nick said, "If there's some kind of a problem, perhaps Miss Baxter should have counsel before answering your questions."

"Are you a member of the family?" Rodriguez asked.

"A friend, a good friend. Is there a charge pending?"

"It's merely an investigation at this point."

Laurel asked, "An investigation of what?"

Detective Rodriguez looked at each of them in turn, his dark eyes lingering on Diana. "Tony Koop's death."

In unison the two women gasped, and Nick asked quickly, "How did he die?"

"This morning his neighbor found him lying on the concrete patio under the balcony of his beach house."

"Tony?" Diana murmured, and sank down onto a chair.

Laurel trembled and felt as though her knees had turned to mush. Slowly she sat down, also. Her fingertips felt like ice, yet her eyes were burning. She realized that her world and Diana's had been in jeopardy before, but now it was crumbling around them.

As he placed a hand on Laurel's shoulder, Nick asked, "What does that have to do with Miss Baxter?"

"Late last night," the detective said, "his neighbor was awakened by an argument coming from the decedent's house, then she saw a woman rush to a sky-blue Mercedes with the initials *D.B.* on the front plate. In the morning she went to complain about the ruckus and discovered his body. It appears he fell from his balcony. When we checked the house, we found the contents of Diana Baxter's financial file strewn about the living room."

Nick glanced at the pallor that had washed over Laurel's face. "Was it an accident?" he asked.

"The man reeked of alcohol, but we won't be sure until an autopsy is done." He fixed his eyes on Diana.

"Miss Baxter, were you at Tony Koop's home last night?"

Laurel jumped up from the chair. "I was there, not Miss Baxter. It was her car that I drove."

Shocked, Diana asked, "You were there? But why?"

Laurel's voice shook when she replied, "We had . . . business to discuss."

"In the middle of the night?" the detective asked.

Just as Laurel's lips parted to respond, Nick said, "You don't have to answer any questions until you're advised by an attorney."

The detective shot him an annoyed look.

"No," Laurel said. "That won't be necessary."

"This is merely an investigation," Detective Rodriguez repeated. "At this point there are no charges against anyone." He faced Laurel. "I would like you to come to headquarters to make a statement, Miss Davis." He gave Nick a sideways glance. "If that's all right with Mr. Malone."

Laurel nodded, and Nick said, "I'll drive you there." When the man started to object, Nick added, "We'll be right behind you all the way."

Diana sprang from the chair. "I'll go with you."

"No, please," Laurel said quickly. "Go back to the gym. Let Ron know where we've gone and why."

In the car, Nick again pressed Laurel not to say anything until she spoke with an attorney.

"Why? I don't have anything to hide. When I left Tony, he was very much alive."

Nick pulled out of the parking area and followed Rodriguez's car down the driveway. "What the hell were you doing there last night, anyway? I thought you were exhausted and went to bed."

"I wanted to ask him about Diana's file, the one we couldn't find in his office."

"The same one that the police found on his living room floor, I gather."

"Yes," she said, so quietly he could barely hear her.

Nick felt himself becoming angrier by the minute, but he knew Laurel didn't need his anger right now. Calming his tone, he asked, "What made you confront him like that? Didn't you realize it might have been dangerous? You could have gotten hurt." Just the possibility of that jarred him. He glanced over at her. "Did Tony have a good reason for taking the file home?"

"Diana's account had been twenty thousand dollars short, but he'd replaced the money and was adjusting the records. Just as you thought, he did have a knack for creative accounting. His latest short-selling scheme backfired on him. The stock went up instead of down. He lost forty thousand dollars when he had to buy the stock back and return it to the broker."

"Where did he get the money?"

"Half of it was his own, and—"

"And the other half was the extortion money you paid," he finished for her.

"Yes, but he promised to return it by next month."

Nick didn't feel any better knowing what Laurel had just told him. If the police found out about the blackmail and Tony's death wasn't an accident, they'd see that she had motive, method and opportunity. If the man had been drinking heavily, a woman could have easily pushed him off the balcony.

He covered Laurel's hand with one of his. "How did Tony learn about Diana and the lawyer who was working for the Las Vegas syndicate?"

Laurel hadn't forgotten about that half-truth she'd told Nick, and although she hated doing so, she had to lie to him again. "I didn't ask him."

He looked over at her dubiously. "You didn't?"

"Well, I was upset, and he was upset."

"The loud voices the neighbor heard," Nick guessed.

"We didn't argue," she insisted.

"Who tossed Diana's file all over the place?"

"It was lying on his desk when I left."

"Do you know exactly what time you left?"

"No, but it was just after midnight when I got home."

"How long does it take to get from Tony's beach house?"

"With little traffic, about twenty minutes."

"So you left around 11:40," he said to himself. "And you two didn't really argue?"

"Well, a little," she admitted. "But Tony swore that the information about Diana would never be made public, and I trust him." Lowering her voice, she corrected herself. "I trusted him."

Trust. Nick wanted to trust Laurel now more than ever, but again he had the uncomfortable feeling that she wasn't telling him everything.

He squeezed her hand and said, "Look, we don't know what's ahead of us. If Tony's death was accidental, there's nothing to worry about, but it if wasn't—" He cut himself off. "Don't you think it's about time you told Diana what's been going on? She's not as weak and helpless as you let yourself believe. Besides, right now you could use her support."

Terrified that he might inform Diana about the blackmail, Laurel slipped her hand from Nick's. His doing so would only raise up a lot of ghosts from the past, and that was the last thing she wanted her mother to cope with right now.

Steeling herself, she said, "There's no reason for Diana to be upset, Nick, and with this extortion business over with, I no longer need a private investigator. When we get back to the house, I'll write you a check, and you can return to San Diego."

Her words came like a swift punch in his gut. "Is that what you really want?"

A flash of wild grief ripped through her, and she had to fight to hold back her tears. "It's not a matter of what I want. It's a matter of keeping my priorities in order, and right now Diana has to be at the top of my list."

"Am I anywhere on that list of yours?"

Barely able to breathe, she didn't respond; she just sat rigidly, her fingers digging into her leather purse.

Agitated by her silence, Nick followed the detective's car and swerved into the parking lot next to the police station. Switching the ignition key off, he faced her. "Well, since I'm no longer in your employ," he said in a clipped voice, "you can have this as free advice. When you have time, take a good look at the way you're living, Laurel. Someday you may wake up and find yourself all alone."

With her eyes stinging and her pulse pounding at her temples, she turned away and murmured, "There are worse things than that, Nick."

Contrary to his advice, Laurel gave her statement to the police without benefit of counsel. When she came out of Detective Rodriguez's office, Nick saw that she was in worse shape than she had been when she entered. Quickly he got her out of the police station and suggested they have coffee somewhere.

Wanting some fresh air, Laurel took him to an out-door café that was within walking distance. At the El Paseo, they sat at one of the umbrella tables near the fountain, and Nick ordered two coffees.

While they waited, he noted the desperate look in her eyes and apologized for what he had said to her in the car. "I'm sorry for butting in and telling you how to run your life."

"I'm happy that you cared enough to be concerned about me," she said, trying not to think of anything other than the shoppers walking by in the sunshine.

Nick wanted to say that he was more concerned than she guessed, but it was obvious that she wanted him out of her life, and he couldn't blame her. Whatever had happened to Tony, he knew in his heart that Laurel had nothing to do with it. And he realized that if he were to stay in Santa Barbara, he would only be a reminder of the reason she'd had to hire him in the first place. To even think that she might care for him as much as he already cared for her was ludicrous. Laurel Davis was a woman used to the good life. A life with troubles, yes, but there were a lot of goodies that went with her job. And what was he? A P.I. who didn't know what short selling stocks was all about. Most likely she handled more money in a month than he did in a year.

Laurel took a long swallow of the coffee that was served, and when she put the cup down she saw that her hand was shaking. "Nick," she said in an equally un-steady voice, "thank you for your help and the support you've given me."

He chuckled dryly. "Help? You're the one who tracked down the extortionist."

"I'm the one who got to him first, that's all." She looked deeply into his eyes. "I know I presented you with an impossible job, and I wish—'' she lowered her eyes to her coffee cup ''—I wish that I could have been more open with you from the start. I honestly do.''

"I'm happy for you that the extortion business is over with. Once the police clear up this business of Tony's death, you can get back to a normal life.''

''Normal,'' she repeated, tracing the handle of the cup with a finger. ''My life's never been normal, nor has Diana's.''

Diana again, he thought, and wrestled with the desire to preach to her once again. ''Well,'' he said, ''I guess she's been like a mother to you in a way.''

Laurel's eyes flicked up, but she quickly averted them. ''Yes,'' she whispered, ''she's been very much like a mother to me.'' She took another sip of coffee and said, ''You're fortunate to have your father. I'm sure you understand some of my worrying so much about Diana.''

Nick looked at her oddly. ''Me, worry about Bob? Why? He can take care of himself.''

''*Worry* might not have been the right word, but I'm sure you're concerned about his well-being.''

''I certainly don't dwell on it.''

''But he's your father,'' she insisted.

''That doesn't make me his keeper. Bob goes his way, and I go mine.''

Her nerves on edge, she said indignantly, ''Well, with an attitude like that about your own father, I can see why you don't understand my concerns for Diana.''

''It's been my experience that most people want to be independent. I certainly do, and so does my father.''

''But how can you be so callous about him?''

''Callous?'' Laurel had upset Nick enough already, and now he didn't understand why she was badgering him about being a concerned son. Confused, he asked,

"How the hell does my relationship with my father have anything to do with your problems?"

"It doesn't," she said in a coolly impersonal tone, feeling she was about to come apart at the seams. "But your cavalier attitude toward him certainly tells me something about you."

Exasperated now, Nick asked, "What do you want to hear, that I worship the ground he walks on? That I worry about him the way you do about Diana? Well, I don't."

Feeling like a tightly coiled spring, Laurel finished her coffee and stood. "I'd better get back. Diana's probably in a state by now."

THE DRIVE TO THE ESTATE was made in silence, with the two of them trying to figure out just why they had gotten so upset with each other. Neither was successful.

When they reached the house, both Diana and Ron met them at the door. Laurel had expected her mother to be upset, but Ron seemed even more nervous as he made her go over every detail of what happened at the police station.

"No, Ron," she said for the third time, "I'm not in any trouble. I saw Tony last night, and he was alive when I left. If he started drinking afterward and fell off the balcony, I'm sorry, but I had nothing to do with it."

Nick asked, "He wasn't drinking while you were there?"

"No."

He filed that information away for future reference.

"What will happen to Tony now?" Diana asked Laurel as delicately as she could. "I mean ... well, you know what I mean."

"Wayne's been notified, and he's flying in from Colorado to take care of the funeral arrangements."

"After the autopsy," Ron said, as though to himself.

The anxiety on his face was more than obvious, but Laurel couldn't understand his concern. She knew that Ron detested Tony and the life-style he had led. "Yes, the autopsy is being done today. You know, I think we all need to try to think about something a little less morbid."

"You're right," Diana agreed. "Why don't we drive up the coast for dinner?"

"Nick's returning to San Diego," Laurel informed her, feeling extremely ambivalent about his leaving. She was surprised when Ron spoke up.

"Do you have to take off right away? Why don't you have dinner with us and leave tomorrow? Getting through L.A. is bad enough anytime, but you'd be hitting it at rush hour if you left now."

Laurel felt an instant quickening of her heartbeat. She hated the thought of Nick just walking out of her life, particularly after the harsh words they had had over coffee. She desperately wanted to be with him, if only for a little while longer. Quickly she said, "Ron's right about the traffic. Why don't you stay over?"

The surprising invitation from Laurel would have been more than enough for Nick, but there was something in Ron's frightened eyes that was almost a plea. "All right," he said, "I will." Looking at Diana's cool expression, though, it was quite apparent that she didn't share the others' enthusiasm.

Not one of the foursome brought up the troubles of the day during the drive to the restaurant, just south of Santa Maria, or while they dined on lobster and white wine. Laurel was particularly grateful for that, but she couldn't forget that in the morning Nick would be gone for good. And that would be the end of another brief chapter in her life.

When they arrived back at the estate, Diana took to her room to study her script, declining Laurel's offer to read with her as she usually did, and Ron headed straight to his garage apartment.

"Looks like we've been deserted," Nick remarked as he and Laurel walked alongside the pool.

"I can stand the peace and quiet, believe me," she said, and looked up at the stars.

"Could you stand a swim? I could probably get a bathing suit from Ron."

Pensively she looked out into the darkness, remembering the way Nick had held and kissed her that evening on Malibu Beach. Tired of fighting her battle of personal restraint, she reminded herself that tomorrow Nick would be but a memory. Facing him, she gave in and said, "That would be relaxing, but there are swimsuits in the bathhouse by the pool, all sizes and colors."

In her eyes, Nick saw a glow so warm and intimate that he began to tingle inside. It puzzled him, however. This afternoon she couldn't wait to send him packing, and now she was looking at him in a way that turned his legs to jelly. "Laurel," he said moving closer, "I'm really happy that all your troubles will soon be over—" he placed gentle fingers on the side of her cheek "—but I'm going to miss you."

"No more than I'll miss you," she said honestly, feeling as if she were drowning in his eyes. Becoming flustered by his touch, she stepped back. "Uh...I'll meet you at the pool in a little while."

Nick watched as she hurried back into the house. Why did his neck feel so hot? he wondered, running his hand over it as he ambled to the bathhouse.

Later, when he came down to the pool, Laurel wasn't there yet, so he tossed his short velour robe onto one of the lounge chairs, ran a few steps and dived in. After swimming underwater to the center of the pool, he surfaced, swung his head to the side to shake off the droplets and pushed back the wet hair that draped over one eye.

As he did, he spotted Laurel coming down the steps leading to the pool area. She was wearing a white swimsuit that was molded to each and every curve of her lovely body. Her hips were slender; her legs were long and firm. The sight of her took his breath away.

Even though the water was cool, he felt a searing heat shoot down deep inside his body as he watched her lithe movements. She moved with the same grace that Diana did, and looked a great deal like her in the moonlight. Possibly it was her auburn hair, he thought.

Entranced, he watched as she stepped up onto the diving board and went to the end of it. He saw her pause momentarily, her hands at her sides, then she performed a perfect swan dive and cut the water as cleanly as Diana had that first day he'd met her. Gauging where Laurel would surface, he swam with long, sure strokes.

When her head pierced the water, she opened her eyes to find a smiling Nick directly in front of her. As she brought her hands up to wipe her face, she felt one of Nick's arms move around her waist. Instinctively her own circled his shoulders for support.

Treading water with his strong legs and his other arm, he said, "This is nice, isn't it?"

"Yes," she agreed, and moved her hands slowly over his wet skin.

Laurel tried to control the flurry of sensations rushing through her body at the feel of her breasts pressing against Nick's muscular chest, the warmth of his skin under her hands and the syncopated movement of his thighs along hers. But pent-up emotion and desire long confined exploded within. She slipped her hands around his neck and brought her fingers up into his wet hair.

Just when her attraction to Nick had developed into something more, into something she had refused to recognize, Laurel didn't know. There was one thing she was certain of, however. The overpowering feeling she had for him at this moment was too strong to restrain. The realization of that was at the same time frightening and exhilarating. It was frightening because she knew there was no turning back; it was exhilarating because she didn't want to restrain herself any longer. In the next instant, she pressed her lips to his and kissed him with an urgency that took him by surprise.

CHAPTER ELEVEN

GLORYING IN their shared kiss, Nick stopped treading water and wrapped his other arm around her. With their lips joined, they slowly slipped under the water. He held her firmly against him, and her tresses flowed weight-lessly around their heads. For what seemed like aeons, they drifted silently, aching desire, burning need and wordless love melding them together as one.

When they did surface, Nick found that he could stand on the bottom of the pool. He was breathing heavily; Laurel was, too. She rested her head on his shoulder, her arms still clasped around his neck. He could feel her taut breasts heaving against his chest.

He moved one hand over her back and eased the other downward to press her closer. "Laurel," he whispered, half out of his mind with longing and desire, "I want you so damn badly. Say that you want me, too... please."

As she rocked her forehead against the side of his neck, she answered just as quietly, "I do, Nick...oh, yes."

When his arms tightened around her, she raised her head from his shoulder. In his face, which was tense and filled with wonder, she saw the man of her dreams, the fantasy embodied. During the difficult times that Nick had shared with her, she had found him to be kind, in-telligent and not lacking humor. In one way, though, he was superior to her fantasy man: Nick was not merely attractive; he was beautiful in more ways than she had ever thought a man could be, both inwardly and in form. The realization that he wanted her as much as she wanted him was overwhelming.

"Oh, Nick," she breathed, and like a woman possessed, she moved her hands slowly down from his shoulders. Down she guided them, over the swell of his chest muscles and around to the sides of his firm waist. Emboldened when he closed his eyes and sighed, she eased her fingers past the flurry of hair under the top of his swimsuit.

Nick groaned his pleasure and covered her hand with his, pressing it onto his burgeoning excitement. He gazed at her, his sparkling eyes mirroring his delight, and he kissed her with a tenderness that bespoke of the depth of his feelings for her.

Hand in hand, they waded toward the ladder at the edge of the pool. Before stepping up, Laurel's eyes held his, and a brief moment of hesitation took hold of her, but then she smiled softly and climbed out of the water.

After they towel-dried themselves, they donned their robes and made their way to Laurel's sitting room. She closed the door and gazed over at him with loving eyes. The moonlight streamed in through the sheer yellow drapery panels over the windows, casting a warm glow over his smiling, tanned face.

Laurel stepped out of her sandals and moved slowly to him, the pile of the green carpet soft under her feet. He cupped her face in his hands and kissed her lingeringly as he undid the belt of her robe. It parted, and he guided his hands up over her waist and slowly traced the swell of her breasts before taking the rosebud nipples between his thumbs and index fingers. When her moan passed between their lips, he drew his head back and eased the robe from her shoulders.

"God, you're beautiful," he whispered, drinking in the fullness of her firm breasts, the slenderness of her waist and the graceful curve of her hips. "You're even more lovely than I imagined you would be."

"So are you," she said softly, sending his robe falling to the carpet below on top of hers. For feverish moments their bodies moved together in an ardent embrace, the semidarkness silhouetting them in the muted light of the moon.

Laurel's skin quivered as Nick's hands wandered gently over her, testing, learning and absorbing the feel of her feminine softness. Her hands moved also, her fingertips drifting and trailing, stopping to squeeze and to memorize his masculine form. A swirling agitation built up in her breast and spiraled downward to her silken core as his excitement, hot and hard, nestled against her soft, warm flesh.

Suddenly she found herself being swept off her feet. She wrapped her arms around Nick's neck and rested her head in the crook of his shoulder. He saw the open door leading to her bedroom. With sure steps he carried her inside and gently laid her down on the quilted floral spread.

The satiny material was cool under her body, a lovely sensation that tempered the sensual fire she felt building deep inside her. Nick placed a knee on the bed and gazed down at her prone figure, but she was anxious to feel him close once more.

When she extended her arms to him, he sat beside her, took her hands in his and kissed each palm. In a husky voice he said, "I want to please you. Tell me how I can."

She smiled languidly. "Just being here with you like this pleases me."

"No, I want you to be ecstatically happy, just as I am. Do you like this?" He leaned down and slowly moved his tongue over the purple-rose tip of one breast and then the other, circling and laving each in turn.

"Yes, oh, yes," she moaned, losing herself in the exquisite feel of the moist warmth of his tongue. She grasped his broad shoulders when he began to suckle lovingly, then dug her fingers into his skin when a flurry of delightful sensations rippled down across her abdomen.

"And this?" he asked. He began a slow trail of kisses down over her stomach, feeling her muscles contract under his lips as he paused to kiss her smooth, white skin.

For a while he lay crouched next to her, his cheek on her warm belly, moving a hand down and then up one slender leg until his thumb grazed her inner thigh. Tenderly he stroked the silky strands that glowed like amber in the moonlit room. He didn't have to ask if that pleased her; under his cheek he could feel her taking short, ragged breaths.

Laurel sighed when she felt his hand settle and he began a slow pressing motion with the heel of his palm. Suddenly she was floating weightlessly, a feeling similar to the one she'd experienced during their underwater kiss. She moaned when his fingers began a sensual, searching probe. Tilting her head back on the pillow, she guided a hand around his neck and ran her fingers through his damp hair. "Nick," she whispered, gasping when he discovered her secret place, then giving herself over to the exhilaration of his loving ministrations.

With great effort, he fought against the overwhelming craving he had to satisfy the delightful agony that pulsated at his groin. Intoxicated with the sensual feel of her, he murmured her name and sunk his lips onto that place his loving strokes had prepared.

She felt a dizzying, voluptuous pleasure spiral through her as his tongue entered and began its sweet caresses. Her toes and fingers tingled, her legs stiffened and she grasped the back of his head and shuddered. Then she was floating once more, drifting aimlessly, happily.

But only for moments. With closed eyes and her arms stretched out over the bedcover, she felt a velvety force slowly ease into her moist cocoon. She gasped again, wadded the quilt in her hands. The shock passed quickly, and she concentrated on the thrilling sensation.

When he lifted his face to look at her, she opened her eyes, smiled up at him and extended her arms to him again. "Now," she whispered, her one-word plea barely audible.

Nick lowered himself slowly, and Laurel's breath caught when a tantalizing thrust filled her completely. Never had she experienced such an elated feeling of oneness with another human being.

"Oh, love," he murmured in a raspy voice, wrapping his arms around her, his eyes aglow with wonder and joy.

"Kiss me, Nick," she pleaded, and welcomed his lips once more.

With each slow thrust, she felt her own excitement build anew, and soon she began to soar once more. How wondrous was the feeling of total unity with the man in her arms, the man who was carrying her higher and higher in their love-locked embrace!

For a long while they lay together in silence, both of them trying to get a grasp on reality. When her thinking cleared, Laurel became truly aware of the situation she found herself in. As wonderful as being in Nick's arms was, she had to ask herself what she might be letting herself in for if she permitted herself to fall in love with him. Of course, she hadn't yet. Or had she? she wondered.

No, she convinced herself immediately. What existed between them was merely an overpowering physical attraction. No more, no less. So what was the problem? she asked herself as Nick stirred.

"Asleep?" he asked softly.

"No," she replied, then slowly moved her hand over his warm chest, delighting in the silky feel of the soft hair under her fingertips.

"I don't know about you," he said, grinning in the semidarkness, "but I feel like I've just been to heaven and back." He kissed her forehead. "I've got an angel in my arms to prove it."

Laurel's lips spread in a serene smile. "That's a pretty lofty image to live up to."

"Not for an angel. Listen," he said in hushed tones, "when this business about Tony's death is cleared up, come down to San Diego for a few days or a week maybe and be my guest for a change. We have so much to learn about each other."

The idea sounded glorious to Laurel, but instantly the reality of the obligations that controlled her life came into play, and she knew that as much as she wanted to, she couldn't accept his offer. "I can't," she said quietly.

Nick raised himself onto his arm and offered her an irresistibly devastating smile. Jokingly he said, "Just because I'm throwing myself at you, I don't want you to think I'm not constantly pursued by lovely ladies in San Diego.''

"I believe that, Mr. Malone, and I'm flattered that you want me instead."

His voice turned serious. "You need some time away from here, Laurel. You're trying to handle too many things all by yourself. You need someone to—"

She placed her fingers on his lips and said sadly, "I don't need anyone, Nick. I'm used to going it alone. As you said—" she had to force the words out "—I'm extremely dedicated to my job."

"Doesn't it bother you that your dedication might cost others a great deal? Please, don't decide about San Diego this minute. Take some time to think about it."

She turned her head to avoid his eyes. "I don't have to. I just can't take time off now."

"Because of Diana?"

"I can't get distracted right now, not when she's so close to getting her career on track again."

"Distracted? Is that what I am . . . a distraction?"

"A bad choice of words," she apologized, looking back at him, "but you know what I mean. You see how much she depends on me."

"You need that, don't you?"

"Need it? Of course not. It's just a fact."

Nick turned away, took a deep breath and exhaled it in one long, tense sigh. "Wanting to help your employer is admirable, but you should be concerned with your own happiness, as well."

With less than total conviction, she said, "If Diana's happy, then I am."

"Are you really so content to live your life vicariously through Diana Baxter?"

Laurel lifted herself onto her elbows and tried to sound reasonable. "I lead an extremely satisfying life."

"A satisfying love life, too?"

"My love life is none of your business," she snapped before she could stop herself. But the moment Laurel realized what she had said, she felt an overwhelming sense of loss.

Nick did, also, and he understood what she was telling him. As far as she was concerned, what they had just experienced together had nothing to do with love. Sitting up, he placed his feet on the carpet and glanced back at her. "You know," he said huskily, "you're a great cure for happiness." He pushed himself up from the bed and stalked toward the sitting room.

"Nick!" she called, but he didn't stop. Jumping up, she rushed to the closet and grabbed a blue silk robe. She shrugged into it as she hurried to the door of the bedroom. He had his robe on and was about to leave. "Wait!" she cried.

"For what?"

"For my apology." She ran her fingers through her hair, sounding confused when she tried to explain. "I don't know why I said what I did, but I've had a bad day, remember?"

"Is that why we wound up—" he nodded toward the bedroom "—in there? Because you had a bad day?"

"I hope you don't really believe that," she said quietly, feeling as though an enormous weight were pushing at her chest.

Nick reached for the doorknob, but then he looked back at her. "What kind of game are you playing? You float into my life, and when I take notice, you have no qualms about putting me in my place very quickly."

Hearing the hurt in his voice, she wanted to rush to him, to hold him and tell him that he meant so very much to her. She wanted to tell him that the time they had just shared together had been the most beautiful in her life. She wanted to, but she couldn't.

Maybe it will be simpler this way, she told herself. Cutting their relationship off quickly and cleanly, Nick would go his way and she would continue on in the only way she knew how—taking care of the responsibilities that life had dealt her.

In a thread of voice, she murmured, "I'm sorry, Nick, so very sorry." Slowly she turned and withdrew to the bedroom.

THE EARLY MORNING SUN streamed through the windows in Nick's room as he finished packing his suitcase. When he heard a knock at his door, he thought that it might be Laurel. Hopefully he said, "Come on in," but his smile evaporated when Ron entered.

"You're leaving?" Ron asked.

"That was the arrangement," Nick reminded him. "Dinner and a bed for the night."

Hooking his thumbs on the waistband of his slacks, Ron asked, "Do you have to go?"

About to give the bathroom cabinet a final check, Nick stopped midway and scrutinized Ron's face. He saw the same worried look in the trainer's eyes that he had noted the previous night when Ron had asked him to have dinner and stay over. Smiling, Nick asked, "Have you really grown that attached to me?"

"I'm thinking about Laurel."

"Laurel? I doubt if she'd want me to stay any longer than necessary."

"Well, it may be necessary."

"What's that supposed to mean?"

"You're a private investigator, and she's your client, right?"

"She was my client."

"Couldn't you just stick around until after the autopsy?"

"Why?"

"Damn it, man! Laurel could be in big trouble."

Nick eyed him questioningly. "She won't be if the autopsy shows that Tony's death was an accident."

"And if it wasn't?"

"Is there something you want to tell me, Ron?"

"I'm just worried about Laurel, that's all. If Tony's death turns out...not to have been accidental, won't the police come down on her?"

"Not if they find that she's told them the truth. You believe she did, don't you?"

"Of course I do. It's just that...look, couldn't you stay on until after the autopsy is finished? That couldn't take more than a day or two, if that long."

Now Nick started to worry. He'd had complete faith in Laurel's story that Tony had been alive when she'd left him, and he'd felt certain the police couldn't prove otherwise. But now Ron had him wondering.

"I could stay if I'm invited, but I don't think that's likely."

"Would you stay if Diana asked you to?"

"I seriously doubt that she would."

"She will. Leave it to me." Ron looked away briefly, then asked, "What makes you think Laurel wants you to leave?"

"What makes you think she doesn't?"

"There's a good view of the pool from the garage. I watched you and her last night."

"For how long?"

"Long enough to think that you care what happens to her," he replied and started toward the door.

"Ron," Nick called, and the man turned. "The people in this house get stranger and stranger. Is it me, or do you see it that way, too?"

"It's not your ordinary household, is it?" he remarked and glanced at the suitcase on the bed. "Might as well unpack, Nick. I'll talk to Diana now."

Nick cocked his head, wondering what Laurel would think.

After unpacking, he went downstairs to find out, but on his way to the library, he saw Carlos let Guy in at the front door.

"Hey, how're you doing?" Nick greeted the other man as he crossed the entry hall.

"Don't ask." Guy scrunched his face. "Have you heard about Tony?"

"Awful, isn't it?" Nick placed an arm around Guy's shoulder and headed him toward the salon. "Got a minute?"

"Only a minute. Sheila's got the bug, so I'm taking her appointments today."

Once inside the salon, Nick guided him to the far side by the windows. "It's a shame about Tony. I understand that you were a good friend of his."

"Hardly. Where did you get that idea?"

"Tony told Laurel that he had loaned you the money for your mobile unit. Only a good friend would do that."

"It wasn't a loan," Guy insisted forcefully. "Tony made some investments for me."

"Oh. I guess he wasn't so generous, after all."

"Tony didn't have a generous bone in his body. Anything anybody ever got from that bastard was earned, and usually the hard way. You know, it's a shame. He had a lot going for him, but, man, inside he was a bundle of nerves."

"Real bad, huh?"

"Bad? The guy could have a nervous breakdown trying to fold a fitted sheet. He popped Valium like Life Savers."

"Valium and alcohol," Nick mumbled to himself. "So, Tony could have fallen off his balcony."

"Who'd have thought he'd die that way? I always figured he'd go out with a case of terminal orgasm." Guy checked his watch. "I gotta run. Diana's waiting for her facial." He patted Nick's arm. "You take care, big guy, and remember to use some conditioner on that hair of yours."

"I'll do that," Nick promised, thinking that the twenty thousand dollars Tony had loaned Guy was a gift now. And wasn't that nice for Guy.

But the information about Tony's Valium habit and the fact that he had reeked of alcohol when his body was discovered made Nick feel a little better. It the autopsy indicated that the drugs and alcohol were in his system, Laurel wouldn't have a thing to worry about—and she was Nick's main concern. Nodding to himself, he went to the library to see how she'd take the matter of his not returning to San Diego just yet.

The door was halfway open, so he stepped into the room. Reva was with her, and he caught the tail end of what she was saying to Laurel.

"...and I'm certainly not going to cry for Tony. He got just what he deserved." Reva saw Laurel's attention go to the door, and she turned. "Hi, Nick. How's the security business?"

"Under lock and key," he joked, then shifted his eyes to Laurel. "Sorry, I didn't know you were busy. I'll catch you later."

"Later? You're not leaving?"

Hoping he was right, he said, "Diana wants me to stay on for a day or two."

That didn't sound like the Diana she knew, Laurel thought. "Reva, excuse me for just a minute." She went to Nick and gave him a look that said *I don't believe that.*

Outside the library, she asked, "What's this about Diana asking you not to leave?"

With an innocent expression plastered on his face, Nick shrugged. "That's what Ron told me."

"Why would she do that?"

"Maybe she's anxious about this autopsy business, just as you are."

"What? Why should I be anxious about that?"

"Just a crazy guess."

"Crazy is right." She glanced back toward the library door. "I've got to finish with Reva. We'll talk later, all right?"

"Sure. I'm your guest here."

"Diana's guest," she corrected him, and went back inside.

Immediately after Reva left, Laurel charged upstairs to talk to Diana. She found her sitting on the love seat, going over her script.

"Did Reva bring the beaded purse?" Diana asked.

"No, she forgot it, but she changed the clasp on the fox trim." Joining Diana, she inquired, "Why did you want Nick to stay?"

"It was Ron's idea. He's worried about this police business, although I don't know how he thinks a security consultant can help."

But a private investigator might be able to, Laurel thought.

Laurel had actually wanted Nick at her side until she was totally cleared of any implication in Tony's death, but after what had happened between them, she hadn't seen how she could ask him to stand by her. Now she was grateful that Ron had.

Diana observed Laurel's expression as it softened. "You really like Nick, don't you?"

"Yes, don't you?"

Lifting her eyebrows, Diana's voice turned chilly. "I did at first, but when he mentioned Garrison's name— Well, I guess it upset me more than it should have." Diana placed her fingers along the side of her throat, then asked, "Just how much do you like Nick? Is it serious?"

"No, not really," Laurel told her, not wanting to think of what might have been.

"Well, good. I was afraid you might be falling in love with him. I should have known better. You haven't really been acquainted that long."

Sadly Laurel lowered her eyes. "No, we haven't been, and love at first sight happens only on the silver screen, doesn't it?"

"It was that way with Garrison and me."

Laurel's eyes darted to her mother's. "Must you keep bringing him up?"

"Darling, I know how you feel about him, but after all these years—"

"After all these years," Laurel interrupted, "are you beginning to forget what he did to you?"

"It wasn't all Garrison's fault. I've told you that it—" The knock at the sitting-room door drew her attention. "Yes?"

Ron opened it. He looked terrified. "Detective Rodriguez is here. He wants to talk to Laurel."

Wide-eyed, the two women glanced at each other. "Find Nick," Laurel said quickly, "and ask him to meet us downstairs."

In the salon, Laurel greeted Detective Rodriguez, and Diana took a seat on the sofa.

"Has the autopsy been completed?" Laurel inquired.

"Yes. I'd like to ask you a few questions."

When Laurel saw Nick and Ron enter, she told them, "The autopsy has been done."

Ron sat down next to Diana, and Nick stood at Laurel's side. "The results?" he asked.

Ignoring his question, Rodriguez asked Laurel, "What time did you leave the decedent's home Monday night?"

"Approximately eleven-thirty or a little thereafter," Nick said.

Rodriguez aimed his steely dark eyes at him. "I was asking Miss Davis."

Laurel said, "Between eleven-thirty and eleven-forty at the latest."

"How can you be so certain?" the detective asked.

"Because I was back here shortly after midnight."

"How shortly?"

"Five minutes after, perhaps. Why?"

"The medical examiner places Tony Koop's death around midnight."

"So," Nick said, smiling, "Miss Davis has nothing more to tell you."

Rodriguez faced him. "Miss Davis and I both speak English very well. There's no need for you to speak for her, unless you're her attorney."

"Nick is right," Laurel said. "There's nothing more I can tell you than I already have. Tony and I had business to discuss. He was fine when I left."

"While you were there, had he been drinking?

"No."

Diana rose from the sofa and clasped her hands in front of her. "Why are you asking all of these questions?"

"I'm sorry, Miss Baxter, but it is necessary." He fixed his eyes on Laurel again. "No appreciable amount of alcohol was found in the decedent's system."

"Any drugs?" Nick asked.

The detective shook his head. "Apparently someone doused his shirt with bourbon."

"Did you check for fingerprints on the bottles?"

"Mr....Malone, is it?" Rodriguez asked calmly, and Nick smiled. "As an interested citizen, you're to be commended, but I've been conducting investigations for almost twenty years. I know how to do my job."

"No fingerprints, I take it."

"The bourbon bottle was wiped clean." He faced Laurel once more. "I'd like you to come to headquarters with me now, Miss Davis."

"Why?" she asked.

"For one thing, a positive identification by the decedent's neighbor."

"And?" Nick asked, placing a hand on Laurel's shoulders.

"The results of the autopsy indicate that Tony Koop was dead before someone threw him off the balcony."

A thundering silence hovered over the group in the salon before Diana rushed to her daughter and took hold of her arm. To the detective, she said, "You can't possibly believe Laurel had anything to do with Tony's death."

"Please, Diana. I'm certain they just want to question me again."

"I'm afraid it's more serious than that, Miss Davis," Detective Rodriguez said. "You have the right to remain silent. If you give up that right—"

"No!" Ron shouted, coming forward. "I was at Tony's beach house after Laurel left."

"Don't say anything," Nick warned him.

Flashing an intense look at Laurel, Ron said, "We had a fight, and I—I killed him."

CHAPTER TWELVE

IN THE DEATHLY SILENCE that followed, all eyes focused on Ron. Diana took one of his hands in hers. "What are you saying?"

Tiny beads of perspiration formed over his upper lip, and he swallowed hard. "I saw your Mercedes pull out of the driveway. I thought it was you, and I followed it." He looked at Laurel, then at Rodriguez. "I saw Laurel rush out of the beach house, and I went inside to find out what was going on. Tony and I argued, and—"

"About what?" the detective asked.

"What difference does it make?" Ron asked curtly. "I hit him, but I didn't mean to kill him. When I saw that he was dead, I sprinkled some bourbon on him, wiped the bottle off, and—and I hoped to make it look like an accident by—"

"By throwing his body over the balcony," Rodriguez completed his sentence for him, and Ron nodded.

After reading Ron his rights, the detective took him into custody.

With terrified eyes, Diana hurried to the window and watched Ron get into the back seat of a car with Rodriguez as another man got in the front and drove down the driveway. Stunned, she turned and scurried to the bar cart that had, in recent years, been used for guests only. She pulled off the crystal top of a decanter and poured herself a Scotch.

Laurel rushed across the room, and in one swift movement she grabbed the glass from her, spilling half of the contents on the carpet. "Getting back to where you were six years ago won't solve anything!" she cried, feeling that she, too, was at the breaking point. "Filming begins next week!"

With one hand on her hip, the other at her forehead, Diana screamed, "To hell with the filming! I'm staying right here to help Ron."

Laurel looked over at Nick with pleading eyes, hoping for his support in dealing with Diana, but he remained silent, watching the two of them. Taking hold of her mother's shoulders, she spoke as calmly as she could. "I'll obtain the best lawyer there is for Ron. By walking out on your contract and messing up your life again, you'll only hurt him. If you really want to help, let him see that his years of work weren't in vain."

"I can't." Diana moaned. "Don't you see that?"

Rushing to the mantel over the fireplace, Laurel snatched up one of the two Oscars Diana had won. With her other hand she grabbed the Tony Award that the star had received years ago for a Broadway performance. Holding the two statues out, Laurel's voice rose in pitch. "You *can* do it. You're supposed to be an actress!"

Nick sympathized with Diana when she slumped against a high-back chair and grasped it with trembling fingers. In a restrained voice he said to Laurel, "There are more important things in life than making a movie."

"Stay out of this, Nick," Laurel shot back. "Nothing or no one is more important to me right now than seeing Diana succeed in *Winner Takes All*." She faced Diana, and her features hardened. "We've all worked too hard to get your career going again."

Diana held out a supplicating hand to her daughter. In a desperate voice she cried, "Why did we? What for?"

Stunned by the questions, Laurel's voice shook when she responded. "Because it was . . . what you needed . . . and what you wanted."

Tormented by thoughts of Ron's arrest, Diana blurted out, "What I wanted, or what *you* wanted?"

Dazed and shocked by her mother's question, confusion disrupted Laurel's thinking momentarily, and a glazed look of despair spread over her face. Almost immediately she explained away Diana's ludicrous accusation by telling herself that her mother was half out of her mind with worry.

Softly Nick said, "Diana has a point."

Laurel's shock yielded quickly to anger, and she flashed him a look of disdain. "You don't know what you're talking about."

"Please," Diana pleaded, "stop it, both of you!"

Nick examined the dejected expression on Laurel's face as Diana rushed from the room. He wasn't certain if it was born of hurt or disappointment. He knew both women were miserable, but his heart went out to Diana a little more when he saw Laurel look at the awards she was holding and grimace.

In a low, tormented voice, she mumbled, "Life has a nasty way of surprising us, doesn't it?" Slowly she replaced the statues on the mantel, leaned an arm on it and covered her eyes with her fingers.

"We don't always get what we want out of life." Nick remarked quietly. When she didn't respond, he moved closer. "I'm sorry things didn't work out the way you hoped they would."

Slowly the fingers that blanketed her eyes slipped down, and she stared at him in silence before saying snidely, "Thank you for your help."

"I'd like to help both of you, not just one or the other. If you're worried about getting another job, you shouldn't be. With your dedication, I imagine that any number of stars would be more than happy to have you run their lives for them."

"A job," she repeated, too exhausted to be angry. "Is that what you think I'm worried about?"

"I hope not."

Laurel sighed deeply and stepped slowly away from the fireplace. She clasped her arms and, as though thinking out loud, said, "Maybe I should just walk away from everything and start a new life for myself." Her low laugh was weak and distorted in sound. "I wouldn't even know how to begin." Her thoughts in turmoil, she asked, "By turning my back on Diana? On Ron?"

"On me, too?"

Laurel was concentrating so hard, she didn't hear his question. She faced him, her expression desperate. "I don't know how to do anything else other than keep Diana going. And if I walk away, she'll fall apart again—and Ron won't be here to help her this time."

"Maybe she won't fall apart," Nick suggested.

"And what do you say if she does? 'Oops, guess I was wrong.' No, I'm going to stick by her, whether she likes it or not."

"Admirable trait, loyalty," he commented, knowing she had made up her mind.

"Somehow, some way," she said, pacing and speaking to herself again, "she's got to do the damn picture." Stopping, she faced Nick, and her brow drew together in an agonized expression. "But how? What do I do?"

He realized that there would be little chance of convincing her to look at things from Diana's point of view. And again Laurel was asking for his help. Feeling about her the way he did, he knew he couldn't refuse her.

"First of all," he said, "we've got to think about Ron. I have a funny feeling about the story he told Rodriguez. Brawn is one thing, but Ron has intelligence, also. It's my guess that he's too aware of his strength to let it get out of control as he said he did."

"You don't believe his story?"

"It's possible he could be covering up for someone."

The shock of his insinuation hit her full force. Amazed, she asked, "You think he's covering for me, don't you?"

"I didn't say that."

"Then for whom?"

"That's one of the other pieces we've got to take a good look at. Maybe we could find some answers at Tony's beach house. And we don't have a great deal of time. You said it yourself—Diana's scheduled to go before the cameras next week."

NICK TIMED THE DRIVE to the beach house that was just north of Santa Barbara. It took exactly twenty-one minutes. Following Laurel's directions, he turned off the highway onto a paved road, then onto a shell-and-rock road that curved around the orange-brown bluffs at the edge of the Pacific.

"It's the second house," Laurel said.

He studied the two homes, noting that they were separated by approximately forty feet. Tony's was a little higher than the first. Both had been built on stilts that now were blue-gray in color and hued by weather and time. Each had concrete patios under wooden decks that looked out over the wide expanse of ocean.

"Look," Laurel said, indicating the yellow police-barricade tape that had been set up around Tony's house. "That means we can't go in."

"It means we shouldn't," he said, and parked in the first driveway. "I hope his neighbors work days."

As Laurel got out of Nick's car, she felt a brisk breeze coming off the water. The afternoon sun was warm on her face. Snowy-white sea gulls and slender-winged terns competed for space along the beach in front of the churning breakers. She glanced up at the few languid clouds that drifted overhead, moving toward the Santa Ynez mountain range, and she thought about how tranquil the scene was. But when she turned toward Tony's house, she thought of the last time she had seen him. It had not been so tranquil then.

Following Nick toward the back of Tony's house, she asked, "What if the police are still here?"

"There are no cars around, but if someone is up there working, we'll be scolded for crossing the barricade tape and told to go away."

At the top of the landing, he knocked on the door and waited. No response. "Where did Tony hide that key?"

"In the lantern there. Reva told me the side panel opens."

Nick grasped the side of the lantern, and when it opened he felt around inside. "Bingo," he said and removed a key. After unlocking the door, he returned the key to its place.

Inside, Laurel asked, "What are we looking for?"

"I don't know."

"You don't know? And you make a living doing this?"

He looked at her over his shoulder. "I've got a car that's paid for and a savings account in five figures." On the wall to his right he noticed several photographs of a man with different people. Diana was in one of them. "That's Tony, I assume."

"With some of his clients."

"Tall, wasn't he? He must have been around six-foot-two or -three. I'd say he was pushing two hundred pounds." He glanced at Laurel's slender body. "Too much for most women to drag around and lift over a railing. From what Rodriguez said, he didn't jump over."

"Nick, don't be light about it. Diana and I liked Tony."

"Not too much, I hope."

"Enough for her to bring him back a jade replica of the Eiffel Tower from Paris." She turned toward the end of the bar along the adjacent wall. Not seeing the replica, she said, "That's strange. Tony always kept it right there on the bar. He was proud of it and said it made a good conversation piece."

Nick scanned the shelves behind the mahogany bar. He didn't see a replica of the Eiffel Tower, but what he saw interested him more. Moving behind the bar, he studied but didn't touch the gold cigarette lighter with the ruby stone in it that lay near an assortment of bottles. "The man must have bought them by the gross."

"Bought what?"

"That cigarette lighter there."

"It's not Tony's. He didn't smoke."

"A lady friend's, perhaps," Nick said thoughtfully.

Laurel went to the desk at the far side of the room and picked up a folder. "It's Diana's financial file, the one Tony showed me to prove that he'd replaced the money."

"Better leave it be. The police probably aren't through here." While he looked around the room, his eyes returned to the pictures of Tony on the wall. "Who'll be taking care of Diana's finances now?"

"One of his partners, if everything is all right after I have her account audited."

"You'll still be out twenty thousand dollars."

"I know," she replied dismally.

Nick scanned the tweed rug carefully, his eyes darting left and right, then he opened the sliding glass door to the deck. At the wooden railing, he glanced down at the concrete some twenty-five feet below and noted the white outline the police had left to indicate where Tony had landed.

When he reentered the living room his searching eyes spotted a nasal inhaler sticking out from under the sofa. He looked back at Laurel, who was standing by the bar. "Did Tony have sinus problems or hay fever?"

"Not that I know of. Why?"

"Just wondering," he said, recalling that Fran had taken a nasal inhaler from her purse the day he had met her at the estate. "Do you know where he kept his personal papers? I'd love to find out who his beneficiary is."

"No, but I imagine he had a safe-deposit box. That's where I keep many of Diana's important papers. Since he never married, Wayne, his father, is probably the beneficiary."

"Maybe so. See if anything looks out of place to you in here while I check the bedroom."

The moment Nick left the room, Laurel dashed behind the bar and quietly opened a cabinet door she'd seen Tony use. There, in a divided rack on a shelf, were a number of file folders, and she went through them until she found a slender one with Diana's name on it. Inside Laurel saw several financial statements that dated back to the year she had been born. Quickly she shoved the file into her tote bag.

"Find anything?" Nick asked when he came back into the living room.

"No. Did you?"

"Only that the man had enough clothes to open his own store. Well, we'd better not push our luck. Let's get out of here."

DURING DINNER, neither Laurel nor Diana had much of an appetite, and while they picked at the roast beef and parsley potatoes, Nick felt a little guilty in doing justice to Elena's delicious cooking.

Toying with her delicate crystal wineglass, Diana asked Laurel in a listless voice, "Did the attorney you spoke with in San Francisco think he'd be able to get Ron released on bail?"

"He said he would try to, but he wouldn't know until he arrived in the morning and had a chance to go over whatever charges the police come up with against Ron."

Attempting to brighten the scenario, Nick said, "His lawyer shouldn't have a great deal of trouble getting him out on bail if the charge is manslaughter. After all, there was no intent. It was accidental. Ron didn't mean to kill Tony."

"Do you think we should phone the lawyer again? Maybe he—" Diana stopped midsentence. "Ron!" she cried out, and rushed to the archway where he stood.

Laurel and Nick followed immediately, all three of them asking questions at the same time.

Looking exhausted—so unlike him—Ron held up a hand. "I'll tell you everything, but you know what I'd love right now?"

"Anything, Ron, anything," Diana said, flushed.

"A cold beer."

"Carlos," she said to the ever-present hired man, "would you please bring Ron one? We'll be in the salon." She latched onto Ron's arm and headed across the entryway.

In the salon they grouped around him, and Nick asked, "Are you out on bail?"

"R.O.R., released on my own recognizance pending charges."

Laurel asked, "What charges?"

"I guess they have to figure that out."

Nick looked at him dubiously. "You mean Rodriguez didn't know what to charge you with?"

When Carlos came in carrying a tray, Ron left the glass and took only the bottle and the napkin. After a long swallow of beer, he slumped down on the sofa next to Diana. Looking up at Nick, he said, "Rodriguez kept asking me exactly how I killed Tony. I told him time and again that I hit him, and he fell down, that I checked for a pulse, but there was none. I guessed he'd either had a heart attack or I'd just hit him too hard and something happened to his brain. Rodriguez kept wanting to know *where* I had hit him and *how* he fell." Ron took another long drink of beer.

"And?" Nick asked.

"I told him that I hit Tony on the jaw." He glanced uneasily over at Laurel, who was seated across from him, listening intently. "Then Rodriguez said he didn't think that I had killed Tony."

"What?" Diana asked, beaming.

Nick noted the surprised expression on Laurel's face as Ron continued.

"He told me that the autopsy report showed no bruises on the face from a fight as I described it, and—" he had trouble keeping his eyes off of Laurel "—and that Tony had died from being struck on the back of the head with a blunt instrument."

"So what possible charges could they have against you?" Diana asked, wanting to believe that everything was settled.

Her smile evaporated when Nick said, "Probably interference with a police investigation and maybe even conspiracy."

Leaning forward, Laurel asked nervously, "Does Detective Rodriguez have any idea who could have killed Tony?"

Ron lowered his eyes. "I don't know. He told me that during his twenty years of investigating murders, he'd come across people confessing to protect someone else. He said it didn't usually work and asked me what really happened." He fixed his eyes on Laurel. "I told him."

"What?" Nick asked, seeing the anxious anticipation on Laurel's face.

Ron placed his beer down on the table next to him, clasped his large hands and began rubbing them together. His eyes slipped nervously over to Laurel. "I did think you were Diana when you drove away, but on the highway I got close enough to see that it was you. I followed you because I thought that wherever you were going, it might have something to do with the—" he almost said blackmail "—with the reason you thought we needed more security around here. When you pulled off the highway, I knew you were heading for Tony's, so I parked on the road above and waited until you came out."

"Then you went into the beach house," Nick concluded.

"No, I started to follow Laurel home, but halfway here, I decided to go back and have a talk with Tony."

"Why, Ron?" Diana asked, perplexed.

Ruffled by the direct question, his voice rose in pitch. "Wouldn't you wonder why Laurel was at Tony's in the middle of the night? You know the kind of a reputation he had. I was worried about her."

Diana looked over at Laurel. "Darling, what *were* you doing at Tony's beach house?"

Laurel had known the question would come up eventually, and she had prepared for it. "I didn't want to worry you, but Tony had been having some financial setbacks in the stock market. I needed to go over your account with him to make certain your investments weren't affected."

"Were they?" Diana asked.

"No, not at all."

"Well, that's good. We really don't have great difficulties, do we?" She grasped Ron's arm tightly. "Oh, but then you found Tony."

Ron nodded. "He was dead, and I thought that—that Laurel had killed him, so I tried to make it look like he'd had an accident."

"You were trying to protect her!" Diana sang out. "Oh, Ron, that was so good of you, but you should have known better. Laurel couldn't possibly kill anybody."

Nick wished like hell that he could prove that, but right now he knew it would be impossible.

Resting back against the chair, Laurel said quietly, "I'm not at all sure Detective Rodriguez would agree with you, Diana. He probably sees me as his number-one suspect."

"Not necessarily," Nick said. "Rodriguez would have been here by now. But I'm sure he'll want to talk to you again and get that positive identification from the neighbor who saw you leave." He looked down at Ron. "Think hard. Do you remember seeing anything near the body, anything that could have been used as the murder weapon?"

Ron shook his head. "The minute I saw him lying there—"

"Where?" Nick asked.

"He was behind the bar. It looked like he'd been going through that cabinet with the files in it."

"Cabinet?" Nick's eyes went to Laurel, and he saw her look away. "What cabinet?"

"The one in back of the bar," Ron told him. "The door was open, and I had to shut it to pick Tony up."

"Oh, please," Diana said, "no more about Tony. Laurel, shouldn't you phone San Francisco and let the attorney know that Ron's been released?"

"I'll do that right now," she said, and headed quickly for the library.

Seeing the tender way Diana was smiling at Ron, Nick followed Laurel out of the salon.

"Ron," Diana said sincerely, "that was so sweet of you to worry about Laurel like that, but you took an awful chance."

He leaned back on the sofa and rested his head against it. "I didn't do it for Laurel. I did it for you. I know how much you think of your personal manager."

Diana heard the bitter tone in his last two words, and a wave of apprehension swept through her. "Don't be jealous of Laurel, please. I want the two of you to be the best of friends."

"How can I feel otherwise?" he asked, tilting his head toward her. "She runs your life, tells you which jobs you can or can't take. She plans your days and even dictates what you'll wear at the damn awards ceremony."

Not wanting him to cause a scene within Laurel's earshot, Diana asked him to go upstairs with her, and when they reached her sitting room, she closed the door.

"I won't have you saying anything against Laurel. Yes, she is important to me, more so than you'd like, perhaps, but she was there for me when no one else gave a damn. If you thought I was a mess when you first arrived here, you should have seen me during the two years that Laurel cared for me almost single-handedly."

She took quick steps toward the fireplace and turned, softening her tone. "Since you've been here, you've seen how she protects me. Without her, I'd still be a basket case. Laurel kept my sights high when the chips were down. She refused to let me take the only work offers that came along at the time . . . the commercials and the shoddy parts in class B films. I was at the bottom of the heap, a real case who avoided reality by washing down pills with Scotch. If it weren't for Laurel, I would have killed myself long ago. So I will never, *never* listen to anyone put her down."

Exasperated, Ron got up from the sofa and took hold of her shoulders. "I understand how good Laurel has been for you, but if she has your interest at heart, she'd also want you to have something more out of life than fame and fortune."

"Fame and fortune," Diana repeated with little emotion in her voice. "Once I thought that success would solve all my problems. It didn't. Success and wealth make very inadequate companions when life gets really tough."

"Exactly. Look how much success and wealth helped you when you finally bent under the pressure. I love you, Diana, and I believe you love me, but I won't settle for a ménage à trois. We either get our relationship straightened out, or I'm out of here for good."

"Don't say that, please," she begged. "I need Laurel, but I need you, too."

"You're not the only one with needs. I have needs, also, and believe it or not, so does Laurel. How the two of you got so stuck together is beyond me, but I can't handle it. Do you love me or not?"

Diana's eyelids lowered, and she nodded.

"Then marry me. Let's get the hell out of this museum and get a normal life going for us in a normal house with normal neighbors who we can have over for dinner on Saturday nights for normal conversation."

Slowly Diana began to turn away, but Ron tightened his grasp on her and spun her back to face him. "Is it me?" he asked, hating the pain he saw in her eyes. "Is there something wrong with me? Tell me. I'll do my damndest to try and fix it."

With her trembling hands cupping his cheeks, Diana pleaded, "Don't even think that, darling. There's not a thing wrong with you. It's me. I'm just so confused I can't think straight."

She slipped her hands around his neck and leaned against his chest. "Please, Ron, give me some time, just a little time. Help me get through this film."

"And then?" he asked.

Doubting that she would ever be able to tell her daughter what was really in her heart, Diana forced her actor's mind on the script she wanted to see. Softly she said, "And then we'll do whatever you want."

"Do you promise?"

Diana stepped back from him. As she eased the dress off her shoulders, she whispered, "I promise."

CHAPTER THIRTEEN

"YES, MR. BELLU," Laurel said into the receiver, "I'll let you know when charges are filed against Ron, and thank you again."

After hanging up, she turned to Nick, who was standing by the window, watching her. Thinking of Ron, she said, "Well, that's one more near catastrophe taken care of. I'm not sure what it says about me, but when Ron told Detective Rodriguez that he had killed Tony, I believed him."

Try as he had, Nick still found that there was no silencing his suspicion that Laurel hadn't told him the entire truth about what had happened at Tony's. What was it that she was hiding from him? he wondered. And if he couldn't trust her, why was he so damn attracted to her?

"Doesn't that seem incredible to you?" she asked.

"That you thought Ron had killed him?"

"Yes, it does to me now."

Nick slipped his hands into his trouser pockets and tilted his head slightly. His eyes fixed on Laurel's white pumps, and his gaze drifted up over her gorgeous legs, past the feminine blue dress with the dainty white flowers, over the smooth skin of her throat and onto that lovely face of hers. No, he told himself, she just didn't fit into a scenario complete with extortion and murder. But she was smack in the middle of it, just the same. He had to force his attention back to their conversation.

"To be honest, much of what's happened since you walked into my San Diego office seems incredible to me."

"I know what you mean," she agreed softly.

"I'm not sure you do."

She looked into his eyes and again noted the intense way he had of looking at her, as though he were trying to read her thoughts.

"For example," he continued, "the most incredible thing is that I could fall in love with you very easily, and I don't want to."

His blunt words echoed in her ears and started a relentless pounding in her heart. She had wanted Nick to express his feelings for her, but at the same time she feared his doing so. Now that he had, she didn't know what to say to him.

"No comment?" he asked. "Not even a 'sonuva-gun'?"

The smile that she tried for barely lifted the corners of her mouth. Looking away, she stammered, "I—I could say that I'm flattered, but I'm still thinking about why you don't want to—" She couldn't quite get the words out.

"To fall in love with you," he finished for her. When she said nothing, he explained. "The reason I don't want to is that it's obvious you don't have room in your life for me."

"Nick," she said, forcing herself to look directly at him, "it's not that I don't have deep feelings for you. It's only that... Well, if we had met at some other time, under different circumstances...."

He nodded, smiling wryly. "It's just not convenient for you right now." After a dry chuckle, he lightened his tone. "Listen, I'm not your average pushy guy who's heartsick. I just needed to get that admission off my chest. Now that I have, let's forget I ever said it. Besides," he added matter-of-factly, "we've got more important things to think about. Like who, other than you and Ron, was at Tony's beach house the night he died."

Laurel turned toward the library door as Reva came in.

"Excuse me, folks," she apologized. "I'm just dropping off this beaded bag for Diana."

Taking the small white box from her, Laurel said, "You needn't have driven out here with this tonight."

"No problem. It was on my way. I'm meeting Sam at the country club."

"That bodes well, I hope," Laurel said.

Reva's brown eyes sparkled. "He took me completely by surprise."

Remembering the gold lighter he'd seen at Tony's beach house, Nick searched his jacket pocket, then asked, "Reva, do you have a cigarette on you? I left mine upstairs."

"I thought you took the pledge," she remarked, reaching into her purse.

"I did, but I'm not the rock of willpower I led you to believe. Thanks." He slipped the cigarette between his lips and checked the nearby tables. "Got a match? All I have is the habit." He watched attentively when Reva withdrew a stainless steel lighter and flicked it.

"Laurel, I have to run," Reva said. "I don't want to keep Sam waiting." Smiling at Nick, she shook her head. "Smoking is a disgusting habit, isn't it?" Then she sailed out of the library as quickly as she had come in.

"When did you start smoking again?" Laurel asked.

Nick snuffed the cigarette out in what he hoped was an ashtray and not an empty candy dish. "Doing this is taking real willpower," he mumbled, and looked over at Laurel. "I wonder what happened to Reva's gold cigarette lighter?"

"The one Tony gave her?"

"Exactly."

"Really, Nick. Can you blame her for not wanting to use it after they parted company or after what happened to him?"

"Remember the lighter we saw on the shelf behind the bar at his house?"

"Maybe she gave it back to him."

"That's possible, but if she did, I'd love to know when."

"So now you've added Reva to your list. You're tired, Nick, and so am I. I'm going to bed."

"I thought you'd never ask," Nick said, his memory presenting him with an instant replay of the time they had spent together in her bedroom.

"Alone," she said as she patted him on the cheek before heading for the door.

"Laurel," he called, and she looked back at him over her shoulder. "Sleep well."

The way he was looking at her, she decided, was tantamount to a good-night kiss, and her arms ached to reach out to him. "You, too," she said softly, her gaze holding his a fraction too long for his comfort.

After Laurel left the room, he closed his eyes and muttered, "I don't want to fall in love with her. I don't want to. I don't want to...."

AT THE LA ARCADA plaza, Nick followed the directions Reva had given him on the phone and made his way through the throng of noontime shoppers to her boutique.

He had expected to find a trendy-type shop with strobe lights and with-it music, but when he walked in, he was surprised. The boutique was elegant. The color coral was predominant in the decor; unobtrusive background music muted the quiet conversations of the salesladies and their customers, some having a beverage, as they discussed outfits being modeled. A smiling, attractive woman greeted him.

"Reva Perlman is expecting me," Nick said.

"Mr. Malone?" the woman inquired pleasantly, and he nodded. "This way, please."

In her office, Reva was leaning against the edge of her desk with the phone to her ear. She smiled at Nick and gestured to the sofa in back of a coffee table. As he sat down, he could tell that she was unhappy about something.

"Damn it, Myra, I was depending on you to approach Macy's and Bloomingdale's with a little more finesse. Their volume sales would have helped me recoup some of the money this project has cost me. Try Saks and Bonwit Teller." She listened briefly. "Well, the Fifth Avenue markup would have made it more difficult for a new line to succeed, anyway." Reva placed her palm over the mouthpiece and told Nick, "I won't be long."

She talked business for a few minutes more before slamming the receiver down. "Not my best day," she said. "Do you mind if we have lunch here? I'm expecting another call from New York."

"Not at all."

She sauntered into an adjoining room and returned with a platter of sandwiches. "I had the restaurant fix these for us. We have chicken and roast beef. Would you like coffee, tea, a cola or something stronger?" Her charm bracelet jingled as she flicked her blond hair back. "I sound like a stewardess."

"A thoughtful one. Coffee is fine."

"What kind of a gift are you thinking of for Laurel?" she asked as she poured two cups of coffee from an urn on a side table.

"That's where I need your advice."

"Well, do you want a personal or an impersonal gift?"

"How personal does personal get?" he asked, placing two halves of a roast beef sandwich on his plate.

"As personal as you want. Anything from lacy lingerie to a scarf pin. How much longer are you planning to be here in Santa Barbara?"

"A few days, maybe."

Her wide mouth formed an insinuating smile. "If I were you, I'd go with the lingerie."

Hesitantly he said, "You know Laurel better than I do."

"I doubt that, unless you're not half the man I think you are." She spread a napkin over her lap and took a bite out of a chicken sandwich.

After a swallow of coffee, Nick asked, "You don't believe that Laurel might think that lacy lingerie would be a little too personal?"

"To get her mind off of that all-consuming job of hers, you'll have to give her something that will get her undivided attention, or you'll wind up being another Brian Cannady." She saw the question in his eyes. "She hasn't told you about Brian?"

Nick shook his head as he chewed.

"Well, Laurel is a good friend, mind you, but she really messed up when she let Brian get away. He was an architect who worked mainly in Beverly Hills. He and his wife now live in St. Louis." She reached for her coffee cup, and after a sip, she said, "The man had positively everything. He had looks, money, and he adored Laurel."

"She adored him, I take it."

"Everyone believed she did, but just after they became engaged, Diana had her breakdown, and Laurel kept postponing the wedding. Finally Brian gave her an ultimatum, but you know how she is about Diana. Well, that was the end of Brian."

"I guess she took it pretty hard."

"With Laurel, you never know. She keeps her emotions fairly private, except when it comes to Diana. Then she can become a raging tigress. That, Nick, is one strange relationship. I don't know what it's all about, and I'm not sure I want to know."

To change the subject, he said, "Let's go with the scarf pin." As though it were an afterthought, he asked, "How was dinner with your ex?"

Reva looked at him curiously before saying, "Sam is acting like he did when he courted me, and I love it."

"I guess he was surprised to hear about Tony's death."

She was quiet for a few seconds, then asked, "More coffee?"

Nick raised his hand. "Thanks, no. I understand that Tony and Francine Gregory had been seeing each other for a while."

"How he ever got involved with that bimbo, I'll never understand," Reva said in a harsh tone. "She has as much warmth as an ice cube."

Grinning, Nick said, "Sounds like his love life kept him pretty busy."

"Too busy, unfortunately for him." She offered Nick a sly smile. "You don't have to talk around the question that you really want to ask. Did Tony and Laurel ever have anything going on between them? The answer is no. She has too much class. Tony had a flair for the more earthy types. He was bound to get his eventually, and he did, didn't he? Apparently he picked on the wrong woman."

Nick reached for another sandwich, mentally filing away Reva's comments.

LAUREL HURRIED from police headquarters in downtown Santa Barbara as fast as she could. Nick had wanted to go with her for the positive identification by Tony's neighbor, but having had other business to take care of, she convinced him that she could handle the situation on her own.

It had turned out to be more of an ordeal than she'd thought it would be. The one positive thing that had come out of it was the woman's statement that she had seen Laurel leave Tony's beach house just after eleven-thirty the night he died. That seemed to have satisfied Detective Rodriguez—for the time being, anyway. But he had yet to make up his mind on what charges would be brought against Ron.

After completing business at her bank, Laurel had lunch with a fellow personal manager, shopped for birthday presents for Rosa, Alicia's daughter, and hurried back to the estate.

She had just placed her packages on the table in the entry hall when she heard Diana call her name. She turned to see her mother coming down the stairway, but the smile on her face froze when she saw that Diana was already dressed in the ivory satin gown with the off-the-shoulder white fox trim. Ron was next to her, wearing his tuxedo.

Laurel glanced at her watch. "I didn't realize we were leaving so soon. I'll dress quickly."

"No need to rush," Ron said. "Diana and I are going into L.A. early. We'll have dinner and meet you at the ceremony later this evening."

"But—" Laurel's eyes shifted to Diana "—we've always gone together."

"Ron," Diana said, more than a little uncomfortable with the change in plans he had insisted on, "maybe we should all—"

Before she could get another word out, he took hold of her arm. "We'd like to have dinner alone tonight, Laurel," he said decisively.

Laurel shrugged to hide her confusion and the sharp sense of betrayal that ripped through her. Peering through the moisture in her eyes, she asked, "Is that what you want, Diana?"

"Well, darling, how often have Ron and I been out together recently?" Nervously, she made a dramatic gesture with her hand. "You know what they say. 'Two's company, three's a crowd.'"

Laurel stepped back, shaken, feeling as though her mother had just slapped her in the face. For the past ten years, she had discounted her own wishes and her own chances for happiness to see to Diana's needs. Now she was being cast aside and made to feel like an outsider, little more than a face in a crowd.

She grasped the edge of the table behind her for support and managed a tenuous smile. "You look lovely." Her eyes drifted over to her mother's escort, his masculine attractiveness magnified by the royal-blue tuxedo he wore. "You look great, too, Ron. I wish you both a wonderful evening." She turned quickly and started to gather her packages.

"Laurel—" her mother began.

"Come on, Diana," Ron said firmly. "We'll be late."

She glanced back over her shoulder as he hurried her to the front door. "We will see you later, won't we?"

Not answering or turning, Laurel fought to control the jagged breaths that racked her chest. With her head bent, she tried to understand just why she was feeling so frightened and so miserable. Her mother and Ron had gone out alone before, and it had been good for Diana. But, Laurel asked herself, feeling angrier by the second, why was her mother cutting her out of her life all of a sudden?

"Damn it!" she muttered, and hit the table with her clenched fist, knocking one of the gift-wrapped packages to the floor.

"Let me."

Her ears vaguely registered the sound of a man's voice. Spinning around, she saw Nick bending down to retrieve the fallen package. "Oh . . . uh . . . thanks."

He handed her the pink-ribboned box. "Pretty. Who are the presents for?" Feeling pleased with himself, he thought of the gold scarf pin he had in a small box in his pocket.

"It's for Rosa. Tomorrow's her birthday."

"Let me help," he offered, and picked up two of the larger boxes from the table.

Nick studied her on their way up the stairs, trying to assess the reason for her touchy mood. "I saw Diana and Ron getting into the Mercedes. They make an attractive couple."

"Don't they," she remarked, her voice tinged with sarcasm.

So that's it, he thought. "I take it they're off to the awards ceremony."

"Yes."

Nick followed Laurel into her sitting room and placed the packages on the table by the settee. "Aren't you going into L.A.?"

Laurel's response dripped with the pain she felt in her chest. "Why? Don't you know that three's a crowd?" Shrugging out of her tan linen suit jacket, she tossed it on a chair.

"How about four? I could go with you if you'd like."

Laurel smoothed a hand over her hair. "I don't feel like seeing a lot of people tonight, Nick."

"I know what you mean. I get spells like that sometimes."

"I'm not having a spell of any kind," she insisted, and stalked to the window to stare out at the Mercedes as it sped down the driveway.

Nick strode to the other side of the window. "Aren't you pleased to see that Diana and Ron are acknowledging their feelings for each other?"

Still upset and bewildered, Laurel mumbled, "I'd be more pleased if she were concentrating on her job."

"As you do," he suggested.

"Exactly. When the movie is finished, then she'll have time for Ron."

He recalled the conversation Laurel had had with Diana's agent. "How much time before her next project?"

"There won't be a next project if she doesn't get through this one." With firm steps, Laurel went to the settee, grabbed her jacket and headed for her bedroom closet.

Nick followed and rested his shoulder against the doorjamb. Realizing he was walking on thin ice, he asked, "Would that be so bad?"

With a hanger in her hand, she turned and sent him an icy stare. "Nick, shouldn't you be sleuthing or something?"

"Why? You found out who the extortionist was."

She closed the louvered door a little harder than necessary. "I mean in San Diego."

"I'm a guest. Just because you won't take any time off doesn't mean I can't."

Curtly she asked, "Exactly why did Ron want you to stay here?"

"Maybe to keep you company while he got to see more of Diana... alone."

"That's not funny."

"I'm not trying to be funny. I'm just trying to figure out why you won't let yourself be happy for the two of them."

"I told you once, Nick," she said, stalking past him and returning to the adjacent room, "stop meddling in our lives."

"Is my caring about your happiness meddling?"

Laurel kept her eyes focused on the fireplace. She didn't want to argue with Nick, but she had a terrible feeling again that disaster was just around the corner.

"Why are you so upset about her going out with Ron? I thought you liked him."

"I do," she said quietly.

"Then what's the problem?"

Facing him, she explained, "Anything that gets in the way of Diana's concentration on the film is bad for her. Don't you see that?"

"Isn't that a decision she should make? She's a big girl now."

"I've known her a great deal longer than you have. Diana can give easily to a thousand people from the stage or to millions in movie theaters across the world, but on a one-to-one basis, she hasn't had much success. In fact, relationships have been disastrous for her, and I'm the one who has to pick up the pieces. I just don't have the strength to go through it again right now. At times Diana is like a child."

"Maybe I'm in a position to see things more objectively than you can."

"And just what is it you see?"

"Two women caught up in a destructive symbiotic relationship, and only one is even attempting to break loose from it—Diana."

Laurel stiffened, thinking that just as her mother had, Nick was turning on her, too. Her annoyance at him increased when she found that her hands were shaking. Her burning eyes met his, but in them she found only a sincere concern. Two conflicting emotions welled up within her: fear for her mother's future and desire for Nick. Slowly her anger diminished, and in its place Laurel felt only an exhausting weariness. Mulling over Nick's remark, she eased her body down onto the settee and murmured, "Is that what you see?"

Nick moved behind her and began to massage her shoulders. Softly he said, "I had a client once, a woman. She had spent most of her adult life caring for her invalid father after his wife had died. The woman had two sisters and a brother. Not one of them ever lifted a hand to help her. She saw herself as a martyr, but in effect she had settled for feeling sorry for herself rather than attempting to make reasonable changes in her life. I can understand a daughter doing that, but not an employee, no matter how dedicated.''

Laurel's neck and shoulder muscles had become so tense that they had ached, but now under Nick's gentle massaging, some of the tension had begun to dissipate. With her eyes closed, her tone was calmer when she said, "Trust me, Nick, you're in no position to draw any conclusions about me or Diana."

"If I'm not, it's because you won't let me."

"I don't know what you're talking about," she said, and she felt him withdraw his hands. Turning her head, she looked up at him. His jaw was taut, and there was a coldness in his eyes that she hadn't seen before.

"You're doing it again, Laurel. You're shutting me out, and I don't understand why. I only want to help you. Don't you see that?"

"Help me," she repeated, and chuckled dryly. "Why does that sound so strange to me, Nick?"

He leaned down and rested his hands on the back of the settee. "Maybe because you've never let anyone help you. Look, I understand how concerned you are about Diana, but I have feelings, too, and so does Ron. What really troubles me is the possibility that you aren't able to empathize with anyone else's feelings except hers. Tell me I'm wrong."

A wave of anxiety swept through her, heralding a renewal of the mental war that had been going on in her mind ever since she admitted to herself that her feelings for Nick were more than just an attraction. But even as her feelings for him had grown, so had the sense of duty she felt to her mother. The clash between the two emotions was more than Laurel could bear. The war had to cease! One side or the other had to be victorious.

Standing, she said quietly, "I can't be all things to everybody."

"I agree wholeheartedly, but we have to make difficult choices at times."

She lifted her eyes to meet his. "Please don't force me to choose between you and Diana."

Nick stood straight and met Laurel's hard gaze head-on. "I'd lose. Is that what you're telling me?" When she nodded and turned away, he said quietly, "That's sad. We might have been very good for each other. I'll return to San Diego first thing in the morning."

Numbed by his parting words, Laurel barely heard the door close after he left the room.

"Might have been," she whispered. That was the story of her life. First Keith, then Brian and now Nick.

As though drugged, she stumbled into the adjoining room, removed her shoes and lay down on the bed. Staring up at the white ceiling, she wondered why Nick couldn't see what was so plain to her: Diana truly needed her. It was that simple. It had always been that way.

With the back of a wrist over her brow, she closed her eyes and sought some kind of peace, even for just a little while.

IT WAS DARK when Laurel awakened. She was disoriented at first, but in seconds reality caught her in its firm grip, and her troubled thoughts tumbled anew. She changed into a gown and robe, went down to the kitchen and prepared a cup of tea. With that in hand, she headed to the library and scanned the day's mail. But she couldn't concentrate.

She tossed the unopened envelopes aside and went out onto the terrace. It was quiet, except for the sounds of night birds down by the pond, their plaintive songs only succeeding in making her feel even more depressed. Glancing up at the house, she saw that the light was on in Nick's room.

How facile it was for him to criticize her, she thought and gazed out over the pond. Didn't he realize that her work obligations were about to smother her, that her responsibilities were overwhelming? And that remark of his, that, except for Diana, she was unable to empathize with others' feelings. That really hurt.

But was there any truth to what he had said? *Was* she overdoing the duty she felt toward her mother?

No, of course not, she decided quickly, and once again she told herself that if Nick knew that Diana was her mother, he would surely understand. Understand what? she mused. Why she couldn't permit herself to fall in love with him? It would be so easy to....

The admission itself opened a floodgate of restrained emotion, and Laurel recalled the wonderful feeling of Nick's arms around her, his caresses and his kisses. She thought of his easy laughter and his smile of wonderment when he told her he had never been happier.

She had never felt this way—not with Keith and not with Brian; they had paled in comparison. Nick was unique, a man so special that she was certain his like would never come her way again. He was totally masculine, but there was an endearing gentleness to him at the same time. He could be stubborn, although she'd never seen his stubbornness be self-serving. Nick was caring, too. He cared what happened to Diana, to Ron and to her. And he could make her laugh, even when she sometimes felt that her world was falling apart around her.

Laurel's eyes drifted back up to the window of Nick's room. She saw that the light had been extinguished, and

she assumed that he had gone to bed. She wondered if
he was thinking of her as she was thinking of him. The
heaviness in her heart worsened until she thought she
was going to scream his name in the darkness. *Get a grip,
Laurel,* she ordered herself silently. *Nick will leave, and
he'll forget you. And you'll forget him.*

"Never," she challenged her inner voice in a whisper.

With a firm resolve, she forced away all thought except the truth: she had fallen desperately in love with
Nick.

A cool breeze whipped over the terrace, and she shiv-
ered, but the only warmth she wanted was Nick's arms
around her—if only for one last time.

And that she would have.

CHAPTER FOURTEEN

LAUREL HESITATED at the door to Nick's room, but only for a moment. Slowly she opened it, and the light from the hallway rayed over him as he lay in bed, his chest bare, his hands tucked behind his head, his eyes open.

Startled, Nick raised himself onto his elbows and peered at the silhouetted robed figure standing in the doorway. "Laurel?" he asked, surprise and intensity in his inquiry.

Softly she closed the door behind her and leaned back against it. "I couldn't let you leave thinking of me as unfeeling and callous."

"I don't, not really. It's just that I'm so damn frustrated. I need you and want you so badly, but I know I can't have you."

"Nick," she whispered, "I need you, too. Will you hold me for just a little while . . . please?"

"For as long as you like," he said, and drew back the covers.

She slipped off her robe, eased down beside him and sank into the wonderful comfort of his embrace. Their mutual sighs mingled as she rested her head against his shoulder and welcomed the kiss he placed on her brow.

"This is where we belong," he whispered, "together like this."

"Yes," she murmured, basking in the contented feeling of having his arms around her. She closed her eyes, sensing the pounding of his heart under her hand, knowing hers was beating just as rapidly. Kissing the side of his neck, she moved her arm around his waist. His warmth caressed her palm and fingers, and a tranquil sigh crossed her lips.

Nick thanked heaven that she had come to him; he knew he wouldn't have gone to her tonight. God, she felt so wonderful in his arms. Her wispy breaths against his throat and her silky nightgown under his fingers was driving him wild. All he wanted to do was to lose himself in her softness. She had come to him! he repeated silently, still amazed by the fact. The realization dispelled the nagging doubts that he'd had and the fear that she didn't really care for him the way he cared for her. And she had actually said she needed him!

Nick smiled in the semidarkness and pressed his cheek against her silky hair. Never, never in his life had he been this content. Laurel needed him, and he made a vow that he would always be there for her, no matter what. If she wouldn't come to San Diego, he'd relocate to Los Angeles, and somehow they would work things out together.

Kissing her forehead, he moved his hand down over the curve of her hip and whispered, "I love you." After silent moments, he realized that she had fallen asleep in his arms, and he tightened his hold on her.

"WHAT AN OVATION Diana received!" Ron said to Laurel and Nick at breakfast on the patio. "I've never seen so many men *and* women stand up and applaud like that."

Diana beamed radiantly. "They were probably numb from sitting during Warren's seven-minute acceptance speech. I mean, really, the man only produced the film, but he sounded as though he'd directed it, starred in it and had written the music score."

She placed her hand over Ron's. "You should have seen the envious stares I received when we first arrived at the theater, especially from Ethel Hobson. I swear, if that woman has one more face-lift, she'll have to wear a choker to hide her navel." She turned to Laurel. "I wish you had come last night. You would have been so proud of me."

Laurel's eyes, still shimmering with an inner light, swept to Nick's for an instant, then she told Diana, "I am proud of you, and I don't need a room full of adoring people to remind me of that."

As she adjusted the cerulean scarf that matched the color of her morning robe, Diana looked across the table to Nick. "In this business, you can be on top one day, and find that the next you can't even get on so-called friends' C lists."

"Excuse me, Miss Baxter."

"Yes, Carlos?"

"Mr. Driscoll is calling. He'd like to speak with you. Shall I bring the phone out here?"

"Please." She grimaced at Laurel. "Would you talk to him? I don't want that worrywart to ruin my delightful mood this morning."

When the butler returned, Laurel motioned to him, and he placed the cordless phone down on the table near her. Greetings completed, she listened to Glen for a while, then asked Carlos, "Was an envelope delivered by courier this morning?"

"Yes, Miss Davis. It's on your desk in the library."

"Would you get it for me, please?"

Diana said, "Just bring all the mail, Carlos."

As Laurel chatted with Glen, Nick poured himself a second cup of coffee and said to Ron, "You two looked pretty great when you left here yesterday."

"Ron was born to wear a tuxedo," Diana gushed. "I was so proud to be with him."

When Carlos returned, he handed the brown envelope to Laurel and the rest of the mail to Diana, who began flipping through it.

"Yes, Glen," Laurel said into the receiver, "the revised shooting schedule arrived." She eyed Diana and smiled. "She'll be prepared...okay, we'll see you at the studio on Tuesday."

Laurel put down the phone and scanned the papers Glen had sent. "They're planning to start with the scene where you discover that David is a jewel thief."

"I like that scene," Diana said, still checking the envelopes on the table. "It has a wide range of emotions." Holding up a white business-size envelope, she commented, "This one has no return address."

Nick saw Laurel's face pale as she jumped up.

"It's addressed to me, darling," Diana said, and used a knife to slit the envelope open.

As she began to read, Laurel watched the blood drain from her mother's face. When Diana gaped at the enclosed document, Laurel realized that what she had been dreading most had happened, but she didn't understand how it possibly could have. She asked Carlos to leave them alone for a while and took the papers from a stunned Diana.

Observing the stricken look on Laurel's face as she read silently, Nick asked, "Another demand?"

Shaken, she nodded.

"The blackmailer?" Ron asked.

Aghast, Diana stared at him, "You know about this?" She looked over at Nick. "And you do, also. Everyone knows but me. Laurel, what is going on?"

Her nightmare of nightmares come true, Laurel raised trembling fingers to her forehead. "Please...let's go into the library."

Ron took Diana's arm, and they left the patio. Laurel was about to follow, but Nick grasped her shoulder. "Don't you think it's time you told her everything?"

"I really don't have much of a choice, do I?" she asked, her voice trembling.

In the library, Nick and Ron watched the two women as Laurel told her mother about the first extortion letter, the twenty thousand dollars she had paid, and the hiring of Nick, a private investigator, to discover who the blackmailer was.

"A private investigator?" Diana repeated, shocked by what Laurel was telling her. Wide-eyed, she looked up at Nick, who was standing next to Ron. "Who was it?"

"Tony," Laurel said quietly.

"Tony? But why? He and Wayne have been like family to me."

After Laurel explained about his reverses in the stock market, Ron asked, "Is that what you two were talking about at his beach house the night he died?"

"Yes," she said quietly, and glanced at Nick.

He asked, "May I see the envelope?"

Handing it to him, she said, "I've already checked the postmark date. It was mailed here in Santa Barbara, but Tony couldn't have sent this one."

Hopefully Ron suggested, "Maybe he mailed it before he died, and it was lost or something."

"And maybe we have a second extortionist," Nick added glumly.

Slowly Laurel sank down on the chair next to her desk and placed shaking fingers over her eyes.

"Dear God," Diana moaned, her face still white as a sheet. An awful thought crossed her mind, and she looked over at Laurel. "Darling," she said, her voice husky, "You . . . you didn't—" She couldn't even complete the question.

"No, I didn't kill Tony."

Diana's eyes searched Ron's face.

"I didn't, either."

"Then who did, and why?" Diana asked, still gripping Ron's hand tightly.

"According to this morning's newspaper, the police don't know," he said. "They're still looking for the murder weapon."

"This second demand puts us in a whole new ball game," Nick said. "May I see what was in the envelope?"

"No," Laurel answered firmly, clasping the papers in her hand.

"Oh, for heaven's sake, why not?" Diana blurted out. "We're being blackmailed, and a man's been killed. Why keep on with the charade? Give Nick the papers."

Nick read the letter and the accompanying photostat of a birth certificate. His eyes widened, and he stared at Laurel. "You're Diana's daughter?"

"What?" Ron sat down next to Diana, who nodded with closed eyes.

"This explains a lot of things," Nick mumbled as he lowered himself down onto a chair.

Experiencing an overwhelming sense of vindication, there was a tone of immense relief in Laurel's voice when she said, "Now you understand why I couldn't tell you the whole truth." She wasn't at all prepared for the warning look Nick shot her.

"It doesn't explain everything," he said flatly. Before she could react, he checked the birth certificate again. "The father is listed as unknown. I take it he was the lawyer for the syndicate."

"Syndicate?" Diana asked. "What syndicate?"

Laurel stood and began to pace nervously. "The syndicate was never involved, Nick," she admitted.

"Oh?" He leaned forward in his chair. "What other lies have you told me?"

"What difference does that make now?"

Nick held up the letter demanding another twenty thousand dollars. "This makes a difference." Seeing that she wasn't going to say anything, Nick turned to Diana. "Isn't it about time the two of you started to level with Ron and me?"

"Diana," Ron pleaded, "let's get this business in back of us. Tell Nick what he wants to know, whatever it is . . . please."

Rising from the sofa, Diana placed her hands in the side pockets of her robe. She averted her gaze from her daughter's anxious eyes, then looked at Nick and back to Ron. "I had only been in Hollywood for a few years, and my head was filled with moonbeams." She turned away and faced the window. "One day between scenes, I was introduced to a young lawyer in the commissary at MGM. He was a friend of Sam Goldwyn's and was just visiting the West Coast. The following evening we were both at the same party in Beverly Hills, and before I knew it I was caught up in a whirlwind romance." Turning to the attentive group, she smiled sadly. "Just like in the movies. Girl meets boy, girl gets pregnant, boy marries another girl."

"Diana, please," Laurel implored.

Her warped smile disappeared. "My own daughter hasn't even been able to call me Mother. That alone should have told me how wrong I was so many years ago, and how wrong I've been to let it go on this long."

Nick asked, "But why the pretense?"

"When I told Laurel's father that I was expecting, he wanted me to have an abortion. You see, he was engaged to a socially prominent woman in Virginia. Her father was a senator." After a distorted, wry laugh, Diana continued. "My predicament certainly wasn't entirely his fault, and I was every bit as ambitious for my career as he was for his."

Diana ran the tip of her tongue over her lower lip. "After he returned to the East Coast, Glen arranged for me to go to his sister's home in a small town in Arizona. It was just across the California border. Frieda and Jerome Davis were childless—" her eyes sought Laurel's "—and they raised my daughter as their niece." Facing Nick, she said, "If that sounds coldhearted to you, remember that social mores were much stricter in Hollywood in the late fifties. Today, if a star has a child out of wedlock and announces it to the world, she's applauded for her courage and caring in deciding not to have an abortion. But look what it did to Ingrid Bergman back then. The entire world turned on her."

Diana's eyes rolled heavenward as she laughed caustically. "Oh, I told myself I'd work something out after I had finished the first major film I was starring in at the time. Then I postponed doing so until after the next picture, and the next. Pretty soon Laurel's father had started his own family, and Laurel was already a beautiful young girl." Diana went to her and tilted her chin up. "Except for you, darling, my entire life has been one big mistake after another."

Taking her mother's hand in hers, Laurel said forcefully, "That's not true. You are Diana Baxter, a talented actress who's loved by millions of people around the world."

Ron moved directly behind Diana and placed his hands on her shoulders. "You're loved by a few more people right here in this room."

She covered one of his hands with hers and whispered, "Thank you, Ron."

Nick cleared the lump in his throat and held up the extortion letter. "What about the Davises?"

"That's ridiculous," Laurel said with conviction. "My foster parents would never do such a thing. Over the years, Diana has been more than generous. They want for nothing."

"What about the car you put the twenty thousand dollars in at the Mission Santa Barbara? You said it had an Arizona license plate."

With a raised hand, Diana said, "Frieda and Jerome would never do anything to hurt Laurel or me."

Ron asked, "Do you think we should tell the police about this second blackmail letter?"

Nick said, "Not yet. If they learn about the first one, it would give them just the motive they'd need to believe that Laurel wanted Tony dead."

Feeling Diana begin to tremble, Ron said, "I'm going to take Diana upstairs. I think she should get some rest."

"I think so, too," Laurel agreed and kissed Diana's cheek. "I'll be up later, and we'll talk."

When Nick and Laurel were alone, Nick attempted to sound lighthearted, "Well now, you're just full of surprises, aren't you?"

Seeing his clenched jaw, Laurel said, "Let's get out of this room. I'd like some fresh air."

As they walked toward the pond, he asked, "When did you learn that Diana was your mother?"

Hearing the word *mother* said out loud still seemed strange to Laurel. It had never really been in her vocabulary when referring to Diana in public. But now that it was no longer a secret, she felt as though she had been exonerated of some hidden crime.

To answer Nick's question, she said, "I've known since I was eight years old. Before that I thought she was Diana Davis, not Diana Baxter, the famous movie star. She told me that I lived with the Davises because her job as a buyer for an L.A. department store made it necessary for her to travel a lot."

"Do you ever see the Davises?"

"Of course, during Christmas holidays and on their birthdays. They're both in their seventies now, but still in fairly good health."

"What about the friends you made in college?"

Laurel shook her head. "Most of them are married and have families. We exchange occasional cards."

Nick decided that Laurel's life certainly hadn't been an ordinary one, and he wondered how she had managed to handle the many conflicts that must have arisen. From what she was telling him, it seemed as though she'd felt she had to break contact with almost everyone she had known in the early part of her life. There was one more person he was wondering about.

"I take it you don't see your father," he said quietly, and watched Laurel's facial muscles tense.

"At first I thought he had died, but just after my eighth birthday, Diana admitted he hadn't. She wanted to let him know that he had a daughter, but I asked her not to.''

"Why?"

She stopped at the edge of the pond and focused on the slender palms on the opposite side. "I was afraid I might have to go to Virginia and live with him, a man I didn't even know, and I doubted that he would want me. As I grew older, I came to hate him.''

"Hate him? Why?''

Laurel glanced at Nick, then began walking, following the rim of the pond. "I realized that Diana was holding on to romantic illusions about her first love, and I still believe that he's been the cause of all of her failed relationships.''

"I'm not taking any sides, but is that really fair to your father? Apparently he doesn't even know you exist.''

"And if he had had his way, I wouldn't exist. Garrison Howard wanted my mother to have an abortion.''

Nick stopped dead in his tracks. "Garrison Howard, the senator and presidential candidate?''

"The same,'' she said bitterly. "However, I am Laurel Davis, not Laurel Howard. As far as I'm concerned, he was nothing more than a sperm donor.''

Nick leaned down and grasped the back of a white wrought-iron chair. "The press would certainly have a field day if this story got out, particularly now. Not only would it not help Diana, but the senator's political career would be down the tubes.''

"And it would wreak havoc with his family. He's been married for more than thirty years. He and his wife have three sons and seven grandchildren. I couldn't care less about his career, and if it concerned only him, I'd let the whole world know just what kind of a man he is.''

"Was," Nick corrected.

"Whatever. But if he goes down, a lot of innocent people go with him, Diana included."

"It could happen. We're dealing with a second black-mailer."

Renewed fear gripped her, and she asked shakily, "Do you think I should pay again?"

"No, you'd never be free of him or her."

"Her," Laurel said, echoing him. "I have a hard time thinking of a woman doing this to another woman. What am I going to do, Nick? The letter threatens to release the birth certificate to the press. Garrison Howard wouldn't have to be implicated, but Diana would suffer."

"If it did become front-page news, he might figure it out for himself."

"And come running to embrace his daughter? I doubt that very much. Nick," she said, placing her fingers on his arm, "thanks for being here. I don't know what I would have done if I'd had to go through these past weeks alone."

He placed his hand over hers. "It seems to me you've done exceptionally well going it alone. I just don't understand how you can be so understanding about the way Diana handled the situation so many years ago."

"What would you have me do...rant and rave about it? As nice as it would have been if she had kept me with her and weathered the storm, she didn't. That bothered me a great deal when I was young, but in my teens I began to realize that Diana's emotional makeup was extremely fragile. Her eventual hospitalization confirmed that. There was no way I was going to abandon her, no more than I would have if she had been physically ill."

Laurel bit down on her lower lip, then suggested they head back to the house.

In the entry hall they found Ron pacing. "Diana is lying down," he said tensely. "I think it would do her good if you went up and talked with her, Laurel."

"That's where I'm going." She placed a hand on the side of his face. "Thanks for understanding," she said, and hurried upstairs.

"Nick," Ron said in a low voice, "I need to talk to you in private. Let's go to the solarium."

In the sunny, plant-studded room on the south side of the house, Ron said, "Diana told me who Laurel's father is. You won't believe it."

"I believe it . . . Garrison Howard."

"Do you think that the blackmailer knows?"

"No. If he did, Howard would be getting all the mail, not Diana, and the going price would be more than another twenty thousand dollars."

"How is it to be paid?"

"We don't know. The letter just said to have it ready and to wait for further instructions."

"So what do we do now?"

"We wait."

"That's it, nothing else?"

"I could send the letter to a friend in the crime lab in San Diego, but just about all of us have our fingerprints on the paper now. More important, something tells me our extortionist probably doesn't have a record."

"How's that?"

"Just a feeling I have. There's something that bothers me about Diana getting a typed letter in the mail that says to get the money and wait. Usually the victim receives an anonymous phone call that can't be traced. And why not a deadline like by tomorrow or next week?

It's pretty certain, though, that whoever sent the second letter knew about the first. But who would Tony have shared his little scheme with, and why? My sixth sense tells me that he was strictly out for the money, but that this second person might have an ax to grind or be someone with a twisted mind. This business of getting the money and waiting—" he weighed his own words "—it's as though someone was enjoying playing cat and mouse."

"With Diana," Ron said.

"Maybe with Laurel, too. Since I've been here, I've gotten the impression that she drives people pretty hard when Diana's interest is at stake. That could bug someone."

Ron asked, "Enough to blackmail and maybe to kill?"

"Let's suppose our second individual wanted to put the squeeze on the ladies again, and Tony didn't want to. Maybe they argued."

"A little too rough, and Tony goes down."

"Then Sir Galahad steps in and has Rodriguez thinking we're all trying to ruin his day."

Defensively Ron asked, "What would you have done if you had thought that Laurel killed Tony?"

"The same thing, probably."

"Did she tell you how Tony found out about her and Diana?"

"No, but that's a good question. If ever you want to change careers, come on down to San Diego. We'll enlarge the firm."

Ron smiled, but almost immediately his expression turned serious again. "Nick," he asked hesitantly, "how do you think Laurel would feel about having me for a stepfather?"

"Has Diana said she'd marry you?"

"Yes, but I can't be sure that she will. Most likely Laurel will have her busy with another project as soon as the film is finished. Those two are so used to depending on each other, I don't think either one could let the other go."

"I think I've got a possible solution," Nick said. "How does a double wedding strike you?"

"You and Laurel?"

"No, you and me and Laurel and her mother," he joked. "God, I thought you were quick. Better forget about the job in San Diego."

Ron lifted his black eyebrows. "I'm just surprised. One of you works awfully fast."

"I said a possible solution. It's been uphill all the way with Laurel, not that I don't admit to having a personality defect or two."

"Don't be telling me about your defects. A stepfather can't be too careful about who he gives his stepdaughter away to."

Nick chuckled. "Boy, would the four of us confuse the minister." He thought a moment before asking, "Does Laurel have any idea that you're yearning to become a family member?"

"I haven't asked her permission, if that's what you mean."

"I wouldn't, not just yet. First things first."

"The damn blackmailer."

"Exactly."

CHAPTER FIFTEEN

AFTER DINNER, while Laurel was with Diana, reading her through the script for the first day of shooting, Nick changed into a comfortable yellow pullover and opened his bedroom door a crack so he could hear Laurel when she returned to her room.

At the dresser, he picked up the little box that held the scarf pin he had bought for her. He opened it, ran a finger over the two small entwined hearts and started to put it in his pocket, but after a moment's hesitation he placed it down again, deciding to wait until just the right time to give it to her.

Leaning back in the easy chair by the window, he went over two nagging questions that kept coming back to him. Was the person who killed Tony and the second extortionist one and the same? And why had Tony shared Laurel and Diana's well-kept secret?

As he drummed the arm of the chair with his fingertips, he thought of Guy and the twenty thousand dollars that he had insisted wasn't a loan. If it hadn't been, what was it that Tony wanted from him? Experience had taught Nick that a man only paid that kind of money to get someone to talk or to shut him up—and the dirt was usually about sex or money.

Then he thought of Reva. She was a woman whose marriage had been destroyed because of Tony, who then, most likely, showed her the door. Good motive there for an outburst of anger, he decided. Reva could have found out about his getting the extortion money and decided it would be an easy way to finance her branching out to the East Coast with her new sportswear line. Had that been her gold lighter he'd seen behind the bar, or another one Tony had been getting ready to hand out? It could have been Fran's.

"Francine Gregory, publicist," Nick muttered. The only connection she'd had with Tony had supposedly ended when he had sold his house in Beverly Hills. If it was her lighter, what would she have been doing at his beach house? Fran didn't strike him as the type to get together with an ex-lover for a drink. Nick didn't know how she felt about Diana, but Fran had exposed the sharp tips of her claws when she had talked to him about Laurel. He knew the woman was working on a biography of Diana, and he wondered how much digging she'd done so far. With a background as an investigative reporter, she'd probably know how to go about it, too. Nick made a mental note to take Fran up on that drink. She'd told him that she was listed in the book in L.A.

Then there was this matter of Glen Driscoll and Lyla Sayer that bothered him again, now that he knew Glen had been the one to arrange for Diana to go to his sister's home in Arizona. Nick shook his head, thinking that this case was turning out to be like a Cecil B. DeMille movie with a cast of thousands.

He heard the light patter of footsteps passing his door and jumped up. In the hallway he saw Laurel, carrying a framed painting under her arm. "Redecorating?" he asked, and she turned, startled to see him.

"Uh...no," she said, and continued toward her rooms.

He caught up with her and glanced at the painting. "The Cézanne."

"Yes," she said quietly, and walked past her bedroom door to the next one.

Nick followed her into the studio and watched her set up another easel beside the covered copy she had painted. "You're thinking of selling the original, aren't you?"

"If I have to." She uncovered the painting and began to study it and the copy.

Nick did the same. "Damned if I could tell them apart."

"A connoisseur would be able to, but Diana couldn't, and that's all I care about right now."

"Aren't you jumping the gun a little, or do you know something I don't?"

Changing the direction of the light from the floor lamp next to the paintings, she said, "If you're asking if I've been told how to deliver the money, the answer is no, not yet. But one way or the other, Diana is going to get through the filming of *Winner Takes All*."

"I'm guessing that your having made a copy of the painting is still our little secret."

"Don't you dare tell Diana or Ron," she warned. "I don't want her worrying about money right now."

Palms up, he said, "You're the boss. I'm back on the payroll."

Laurel smiled softly. "Why don't I feel like your boss?" She slipped her arms around his waist and let her body lean against his, as though she was trying to draw strength from him. Resting her head on his shoulder, she said softly, "Sometimes I feel as if I'm coming apart, Nick. So many awful things have been happening, one after the other, and I know there's more to come. I try

232   A PRIVATE AFFAIR

to put up a good front for Diana's sake, but I don't know how much longer I'll be able to."

"You're carrying too heavy a load all by yourself. You've got a dozen people depending on you, but who do you depend on? And this deception that you and Diana have been living with ... well, it's bound to have been festering inside you for a long time."

"You're right. It has been difficult pretending all these years, but it was something we both decided would be best. There was Diana's career to think about, and I certainly didn't want a custody battle to take place. Children are more resilient than we think. At least I was, and I was happy with the Davises. I also grew to understand Diana. Sometimes I thought of her as an errant, older sister."

Laurel drew back from Nick, feeling a surge of renewed strength that lessened her despair. Confidently she smiled. "Now you understand why I've been so protective of her."

"No, Laurel, I don't understand," he said with conviction. "I still think you've been too self-sacrificing. Diana is a lot stronger than you give her credit for, and she has Ron now."

Nick's words came as a violent shock to Laurel. She had been positive that once Nick knew she had been trying to protect her own mother, he would not only understand, but praise her for it. How could she have been so wrong? she wondered. All she could do was to stare at him as he continued to admonish her.

"In making Diana so dependent on you, you've become as dependent on her for your own happiness. Whether you realize it or not, each of you is suffocating the other emotionally."

Laurel's expression darkened, and she felt a terrible tension grip her body. Her mood veered sharply to anger, and she lashed out at him. "That description of a mother-daughter relationship is exactly what I would expect from a man who couldn't care less about what happens to his own father."

"Now wait a minute. Bob and I have—"

"No, you wait a minute," she ordered. "Several times you've made it quite clear that you have your own life to live and your father has his."

"He's an extremely independent man."

"Isn't that nice for you? It relieves you of any responsibility, doesn't it?"

Stung by the tone in her voice, Nick said, "We have a damn sight healthier relationship than you and your mother have."

"There's nothing unhealthy about our relationship!"

"Oh, no? Then why can't she accept the fact that Ron happens to be in love with her? And why the hell can't you see that I'm in love with you!"

Laurel's mind whirled at the intensity of his admission. Again mixed emotions sent her mind spinning. She'd spent her entire adult life feeling she was obligated to care for her mother, but now Nick was causing her to review her wisdom in doing so. But the bond that time had created between her and Diana was too strong to be severed by a split-second decision. Laurel had bypassed her own happiness before and survived; now, though, she wasn't at all certain she even wanted to survive without Nick.

Trying to mask her inner confusion with a deceptive calm, she said quietly, "If you love me, you have an odd way of showing it."

Nick took hold of her arms and searched her face. "You're not always the easiest person in the world to talk to. In fact, there are times when I just want to shake you." Seeing the confusion in her eyes, he lowered his voice. "I have to be in court in San Diego Monday morning. Come with me. We both need some time alone to get a perspective on what we're feeling."

Laurel sighed uneasily. "I'd like to, Nick. I really would, but I can't. I've got to be with Diana day and night now. Perhaps after the movie is finished...."

His hands slipped down her arms, and he turned away. "I've got this gnawing feeling that just as Diana put off telling the truth about having a daughter, you'll put off coming to terms with how you feel about me. Just one more picture, you'll tell me, and then you'll decide. Then it will be just one more and another after that." Facing her, he said, "I'm not as patient a man as Ron is. I won't wait forever to find out if you can make room in your life for me."

Believing she would really lose him this time, her words came in a weak and tremulous whisper. "I guess that means you won't be coming to L.A. with us. We're driving down on Sunday. Elena and Ron are coming, also, but the apartment is roomy enough for all of us," she added hopefully.

Nick immediately sensed just how vulnerable Laurel was at the moment. Not particularly liking the fact that he was taking advantage of it, he said, "I'll go to L.A. on one condition—that you spend the weekend with me in San Diego."

ON SATURDAY MORNING, Laurel checked and re-checked everything that had to be done to make the move from the house to Diana's apartment in Bel Air on Sunday as smooth as possible for all concerned.

"Carlos will drive Elena in early tomorrow," she told Diana for the third time, "so everything should be ready by the time you and Ron arrive."

"Really, it's not as if we haven't done this before."

"I know, but it's been a while." Almost to herself, she added, "I still don't think I should go to San Diego."

"Go, and try to relax. Tony's death and this black-mail business have unnerved us all. If I could, I'd get away myself for a few days, but—" she held up her copy of the movie script "—business before pleasure."

"Exactly. I should be here to do my job."

"Good God, what is there left to do that you haven't taken care of already? Now find Nick and leave. I'm sure he thought the two of you would be halfway there by now."

Diana was right. When Laurel descended the stairs, carrying her suitcase, Nick was pacing in the entry hall.

"Ready?" he asked, beaming up at her.

Laurel took in the casual outfit he was wearing: a short-sleeved blue chambray shirt and white duck pants. "I'm glad you told me to dress comfortably," she said with a smile.

"You look lovely," he complimented, and took her suitcase.

As they drove away from the estate, Nick glanced over at her. "I had hoped you could meet my father, but when I phoned him last night he said he was leaving for San Francisco on a new case. Instead, how does a din-ner-and-dance cruise on San Diego Bay sound to you?"

"It sounds wonderful," she said, hardly able to be-lieve that she and Nick would finally have a chance to be together—alone.

As they continued the four-and-a-half-hour drive, Nick regaled Laurel with stories of the more comical situations in the private investigation business that he, his father and the two investigators who worked with them had experienced. In turn, Laurel told Nick about growing up in Arizona and about some of her college experiences, including Keith Dunbar. For the first time in ages, she began to truly relax, and she was almost able to forget all the problems she had left behind.

Later in the evening, as Laurel and Nick walked on the deck of the cruise ship, he led her to the starboard side, from which they could view San Diego.

Laurel leaned against the railing and inhaled the tangy smell of the Pacific. The cool evening breeze felt good on her face, and she gazed at the myriad sparkles of night lights illuminating the city in the distance. The high rises appeared to be glistening stalagmites against a background of dark hills; lights also flickered along the rim of the harbor. Glancing to her left, she saw several sailboats and watched as their colorful sails dipped in unison into the night wind.

"It's peaceful out here, isn't it?" Nick remarked contentedly, slipping his arm around her waist.

"Yes, it wouldn't be hard for me to fall in love with your city." She tilted her head toward him and smiled softly. "I'm glad I came with you."

"I'm ecstatic." He placed her fingertips against the inside of his wrist. "Just feel my pulse. It's pounding with joy."

"Are you sure it's not the wine you had with dinner?" she teased.

"Uh-uh. Wine just goes to my head and makes me feel lovey-dovey, like I'm feeling now."

When he started to move his other arm around her, Laurel took hold of his hand. "I thought this was a dinner-and-dance cruise. So far we've only had dinner."

"Spoilsport," he chided. "Well, at least I'll get to hold you in my arms, even if we are surrounded by people."

"I've always heard there's safety in numbers."

"Don't plan on it when we get home."

"Is that a threat, Mr. Malone?"

"No, it's a promise."

Nick was true to his word. A little after midnight they were lying in each other's arms in his bed. Slowly and tenderly they made love, savoring each moment and each breathless release with no thought except of the other. Finally Laurel drifted off to sleep, peacefully and comfortably snuggled in Nick's embrace.

On Sunday morning, he hustled her out of bed early, and they had breakfast at a beach restaurant in Mission Bay before visiting Sea World. After a speedy cross-town drive, they boarded the fire-engine-red Tijuana Trolley to the Mexican border. In Mexico, they lunched on tacos and guacamole salad before Nick guided her on a whirlwind spree in the duty-free Plaza Rio Tijuana shopping center. It was dusk when they arrived back at his car, lugging their packages and wearing wide-brimmed sombreros.

On the way to his house, Nick said, "I thought we'd have dinner at La Chaumine on Pacific Beach, that is if you like French food. Then we could take in the floor show at the—"

Laurel placed her hand on his arm. "I don't know about you, but I'm exhausted. Couldn't we spend a quiet evening at home?"

Grinning broadly he confessed, "I was hoping you'd suggest that, and if you're really tired, I know just the thing to relax you."

LAUREL LEANED BACK against the side of the sunken hot tub on the cedar deck at Nick's house and sighed her contentment. Grasping the edge of the blue fiberglass, she let her aching feet rise toward the surface of the whirling water.

"Mmm," she moaned, delighting in the buoyancy.

"Relaxing, isn't it?" Nick asked as he set two glasses of red wine down next to the hot tub.

With her eyes closed, she murmured, "That it is, but I feel guilty being so comfortable while you're doing all the work in the kitchen."

Nick lowered himself onto his stomach and rested on his arms. "What work? I took two packages of frozen fish Mornay and macaroni and cheese from the freezer. Dinner can be ready whenever you are." After handing her one of the wineglasses, he picked his up. "A toast, to frozen dinners and microwave ovens."

Laurel sipped from her glass, her eyes never leaving Nick's. "I'd like to make a toast now," she said softly, unspoken love shimmering in her eyes. "To a perfect weekend. I wish it never had to end."

"It doesn't have to," he said quietly.

As though not hearing what he had just said, Laurel lowered her eyes to the swishing water in the hot tub. "It's been so wonderful. I've enjoyed doing the things that I don't usually have time to do." She looked back up at him. "I'll always remember this weekend."

"I will, too. I've done the same things many times, but they all seemed new today, as if I were doing them for the first time." Slowly he ran the back of his fingers over her arm. "I could lie here forever and just look at you, but—" with athletic grace he pushed himself up from the deck "—I've got a better idea."

He went to the kitchen door, reached inside and pushed a button on the wall. Louvered blinds descended from the overhang, giving them complete privacy. After dimming the lantern lights and raising the background music a little, he undressed and slipped into the hot tub.

"You don't need this on," he suggested, and eased the straps of her bathing suit off her shoulders. Moments later the suit lay next to the two wineglasses, and he took her in his arms.

Laurel's relaxed feelings gave way to the exhilaration that she experienced whenever Nick embraced her. But this time it was even headier and more powerful. She felt an intense joy that left her almost breathless, and when his hard, masculine body pressed against hers, her entire being burned with the need for him. As his hands caressed her, the prolonged anticipation became unbearable. Guiding her arms around his neck, she said softly, "Make love to me now, right here." She drew his head down and kissed him long and hard.

Nick's own excitement surged as her tongue sought and probed his. Reaching down, he took hold of her slender thighs and placed her legs around his waist. He could feel his heart pounding in his chest as he entered her. When she groaned, he clasped his arms around her and deepened his penetration, never feeling the fingernails that raked his shoulders.

Their excited moans mingled with the whirling water and the music floating in the air above them. They held each other hungrily, each whispering endearments as

Nick drove into her again and again until together they both soared over the edge.

The frozen dinners defrosted on the kitchen counter sometime during the night as Laurel and Nick lay side by side in his bedroom upstairs, each realizing that time was slipping away from them—all too quickly.

ON MONDAY MORNING, Nick made his appearance in court and gave his testimony at the Peters embezzlement hearing, then he and Laurel drove the hundred and forty miles to L.A. In time they reached the apartment in Bel Air—a study in French Provincial—and Laurel was in the process of unpacking in her room when Diana entered.

"How was your trip, darling? From the glow on your face, I'd say you enjoyed it."

"Am I really glowing?" she asked, still remembering the feel of Nick's arms around her during the night.

"Like a woman in love. Are you in love with Nick?" she asked tentatively.

Laurel guarded her words. "I'm very fond of him."

"No more than that?"

Casually Laurel remarked, "Really, there are so many other things I have to think about and to do. When would I have time to fall in love?"

Laurel recalled waking this morning to find Nick resting on his arm and smiling down at her. When he had asked her to stay in San Diego and to marry him, she had thought her heart would burst with joy, but time had conditioned her too well, and Nick had received only a vague answer mentioning postponement. Ever since, though, she had permitted herself to hope that she and he might work out a way to share their lives.

Hesitantly she told her mother, "If I allowed things to become serious, I'm sure Nick would want me to move to San Diego."

"Oh." The smile vanished from Diana's face. She slipped her hands into the pockets of her slacks and faced the window.

Still terribly insecure, she was terrified of the inevitable changes that would occur if her daughter ever left her. Despite the pressure Ron was putting on her to sever the comfortable bond—and she was trying to—Diana's fear of becoming ill again was too strong to chance change of any kind.

Suddenly she spun around with a newly formed cheery mask on her face. "Well, San Diego is only a short drive from here, and Nick is very special."

Hardly hoping that Diana would be so quick to give her her blessing, Laurel's heart skipped a beat. Anxiously she said, "You're special, too, Mother."

"Am I really, darling?"

"You know you are," Laurel assured her, trying to sound calm as she hung her robe in the closet. All the while she was wondering how best to tell her of Nick's proposal.

"Does Nick love you?" Diana asked, her question tinged with an ominous tone.

Laurel pulled open a dresser drawer, but, alerted by the raspy quality of her mother's voice, she paused before replying, "He says he does."

"Has he asked you to marry him?"

"Yes, he has," she admitted, steeling herself for the oncoming pain.

"I see. Well, I certainly wouldn't rush into anything. But an occasional weekend with him in San Diego might be good for you."

Laurel felt a cold chill run down her spine. "Are you suggesting that it's all right for me to have an affair with Nick as long as marriage is not in the cards?"

"Nothing of the sort," Diana objected. "I just wanted you to know that I understand. Nick is extremely attractive, and you both have . . . needs. It's just that I'm not convinced the two of you would be happy together over a long period of time. He has his private investigator work in San Diego, and you're used to a different life-style here, where your career is. And right now, Laurel, I need you desperately. You realize that, don't you?"

Turning away, Laurel said quietly, "Yes, I do."

Diana moved behind her daughter and placed a hand on her shoulder. "You know I'd never get through the filming without you. I'd die if you abandoned me. I depend on you so much."

Laurel nodded slowly. "And I—I depend on you, don't I?" she asked in a broken whisper.

In that moment, Laurel's brief hope that her life would change disintegrated, leaving her with a heaviness of heart that numbed her.

PROMPTLY AT SIX-THIRTY on Tuesday morning, Laurel and Diana left in the limousine for the on-camera rehearsal at Universal Studios, just north of greater Los Angeles. Nick and Ron were to meet them later in the star's trailer, which Laurel had insisted on in the contract. She had arranged for it to be wheeled onto the far end of the soundstage, and she'd filled it with Diana's personal things. She had known that her mother would feel more secure in familiar surroundings than in the dressing cabana that would have been provided.

As Peg, the studio stylist, worked on Diana's hair, Laurel tried to reassure a nervous Glen. "Yes, everything is in order for the trip to Hawaii."

"Only eleven days to shoot there," he mumbled, running a hand across his forehead, "and it will probably rain for a week before we even get started."

Laurel smiled. "It's not going to rain. The chamber of commerce wouldn't permit it."

"Glen," Diana said from her chair in front of the vanity, "please go somewhere else and be pessimistic. The weather is something I don't need to worry about right now."

He got up from the chair by the trailer door. "No need for you to worry about anything. I'll do it for both of us." With one hand on the doorknob, he looked back at Laurel. "Fran really did a good job with the picture spread on Diana for *People* magazine, didn't she? You can't buy publicity like that."

"Fran always does a good job," Laurel complimented. "Now go somewhere and relax."

No sooner had Glen left than Fran arrived with a photographer to take pictures. "Just a few more minutes, Fran, and Diana will be ready," Laurel informed her.

"Good," Fran said, tossing her attaché case and a newspaper onto the floral-print sofa. "Ben gets paid by the hour." She sniffled and withdrew a nasal inhaler from her purse. "Did you clear our taking some shots on the set?" she asked, and held the inhaler to her nose.

"I thought about that and decided against it because the shooting schedule is so tight. Besides, you're not submitting a photo layout. They'll only use one picture. Why not take as many as you want in here and send the best?"

A shadow of annoyance settled on Fran's face. "Really, I wish you'd stick to your job and let me do mine."

Laurel was taken by surprise at the harsh tone in the other woman's voice, and she saw that her wide mouth was twisted in irritation. At another time, she would have informed Fran that anything to do with Diana was her job, but right now she didn't want her mother upset by a scene.

"Sorry, Fran," Laurel apologized pleasantly. "I thought I was simplifying things for both of us. Why don't you have Ben take some shots of Peg doing Diana's hair?"

Fran waved a finger at the overweight photographer, and he went to work with his camera.

Peg, a young, pretty blonde, capped the can of hair spray she'd just used and glanced over at the newspaper Fran had brought in. "Did you read 'Behind the Scenes' this morning?" she asked.

Fran's face came to life. "I always begin my day with Verna's column."

Diana grimaced. "Verna probably begins her day by swallowing mean pills. What's she up to now?"

"A rather intriguing little bit of gossip," Fran said, and opened the newspaper. "Listen to this. 'Rumor has it that a still sexy, very much loved screen star has been a mother for many years. Why all the secrecy?'"

Laurel felt a weakness in her knees, and she saw Diana's face go ashen, despite her heavy makeup. At a sudden knocking on the trailer door, her head jerked toward it.

"They're ready for you, Miss Baxter," a man's voice announced.

"Okay, everyone, out," Laurel ordered, and opened the door. "She'll be right there, Doug," she told the man, and he gave her an okay sign with his fingers.

"I'll leave the paper here," Fran said, smiling broadly, then she followed the others out of the trailer.

Laurel shut the door and bounded across the narrow room. She grabbed the newspaper and read out loud. "'Why all the secrecy? And who's the lucky father? Keep reading, my dears, for further details.'" She let the paper drop onto the sofa and looked over at her mother, who had begun pacing in front of the large mirror edged with light bulbs.

"She knows!" Diana moaned, wringing her hands. "Verna knows! Pretty soon everyone will know."

"No one knows a thing," Laurel insisted. "Verna could be talking about any one of a hundred actresses."

Not listening, Diana continued walking to and fro, her eyes glazed. "The media will blow it up, and Garrison will realize you're his daughter."

"Let's not worry about him right now, please. They're waiting for you on the set."

"He's not the kind of man who would just ignore it and try to protect himself. I don't know what he might do, but I don't want to be the cause of hurting his family or destroying his career."

"Mother—" the very word jarred Laurel, and she lowered her voice "—if the truth creates a problem for him, he's brought it on himself."

"You're talking about your father."

"Only biologically!"

A harsher knocking was followed by, "Miss Baxter, they're waiting for you."

"Just a moment, Doug," Laurel called, and faced Diana. "Will you please get a hold on yourself? A cast and crew are waiting for you on the soundstage."

"How am I supposed to go before the cameras now and play high comedy when I'm about ready to cry?"

Laurel took a firm hold of her mother's shoulders. "You do it by using every bit of talent and experience you have, that's how! You're not going to let yourself down, and you're not going to let me down. You are a *star*. Now act like one!"

Diana braced herself, straightened her shoulders and took unsteady steps to the vanity. She pulled a tissue from a box, looked into the mirror and carefully dabbed at the tears that glistened in her eyes. Speaking to her reflection, she said in a choked voice, "I feel so old right now, so very old and tired." Turning, she tugged at the jacket of her gold blazer and forced a weak smile. "'Laugh, clown, laugh.' Isn't that how the saying goes?"

Laurel closed the door slowly after Diana left and leaned back against it, her heart thudding painfully in her chest. She could feel the same fear, tension and exhaustion her mother was obviously feeling. And she hated herself for having been the one to order her to work.

The sound of wild applause filled Laurel's ears as she supported herself against the trailer door, and she realized that the cast and crew were welcoming Diana Baxter back to the world of make-believe.

Cradling her face with her hands, Laurel gave vent to her tears, her sobs shaking her body as the echo of the applause resounded in the trailer.

CHAPTER SIXTEEN

NICK AND RON WATCHED from an unlit adjacent set as the director blocked the scene with Diana and her on-screen lover.

"She's fabulous, isn't she?" Ron whispered.

"That she is," Nick agreed, observing the admiration in his eyes.

When the director began the first take, Ron led Nick farther away from several of the crew, who were also captivated by Diana's performance. Quietly he said, "I just learned that Lyla Sayer left for New York to begin filming a movie. Does that take her off your list of suspects?"

"No, but she and Glen have been near the bottom for a while now."

"Busy Hollywood tongues are saying that Glen and Fran are a new item."

"Now that's interesting. What are they supposed to have in common?" Nick asked.

"Word has it that they both like French films without subtitles."

"Intellectual types, huh? That should make for some pretty thrilling evenings."

Ron looked past the cameras and over to Diana as she accused her leading man of being a jewel thief. "I don't know how she does it. This waiting to hear from the extortionist is nerve-racking. Isn't there anything we can do?"

"Don't look for trouble. It'll find us eventually. What you just said, though, makes me feel even more strongly that money isn't the only reason behind the blackmail."

"What do you mean?"

"If waiting to hear where and how to deliver the money is making you nervous, think of how it must be affecting Diana and Laurel. It could be that our extortionist is getting some kind of kick out of having them wait. The thing that worries me is that he or she could be someone we haven't even thought of. Whoever it is, though, sure isn't helping my relationship with Laurel."

"Nor mine with Diana. You know, we still have a problem with those two. It's one that I've been living with for a few years now. I didn't understand the reason that they were so close. Now that I know, I'm not sure there's anything you or I can do to change things."

"I'm all for trying," Nick assured him. "I'm going to have a little talk with Diana this evening. When she goes on location to finish the film in Hawaii, I'll ask her to go without Laurel. Speaking of Laurel, doesn't she usually watch rehearsals?"

"Always."

"I think I'll see what she's up to," Nick said, and headed for Diana's trailer.

He knocked on the door lightly and opened it. "Laurel?" When she looked up at him, he could tell she had been crying. Stepping inside, he closed the door and went to her. "What's wrong?"

"This," she said in a low voice, and pointed to the gossip column in the newspaper Fran had left.

After reading the item, Nick asked, "Did you buy this paper?"

"Fran had it with her."

"And she brought the item to your attention?"

"No, the studio hairstylist did, but what difference does it make? It's in there for everyone to read."

"There's nothing that points a finger at Diana."

"Always the optimist," she intoned morosely.

"It doesn't hurt to be one. Listen, Diana's out there doing her best. Let's not tell her about this yet."

"She already knows about it." Laurel shook her head, feeling that the tears were about to begin again. "I don't know how she's doing it. She's more upset than I am."

"Yes, I'm sure she's hurting, but she's getting through it. That should prove something to you."

"Like what, for instance?"

"That she's stronger than you think."

Before she could stop herself, Laurel cried, "For God's sake, please don't start psychoanalyzing Diana and me again!" Seeing the hurt look on Nick's face, she went to him and placed her arms around his waist. "I'm sorry. I didn't mean to snap like that. It's just that my nerves are shot. I guess I'm not the pillar of strength I pretend to be."

Nick closed his arms around her and rocked her gently. "Where is it written that you're supposed to be a pillar of strength?" He felt her breasts rise against his chest as she sighed deeply.

With Nick holding her in his embrace, Laurel remembered how wonderful she had felt during the weekend in San Diego, and she suddenly realized that, right now, she didn't want to have to think of anything or anyone other than him. She wanted to give to him in every way that she could, and she wanted to lose herself in the love he offered her.

No, she reminded herself almost immediately. That was only a beautiful dream that couldn't possibly compete with the reality that faced her....

AFTER A LATE DINNER at the apartment, while Laurel was on the phone with Glen, Nick suggested that he and Diana go out on the balcony. She asked Ron to join them, but he saw Nick shake his head, and he said he wanted to catch up on some reading.

As Nick closed the sliding glass door, Diana sauntered to the black wrought-iron railing. Holding on to it, she tilted her head back, saying, "Isn't it a glorious evening?"

Joining her, Nick smiled. "You were pretty glorious yourself today. How do you remember all those script changes they give you and manage to wind up exactly where the director and lighting people want you to?"

Her long silk robe swished as she turned. "Experience, Nick, experience. I've been acting in films for most of my life. The soundstage is my natural habitat. The work becomes difficult only when I'm asked to do something that I instinctively know is wrong for the character I'm portraying."

"You love your work, don't you?"

"Does it show?"

"It does, but I'm not sure that Laurel loves it quite as much as you do."

Diana looked at him in silence, then gazed out over the lights on the hillside below. "Did she say so?"

"She could never bring herself to do that." After a lingering silence, he said, "I know that acting is your life, but does it have to be Laurel's, as well?"

Diana whirled around. "Acting is not her life. Laurel is a businesswoman, an extremely competent one. Being my personal manager is a career that she's chosen."

"Diana, the cameras are shut down for the day. This is real life we're talking about. I love your daughter, but I can't get her to break away from you so that she can create a life of her own."

Sharply she asked, "And you think I'm stopping her?"

"Prove you're not by going to Hawaii without her. You'll have Ron with you."

Stunned by the suggestion, Diana took quick strides to the opposite end of the balcony. She stopped by the potted palm and glared sideways at Nick. "For the past ten years, Laurel has always been my companion. I need *her* for support, not Ron."

Nick took slow, measured steps toward her. "*You* need? When are you going to consider your daughter's needs and start standing on your own two feet?" He braced one hand on the railing and shoved the other in his trouser pocket. "I know about Keith, the man who wanted to marry her, and I know about Brian Cannady."

In a mildly interested tone, Diana said, "Laurel never told me about anyone named Keith."

"Keith Dunbar," Nick supplied. "He was a young man she loved in college, a man she gave up to take care of you."

Diana lowered her eyes and looked out over the railing.

"Don't you see?" Nick asked softly. "You and Laurel are suffocating each other without realizing it. Your daughter has a great deal of love in her that she's never allowed herself to give to a man."

With her fingers nervously stroking the pearls at her throat, Diana said with staid calm, "I understand that you want to marry Laurel."

"More than anything else in life, but she gave me the same lines she handed to Brian Cannady."

Diana began to wring her hands. After long, difficult moments, she said in a strained voice, "Nick, I don't know if I can make it without Laurel."

"You made it today. You were out there in front of those cameras all by yourself. Laurel wasn't with you then."

"No, she wasn't," Diana admitted, seeing Nick's point but feeling torn. Nodding, she said, "You're right, though. No matter how many people are in a scene, when you're acting you really are alone, wrapped up in the character you've become."

"That's Laurel to a T. She's completely wrapped up in the part she plays so well, but it's only a supporting part, Diana. Only you can let her be the star of her own life."

She looked deeply into Nick's eyes. "Do you realize what you're asking me to do? It's only been in these past ten years that I've had my daughter with me. I made a terrible mistake when I left her with Frieda and Jerome. I can't give her up now."

"Try thinking about Laurel. Why continue to make her pay for your mistakes?"

Nick's words weighed on Diana heavily, choking her, filling her with guilt and forcing her to realize just how self-centered she had been. As great as her fear of change was, her fear that someday her daughter might come to hate her was even greater. At that moment Diana decided that any disaster that should come her way wouldn't be as bad as Laurel's hatred.

With raw pain in her eyes, she faced Nick. In a teary voice she admitted, "I have been making her pay for my mistakes, haven't I? But I never meant to be so thoughtless and selfish. I guess it was just so easy to let Laurel take care of everything, and . . . it—it was a way of having her with me finally."

When Nick heard the sliding glass door open, he whispered, "Please think about Hawaii."

"There you are," Laurel said cheerfully. "I just got off the phone with Glen. He and the director are ecstatic." She took hold of Diana's hands. "And rightfully so. You were marvelous today."

Creating a smile that hid her pain, Diana said, "I was, wasn't I? Just wait until tomorrow. Where's Ron?"

"In his room. Shall I get him?"

"No, no. I'll go. I want to talk to him about the on-location shoot." Diana took a deep breath. "Darling, I've been thinking. Would you be terribly disappointed if Ron and I went on to Hawaii alone? We've never really been away together, just the two of us."

Laurel took an uneasy step backward, then froze, feeling as though her blood had changed to ice water. Again she felt betrayed and discarded, just as she had when her mother had attended the awards ceremony without her. Suddenly she was a frightened little girl alone in the darkness, wanting to cry out for help, but knowing no one was there to hear her.

"We're only scheduled to be in Hawaii for a little more than two weeks," Diana said, then turned abruptly and sailed into the living room, where she folded her hands over her heart to still the pounding.

"Two weeks," Laurel repeated weakly before following her mother into the apartment. "Why the sudden change in plans?" she asked in a desperate tone.

"That would give you a little vacation of your own. Perhaps you and Nick could do something together."

Laurel turned and stared daggers at Nick, who was standing by the doorway to the balcony. "This is your idea, isn't it?"

"I only wanted—"

"*You* wanted! What right do you have to want anything from Diana or me?"

"Please, Laurel," Diana intervened, "be reasonable. You and I should have a life outside of our jobs. We both deserve a chance to find happiness."

"I thought we were happy," Laurel insisted.

"I'm talking about a different kind of happiness than we have now. I mean . . . with Ron and Nick."

"Nick?" Laurel exclaimed in a harsh, raw voice, and she glared back at him. "My, but you have been busy."

Just then Ron came into the living room. "What's going on? I could hear you through my closed door."

With clenched teeth, Laurel informed him, "Nick has been busy rearranging our lives to suit himself."

"Ron," Diana said quickly, "would you go over tomorrow's script with me?"

"But I've always done that," Laurel said, feeling yet another shock wave rock her brain.

On the verge of tears, Diana said quietly, "I know, Laurel, I know. I've always let you do too much, haven't I?" Forcing a smile, she reached for Ron's hand and said to her daughter, "We'll talk more about Hawaii another time."

Feeling as though her heart was breaking, Laurel watched them leave the room. Heat surged up her neck and over her face. In the next instant she was numb with confusion and rage. As she faced Nick, her first impulse was to lash out at him again, to tell him to mind his own business, to let her and Diana be. But when she saw the concern on his face, she began to question her own mental disarray.

Dear God, she thought, turning away, weren't things difficult enough without continually feeling torn between her mother and Nick? Earlier she had cherished the hope that she and Nick could spend the rest of their lives together, but this underhanded maneuvering was beyond toleration.

Did he actually think that Diana could survive without her? Yes, he had shoved that piece of advice at her often enough. She looked back at him and saw the determined look on his face, an expression that said he was prepared to have it out with her right now. It was the same look that she had seen on Brian's face that evening he had given her an ultimatum: marry him or else. And she had sent him away. But some force inside her warned her about doing the same thing to Nick. The force was so powerful that her anger began to melt away. In its place, she felt an equally powerful longing to make him understand how much he and Diana both meant to her.

Years of self-denial, however, took hold of her again, and the balance tipped in her mother's favor once more. Only half aware of her words, Laurel said, "Rather than be preoccupied with Diana's travel plans, I'd appreciate it if you'd spend more time doing the job I hired you to do."

Nick stiffened at her verbal jab. "A job that you've made almost impossible from the very beginning."

"You know why I had to."

"I know why you chose to, and you're very good at making choices, almost as good as you are at keeping things from people."

"You sound as if you believe I enjoy it."

He saw the stress in her eyes and softened his tone. "No, I don't think you always enjoy it, but I do think it's become a way of life for you. You probably couldn't change if you wanted to."

Laurel could feel Nick slipping away from her, but she didn't want him to. As calmly as she could, she asked, "What is it you think I'm keeping from you now?"

"For one thing, the night you were at Tony's, you found out how he learned that you were Diana's daughter, didn't you? You're too smart not to have asked."

As painful as it was to rehash that evening, Laurel did so, quietly. "Tony had gone through some of his father's records. He came across old financial statements that Wayne had drawn up years ago, transactions that indicated he had transferred money from Diana's account, money he sent periodically to the Davises in Arizona. Later transfers were made to me at the University of Arizona. Tony guessed why."

"And you didn't think it would be important that I know any of this," he commented dryly.

"Nick, I didn't see what difference it would make. At the time, you didn't know I was Diana's daughter."

He shook his head slowly. "Well, Miss Davis, knowing you has been an experience, one I'll try like hell to forget as soon as this business is cleared up. Right now I need to take a long walk, or I'm liable to say things I'll be sorry for."

Nick started for the door, but unable to control himself, he faced her again. "Things like I don't trust you. I never have been able to. Every time I turn around I learn about something else you've kept from me. I never know what I might learn tomorrow or the next day. It's a hell of a way to operate."

Laurel's heart sank as Nick stormed out of the room, but shortly he was back.

"Here," he said, thrusting a small box in the palm of her hand. "I've been waiting for the right time to give you this, but it doesn't look like that time will ever come."

After the door to the apartment slammed shut, Laurel opened the little box and withdrew the gold scarf pin. She wiped away the teardrop that fell on the two entwined hearts, closed her fingers around the pin and held it against her breast.

Standing alone in the middle of the room, she whispered, "Thank you, Nick."

CHAPTER SEVENTEEN

THE FIRST THING that Laurel did in the morning was to check the newspaper. Her heart sank as she read the gossip columnist's update that stated the mysterious mother-and-daughter team were currently in Los Angeles, and their names would appear in Monday's column.

"Monday," Laurel moaned, realizing she would have to tell Diana, who was certain to hear about it at the studio.

Since Nick hadn't returned to the apartment until well after midnight, Laurel decided not to wake him. After showing Verna's column to Diana and Ron, they left for the studio in the limousine on schedule.

To Laurel's amazement, the day's shooting went smoothly. Diana held up exceptionally well under the strain. Her performance before the cameras strengthened with each scene. Laurel had to attribute much of Diana's success to Ron's constant caring support. But as much as she liked him and appreciated what he had done and was doing for her, Laurel couldn't bring herself to forgive him for using the same tactics that Nick had to separate her and her mother.

In the limousine on the way back to Bel Air, Diana suggested they have dinner out: she needed to get her mind off Verna's column. Both she and Ron were surprised when Laurel announced she would remain at the apartment. In reality, she was anxious to see Nick. Several times, she had phoned the apartment to thank him for the scarf pin, but each time, Elena had reported that she hadn't seen him since she'd prepared his breakfast.

After Diana and Ron left the apartment, Laurel tried to busy herself by going over the auditor's report on Diana's financial situation, but neither her heart nor her head was in it. After a cursory check and deciding that all was well, she placed the report back in the desk drawer in the living room and looked up when Elena came in.

"Can I fix you something before I leave, Miss Davis?"

Laurel smiled pleasantly. "Thank you, no." She glanced at the digital clock on the desk. "You'd better get ready. Carlos will be here any minute to pick you up."

"Are you sure you don't want me to stay?"

"No, you go on to Santa Barbara, and we'll be back at the estate tomorrow for the weekend. Say hello to everyone, and give Rosa a kiss for me."

"I will. Good night, Miss Davis."

"Good night."

For a while, Laurel wandered around the quiet apartment, wondering where Nick was. She had the sinking feeling that he might have returned to San Diego. If he had, she decided that she couldn't blame him. To busy herself, she fixed a cup of tea and curled up in a corner of the sofa.

The opening of the apartment door startled her, and she jumped up, a smile brightening her face when she saw that it was Nick. Barefoot, she ran to him and threw her arms around his neck. "I'm so glad to see you!" she cried.

Nick grinned and cocked his head. "Let me know what I've done to merit a welcome like this, and I'll make a habit of it."

"Where have you been?"

He drew her arms from around his neck and stepped back. "Doing the job you hired me to do," he said with a smile, reminding her of her own words. Walking into the living room, he said, "Following Fran around is like following a comet. And I thought traffic was bad in San Diego."

After silently thanking God that he hadn't returned home, she asked, "Did you learn anything?"

"Yes," he said, tossing his jacket on the chair across from the sofa. "The LAPD takes their No Parking signs seriously. I got a ticket, but it was worth it. Fran made a visit to Verna's office."

"But sometimes she plants items in the gossip columns for publicity reasons."

"She may also be the one feeding Verna the information I read in her column this morning. You did, too, I'm sure."

Laurel nodded and asked, "Would you like something to drink?"

"A bourbon and water would be nice."

While Laurel fixed his drink, Nick asked, "Have you ever seen the manuscript of the biography Fran's doing on Diana?"

"No, but she knows I have to approve whatever she writes. Why do you ask?"

Nick loosened his tie and unbuttoned the collar of his shirt. "Today I was thinking about that file you told me you found in the cabinet at Tony's beach house. What if he was sharing that information with Fran, helping her to do her research?"

Handing Nick his drink, Laurel said, "But Tony promised me that he would never give that information to anyone."

"I'm afraid Tony Koop would never have received an award for honesty."

"He might have been fooled, though," she said reflectively. "Fran could have told him she wanted to see Wayne's old records to corroborate dates of contracts. For the book, she had to know where and when Diana had made films. Fran also wanted to collect data regarding Diana's incomes and major expenditures. He wouldn't have known that I had already given her that information."

"Fooled or not, I'm guessing that Fran could have gotten Wayne's records from Tony. Why else would he have taken ancient files home with him? He didn't need them to do his job. Fran could have been the third visitor Tony had that night. She might even have been there all the time you were and left before Ron returned to the beach house."

"Are you saying that Fran could have killed Tony?"

"Maybe she didn't mean to. The neighbor said she heard an argument. Perhaps she really heard two, one that he had with you and a second with Fran. She could have hit him with something, panicked and run."

Laurel folded Nick's suit jacket and draped it over the arm of the easy chair before sitting down. "Fran, a murderer and an extortionist?" she murmured.

"It's only a possibility," Nick said as he leaned forward and interlaced his fingers. "The day we were at the beach house I also saw a nasal inhaler. It and the gold cigarette lighter could belong to Fran. Let's speculate that she was there when you arrived and overheard Tony tell you he wouldn't broadcast what he'd found out. What if she wanted to use it in the biography?''

"But—" Laurel interrupted.

"Wait just a minute. I'm only hypothesizing. Maybe Tony meant to keep his promise to you. They could have argued, and she might have hit him with something."

"The jade replica of the Eiffel Tower that Diana gave him! Tony always kept it on the bar, and it was gone."

"If the police had found it, forensics could have detected minute traces of blood and perhaps partial prints, even if it had been wiped off."

"It could be somewhere in the Pacific Ocean by now," Laurel said mournfully.

"I imagine a good-size jade piece would be expensive."

"It was expensive, too much so to be thrown away." Laurel's mind was reeling. "But that's a lot of what ifs, Nick. Why would Fran do the things you're suggesting?"

"Greed, revenge, some kind of high she might get out of it."

"But how could we prove any of this?"

"We couldn't. Not yet. What kind of financial arrangements were made with Fran for the biography?"

"The profits from the book are to be divided fiftyfifty between her and Diana."

Nick leaned back, extended an arm over the sofa and began tapping his fingers on it. "If the fact that Diana had had a love child were to be in the book, talk-show hosts here and abroad would be begging for Diana or Fran to appear on their programs. That sure wouldn't hurt book sales."

"But Fran knows I'll be checking the galleys."

"One chapter could be substituted for another, and after the book came out, I doubt that Diana would deny that you were her daughter. Certainly she couldn't sue Fran for telling the truth. I'd sure like to get a look at that manuscript."

So would I, Laurel thought as she stood up. "I could tell her I wanted to check what she's written so far for accuracy."

"And as Tony did with the financial statements, she'd show you only what she wanted you to see."

Nick's gaze drifted over Laurel as she stood there, still barefoot, looking as though her thoughts were a million miles away. He had been thinking about her all day long. Try as he had, he couldn't get her out of his mind, let alone out of his system. And the instant he had seen her, he had felt an inner peace and contentment he had come to need every bit as much as he needed air to breathe. Thinking how quiet it was in the apartment, he asked, "Where is everybody?"

"Diana and Ron have gone out to dinner, and Elena went back to the house in Santa Barbara."

"Leaving you here alone."

"I was anxious to see you again," she admitted honestly.

"I missed being with you today," he said, then stood and took her in his arms. With his cheek against the side of her head, he inhaled deeply. "Your hair smells wonderful, and you feel so damn good."

She placed her hands against his back and let her fingers slip down to his waist, the warmth of him penetrating her hands. In a soft voice, she said, "Thank you for the pin, Nick. It's lovely. I'll treasure it always." She kissed the side of his throat.

"Umm," he sighed, then whispered, "I want to make love with you."

She drew back from him and looked into his eyes. In them she saw the reflection of her own desire, her need and her love. She took his hand and led him from the living room.

Minutes later they lay in his bed, wrapped in each other's arms. He kissed her eyes, her cheeks and her lips. "What am I going to do about you?" he asked quietly. "I had a hard time keeping my mind on the job today."

"Really?" she asked dreamily, luxuriating in the feel of his lips as they trailed up the side of her neck and caught hold of her earlobe. The slow movements of his hands over her sensitized body weren't helping her think clearly, either.

"A man's got to be able to do his job," Nick murmured.

"We both have jobs to do," she whispered, and kissed him long and deeply.

An hour later, as Nick slept soundly, Laurel rose from his bed and went to her room. For some time she had lain awake beside him, thinking about going to San Diego as he had again asked. As she had weighed the possibility, she'd had to admit that perhaps Nick was right; maybe her mother was stronger than Laurel believed. Her work before the cameras at the studio was certainly going exceptionally well.

Still wearing her robe, Laurel peered out the window in her room. If only the blackmail business was over with, she thought in frustration. That would make a decision so much easier. She thought of what Nick had said about Fran and the manuscript.

A glance at the clock on her nightstand told her it was a little after 9:00 p.m. Wondering if Fran was at home, she picked up the phone and called her apartment. After listening to the beginning of a taped message, she replaced the receiver and quickly changed into a gray plaid suit. Minutes later she was in a taxi, heading toward Fran's apartment on Bristol Avenue in Brentwood.

"GOOD EVENING, Miss Davis," the uniformed man said as he opened the cab door for her.

"Hi, Warren. Is your wife feeling better?"

"Agnes is fine. It was just a touch of the flu. Are you here to see Miss Gregory?"

"Yes."

"I'm afraid she's not in. She left about two hours ago."

Laurel made a show of checking her watch. "I guess I am early. I'm to meet her here. Do you think it would be all right if I waited in her apartment?"

"I'm sure Miss Gregory would want you to." He opened the front door to the building and tapped three numerals on the wall phone. "Agnes, would you come to the lobby and take Miss Davis up to Miss Gregory's apartment? I put the passkey back on the rack."

Laurel exchanged a few pleasantries with Warren's wife as they rode the elevator to the sixth floor. As soon as the woman let her into the apartment and closed the door, Laurel went directly to the den and started going through the file cabinet next to Fran's desk.

She checked drawer after drawer and was surprised at the number of projects the woman seemed to be working on, but there was no trace of the manuscript. The last drawer proved equally disappointing, so she went to the desk but found that the drawers were locked. Remembering the afternoon she had seen Fran place something under the desk clock before they'd left to have lunch together, she picked up the clock and smiled when she saw the key.

Quickly she unlocked the desk and began going through the drawers. In the bottom left one she found a hanging file rack. All of the labeled folders contained newspaper clippings, magazine articles and handwritten notes on various aspects of Diana's life and career. Still no manuscript, though.

After thoroughly searching the desk, she locked it, replaced the key under the clock and began to check the credenza near the typewriter.

"The manuscript!" she cried aloud when she found it.

Her eyes raced over the pages as she reviewed her mother's early years growing up in Texas, the beauty pageant she had won in 1950 and her leaving home to go to Hollywood. Flipping the pages over, Laurel searched for events that took place the year she had been born. She read about Diana's sixth movie that year and about a supposed vacation in Europe. The biography picked up with her seventh film in Hollywood the following year.

Laurel sighed with relief, but then she noticed a faint pencil mark between two paragraphs. She held the piece of paper up under the desk light and tilted it until she could make out an arrow that had been almost completely erased.

"An insert?" she asked herself in a quiet but troubled voice.

She remembered that Nick had said Fran would show her a manuscript that contained only what she wanted it to. Hastily she rummaged through the credenza for any signs of other material to be included. She found nothing.

Laurel thought for a moment, concentrating on where she would put things she didn't want seen, items like birthday presents. The shelf in her closet was one place.

She went to Fran's bedroom and had to force herself to further invade the woman's privacy when she opened the closet door. On the shelf she saw the usual boxes that she herself had at home in her closet. To the left was a built-in chest of drawers. Checking each one, she found sweaters and other apparel. In the bottom drawer, however, a folded towel covered something hard that was wrapped in a blue plastic shopping bag.

In her crouched position, Laurel felt a cold shiver ripple down her spine, and she jerked her hand back from the package. After a deep breath, her trembling fingers moved across the slender tip of the wrapped object to a broader rectangular base. Slowly she peeled back the plastic cover.

"My God," she gasped, staring down at the jade replica of the Eiffel Tower that Diana had given Tony.

"Pretty, isn't it?"

Laurel's head snapped up, and she saw Fran looming over her. The woman's cold green eyes bore into hers; her mouth was twisted into a thin-lipped smile.

"Fran! I—I—"

"Save your breath. There's nothing you could possibly say that could excuse what you're doing."

Still holding the jade piece, Laurel pushed herself to a standing position and ran nervous fingers through her hair. "I realize that only too well, but I had to know."

Fran glanced at the replica and crossed her arms. "Just what is it you had to know so badly that you'd lie to Warren and search my apartment like a common thief?"

Laurel kept her eyes on Fran and stepped cautiously from the confines of the closet. She moved past the scowling woman and placed the jade replica on the dresser near the door to the living room. Steadying her voice, she said, "I was looking for the manuscript of Diana's biography."

"In my closet?"

"I know that sounds strange, but it's the truth."

Fran scrutinized her visitor's face before striding into the living room. When Laurel moved to the doorway, she saw her go to a side table and pour a drink into a small crystal glass.

After taking a long swallow, Fran plunked down the glass and peered over at Laurel. "I wouldn't have thought you'd confuse an objet d'art with typing paper."

Frightened and embarrassed, Laurel summoned all her courage. "Where did you get the jade replica?"

"Don't be coy. We both know where I got it."

"From Tony's beach house," Laurel said, thinking her heart was going to stop. She wondered how far to go with her questions, knowing that if Fran admitted to killing Tony, the chances of the woman's letting her walk out of her apartment were pretty slim.

With the glass in one hand and her other braced against her hip, Fran sauntered over to her desk and leaned against it. "If you wanted to see the manuscript so badly, why didn't you just ask me for it?"

"I should have. I realize that."

"Do you, now?"

The arrogance in Fran's voice and expression got to Laurel and bolstered her courage. "I didn't trust you to show me all of it."

Fran's eyes narrowed. "You don't trust many people, do you? But you did trust Tony." A wry peal of laughter traveled across the room. "You were even a greater fool than he was."

"Is that why you killed him?" Laurel asked before she could stop the words from coming out of her mouth.

"*I* killed Tony?" She snickered, took a cigarette from a cut-glass box on the desk and lit it with a gold lighter. After blowing a strong stream of smoke from between her lips, she asked, "When did you dream up that ridiculous idea?"

"How do you explain having the jade piece Diana gave him?"

"Tony was quite generous. I admired it, and he said I could have it. It's as simple as that."

"Is that why you're hiding it in your closet?"

"Only until I have it appraised and insured. Don't tell me you think it's the murder weapon the police are looking for."

"It could well be."

Fran smiled. "You'd better hope not. It has your fingerprints on it now. It would be a simple matter for me to tell the police that I was in Tony's bedroom the night you were there. I could say that after you left, I went into the living room and found him dead. The jade replica was on the floor next to him." Fran's voice turned into a simper. "I know I shouldn't have taken it, but I was only trying to protect Laurel . . . my friend."

Laurel felt another jolt in the pit of her stomach and tried to convince herself that the police would never accept that as proof that she had killed Tony. But maybe they would.

After taking another long puff of her cigarette, Fran asked, "What is this sudden interest you have in playing detective? Don't you have enough to do keeping Diana together, at least until I finish the biography?''

Laurel met Fran's accusing eyes. "You won't be finishing it, but you will be well paid for the effort you've already put into it."

"Oh, no, you don't." Fran crushed her cigarette out in the ashtray on the desk. "That book has cost me a great deal. I've put too much sweat and time into it to let you take it away from me now. I have enough material to finish it as an unauthorized biography. In fact, I plan to liven things up a bit, make it a little juicier for the reading public, and there would be no splitting of royalties with Diana."

Nick's suppositions came back to haunt Laurel as she stared at the wild look on the woman's face. Cautiously Laurel reached for her purse. "You've never liked me, have you, Fran?"

"No," she answered with clear contempt. "You're like a princess in a fairy tale. You didn't have to claw your way up in the business world like I did. You breezed through college with all your expenses paid and walked right into a plum of a job. You even have the effrontery to tell me how to do mine. That's what really rankles!"

The bitterness in her voice seemed like a tangible force striking at Laurel. She wasn't sure whether to detest Fran or to pity her. In as calm a voice as she could manage, Laurel said, "Despite what you may think, my life hasn't exactly been that of a princess. As for having told you how to do your job, I never saw it that way. I assumed you realized I was only doing mine. I guess I made the mistake of believing we both had Diana's interest at heart."

"Let's just say I'm not quite as concerned as you are about your—" Fran pulled her mouth into a sour grin "—employer."

She knows! Laurel thought, the shock of the realization holding her immobile. With false bravado she lifted her head high. "I don't see how we can work together anymore, Fran. I think it's best that we end our business relationship right now. You're fired." She edged her way to the door. "As for the unauthorized biography, I'll see to it that Diana sues if you write anything that you can't prove in court."

Fran moved slowly toward her. "Don't worry, princess, I learned long ago how to do my homework. And there's enough sensationalism in Diana Baxter's life to make *my* book a bestseller."

"If you get to finish it," Laurel said curtly, and hurried from the apartment.

Once outside the building, she walked blindly down the avenue, her heart beating furiously. She never saw the man's shoulder she bumped against, nor did she hear car brakes being slammed on or the driver curse as she crossed the street.

If only she could calm down, get things into perspective and figure out what to do. She dared not go to the police. What could she tell them? That Fran might be blackmailing her, that she might have killed Tony? There was no law saying that he couldn't give the woman a gift someone had given him. And there was no way Laurel could prove that Fran was at the beach house the night Tony died. As for the unauthorized biography, she wouldn't be the first writer to sell one to a publisher.

Nick. She had to get back to Nick. He'd know what to do.

CHAPTER EIGHTEEN

IT WAS ALMOST MIDNIGHT when Laurel quietly opened the door to the apartment in Bel Air. She was exhausted, physically and emotionally, but she knew that the moment she saw Nick, she would feel much better.

"Where the hell have you been?" he growled in hushed tones.

From the entrance, she saw a scowling Nick standing in the living room, wearing his velour robe. "I was out," she whispered inanely.

"That's obvious, but at midnight and alone? You did this to me once before, and a man was murdered. I'm afraid to ask what happened this time."

Her steps uneasy, she entered the living room and dropped her purse onto a chair. "Please, Nick, don't be angry with me."

"Angry? I passed anger an hour ago. I'm well into rage. Don't you realize that I care what happens to you?"

Laurel slipped off her jacket and tossed it on top of her purse. "Thank you for caring."

"Diana and Ron have gone to bed. I told them you had, too. I didn't want them walking the floor with me. Just where were you?"

"Let's go into the kitchen," she suggested.

There, she slumped down on one of the leather-covered benches in the breakfast nook. "I went to Fran's apartment to try and find the manuscript."

The crisp sound of the slap of his palm on his forehead made her jump. "You know, lady, you're a personal manager, not a detective."

"I had to do something! I couldn't just wait to see if Verna names Diana and me in her column on Monday. Besides, I was just trying to help."

"Help? You didn't have the slightest idea of what you might have walked into. Damn it, you could have gotten hurt! You're not, are you?"

"No bruises, if that's what you mean."

Sitting across from her, he asked, "What possessed you to take off like that without telling me? Did Fran phone you?"

"I called her, but she wasn't at home."

His eyes narrowed with suspicion. "How'd you get in?"

"I know the doorman."

"And?"

"Fran caught me going through her closet."

Nick's back hit the wall behind him with a thud, and he muttered a curse. "Everybody wants to be a P.I., but nobody has the patience it takes. I suppose you told her you were collecting clothes for charity."

Exasperated, Laurel blurted out, "Will you be serious!"

He smiled blandly. "Changing your mind about wanting a man with a sense of humor?"

"Right now I need your common sense. I found the jade replica of the Eiffel Tower hidden in her closet."

"Then we can go to police."

Her long lashes flickered a few times. "That's not a good idea. It has my fingerprints all over it now."

"And if forensics should find Tony's blood on it—" He didn't bother to finish. "I'm guessing that Fran said she either bought it from him or he gave it to her."

"The latter."

"Did you find the manuscript?"

She nodded. "Nothing damaging, but in the section covering the year I was born, I noticed a penciled arrow that had been partially erased."

"It could mean nothing, or it could have been a place for added copy later on."

"I thought the same thing, and that's what I was looking for when I found the jade piece. Nick, I'm sure she killed him, and I think she knows about Diana and me."

"Did she say so?"

"Not exactly, but we had an awful scene, and I fired her. Now she's threatening to write an unauthorized biography."

"If we could prove that she was at Tony's beach house that night, Rodriguez would take over from there."

"How could we do that?"

"Beats the hell out of me. Do you have any idea where she was supposed to be?"

Laurel racked her brains. "That was Monday night, the seventh. Fran was at the house that morning, and she said she had a meeting in L.A. that evening. But where?" She thought hard for several moments, then her eyes lit up. "She had an International Association of Business Communicators meeting. It's a public-relations organization."

"Is there some way you could find out if she attended?"

"I know Jim Wright, the secretary. He'd have the minutes of the meeting. But what if Fran didn't show up? That wouldn't prove *where* she was."

"That's the way investigation work goes. You track down one thing at a time. It's like my new interest in gold cigarette lighters. Reva doesn't seem to have hers. I wonder if Fran still—"

"Nick," Laurel interrupted him, "I didn't think about it before, but Fran used a gold lighter tonight."

"She did?" Nick leaned forward and cupped his hands over Laurel's. "See how nicely things turn out when we work together? For the sake of my sanity, promise me you won't go prowling around alone at night again. It makes me nervous."

Smiling for the first time in hours, Laurel said, "I promise." She saw the sudden change in his expression and asked, "What's the matter?"

"My sixth sense is giving me trouble."

"About what?"

"Your friend Reva. It was something she said when I visited her shop the day I bought the scarf pin for you. It keeps coming back to me."

"If I knew what you were talking about, it would make a lot more sense."

"She said that Tony had apparently picked on the wrong woman. Wasn't Reva his last fling?"

"Well, yes, as far as I know, but even if Reva could have done such a horrible thing to Tony, I'll never believe that she'd blackmail Diana and me."

"That's why I have to keep reminding myself that his murderer and the extortionist may not be the same person. It could be that we're dealing with two different people."

"Nick, I honestly hope the police find out what happened at Tony's, but right now I'm more concerned about who's trying to blackmail Diana and just what Verna is going to write for her gossip column on Monday."

"Yes, Monday's getting closer, isn't it? Listen, I have a hunch, but I'll need your help."

"I'll do anything that will bring an end to this nightmare I've been living."

"Good. Do you think you could find out where Reva was the night Tony died?"

"I know where she was...at her boutique. She looked exhausted Tuesday and told me she'd been up until one in the morning taking inventory."

"Until one, huh? Well, I need time to check out a few things, but here's what I have in mind...."

NICK LEFT THE APARTMENT early Friday morning, saying he would meet everyone in Santa Barbara later in the evening. At noon, after the director at the studio gave the instruction to wrap it for the week, Laurel went to see Jim Wright to check on the meeting Fran had supposedly attended. And as soon as she arrived at the estate in Santa Barbara, she made a phone call to L.A.

"Fran," she said when the woman answered, "this is Laurel. We need to talk."

"I thought you said quite enough when we met last. If you're concerned about my pressing charges against you for burglarizing my apartment, don't be. I haven't the time for it."

"It's not that. I wonder if you'd consider taking Diana back on as a client."

"So, you're having second thoughts about having fired me."

"It's something I'd like to discuss with you. Could you come to the house at eight o'clock tomorrow night?"

"For an apology?" Fran asked, self-satisfaction obvious in her question.

Laurel bit her lip and said, "Yes."

"Well, Miss High-and-Mighty, even hearing you apologize wouldn't make the drive worthwhile."

"It's not just that," Laurel said quickly as she fidgeted with the phone cord. "I want to talk to you about Diana's biography."

"Why can't we talk about it now?"

"Because it's rather complex, but believe me, it could really affect sales when the book is published."

"I doubt if it would be anything new to me."

Knowing it was necessary to get Fran to the house if Nick's plan was going to work, Laurel decided to go all the way to lure her there. "It's about Verna's recent columns."

After a lengthy pause, Fran queried, "And you're willing to talk about it?"

"That and more."

"I'll be there, but be prepared to renegotiate my salary."

Laurel jerked the receiver away from her ear when Fran slammed hers down. The next phone call she made was to Reva.

ON SATURDAY EVENING, Ron took Diana to the country club as Nick had asked him to do. At eight-fifteen, while Laurel and Nick waited in the salon, he asked her, "You told them both eight o'clock, didn't you?"

"Yes, and they said they'd be here."

Nick checked the clock on the mantel again. "Experience has taught me that when people's emotions are agitated, they have a hard time guarding their words. If I'm any judge of character, those two will be more than willing to go for each other's jugular."

"It's true Fran and Reva can't stand one another, but I don't know. I hope your plan works."

"So do I, for a number of reasons."

In a deceptively calm voice, she said, "I guess you're anxious to get back to San Diego."

"That's not one of the reasons. I'm anxious for you to get this mess behind you, so you can start making plans for a life of your own."

"After she renegotiates my salary," Fran said sharply as she sauntered into the room. She sent Nick a hard look and asked, "Where does he fit in with our little talk?"

"It's always a pleasure to see you, Fran," Nick said, smiling.

"I'm not here on a pleasure trip, but if Laurel wants to air her dirty linen in public, that's her business."

Fran took heavy steps to the table off to the side of the door and tossed her purse down on it. As she reached inside for a pad and pen, a smiling Reva entered, not seeing her.

"Okay," she said to Laurel, "let's get this discussion about Diana's wardrobe for Hawaii over with. I don't want my Saturday night to be a total loss." She glanced at Nick and examined Laurel's taut expression. "What's up? The two of you look as guilty as sin."

"Well, Laurel," Fran remarked snidely, "you're not too particular about who you invite into your home, are you?"

Reva's earrings jangled as her head jerked toward
Fran. "Apparently she isn't." Sending Laurel an inquisitive look, she asked, "What does she have to do
with the clothes Diana's going to be wearing in Hawaii?"

"Reva, dear," Fran simpered, "I would have thought
you would have changed professions by now. I hear that
every shop in New York has turned down your new line
of sportswear. You might want to try Alaska. Your cre-
ations might have a chance of success there... as oddi-
ties." She aimed hostile eyes at Laurel. "If you want to
talk to me, we'll do it in private."

"We're not going to discuss your job or Diana's
wardrobe," Laurel said calmly.

"Then for God's sake, why did you drag me all the
way here from L.A.?"

"And ruin my Saturday night?" Reva added.

Laurel cast doubtful eyes at Nick, then informed her
guests, "Nick isn't a security consultant. He's a private
investigator, and he believes that one of you is an extortionist and possibly a murderer."

"Are you out of your mind?" Reva asked, obviously
shaken by Laurel's accusation.

"Either that," Fran said, "or you've been sampling
happy pills." She reached down and grabbed her purse.

Quickly Nick said, "I suggest that you stay, Fran. You
can either come up with a few answers now or at police
headquarters, later."

"Laurel," Reva asked, seemingly astonished, "what
is this all about? Why drag me into this? I thought we
were friends."

"I'm sorry, Reva," she apologized, feeling worse than
she had when Nick had told her of his plan, "but I've

been going through hell this past month, and it's got to end."

"Fran," Nick asked, "Where were you the night Tony died?"

She tugged at the strap of her purse. "I was at a meeting in L.A. Why?"

"You showed up," Laurel corrected her, "but you left before the voting. I checked the minutes, Fran, and Jim said he saw you leave around eight-thirty. You would have had time to get to Tony's beach house before I arrived there."

"Reva," Nick asked, "where were you?"

"I don't see that it's any business of yours, but I was in my shop, taking inventory that night. The guard can verify that I was there until one in the morning."

"Nick has already checked with him," Laurel said in a hollow voice. "The night guard's records show that you left at ten-thirty and returned a little after midnight. He said that at one o'clock you asked him if he would like a cup of coffee."

Nick observed Reva's hands and saw her fingernails dig into her palms. "He keeps excellent records, Reva. He saw you drive away at ten-thirty."

Reva's fair complexion turned a fiery red, and she turned briskly toward Fran. "If you're looking for an extortionist and a murderer, Laurel, you're coming down on the wrong person. Your publicist here just about went to pieces when Tony dropped her for me."

Fran bristled. "Tony told me you threatened to kill him if he didn't marry you." She moved closer to Nick. "Sam found out about the two of them and divorced her—" her wild eyes flashed back to Reva "—and she couldn't take being dumped by two men at the same time."

"If I were planning to murder anyone, Fran, it would have been you! Ask her, Laurel...ask her why Tony ditched her. She's sick. She thinks everyone is trying to put her down and keep the world from finding out just how *brilliant* she is. Ask her why she was fired when she worked at the newspaper in L.A."

"I wasn't fired—" Fran pounded the table "—I quit! After three years, I got sick of the clubbiness of the male editors and male investigative reporters. None of them would give me the chance to show them that I could do the job better than any man could. All I got was condescending smiles and a lot of patronizing pats on the back, but none of the real juicy assignments. They never gave me the opportunity to prove that I was tough enough to hold my own even in a dangerous situation!"

Laurel saw the anger and the pain in Fran's face, and she looked at Nick as though to say "enough." When he slowly shook his head, she lowered her eyes.

In a mocking tone, Reva countered, "You're a liar, Fran. You were fired because you couldn't get along with anyone! You were just too tough." She chuckled bitterly. "Tony told me you were pretty tough in bed, too, and that he preferred a more feminine partner. Maybe he said the same to you, and that's why you killed him. As for your being a blackmailer, that's highly likely, also."

Bent over, with her palms flat on the table, Fran eyed Reva darkly. "You're the one who needs the money, now that your sportswear venture is a bust, and you're the one who's been so buddy-buddy with the princess, here! Don't try to say that you didn't know Diana was her mother!"

The moment she said that, Fran's expression turned grim, and her eyes became hooded. Slowly she tilted her head toward Laurel, her copper-colored hair draping over one eye. "So, now it's out, isn't it?"

"Laurel?" Reva asked, sinking onto a chair, "is that true? Is Diana your *mother*?"

"Yes, Reva, she is." Laurel faced Fran squarely. "Tony told you, didn't he?"

Fran laughed hideously. "I was the one who told him after he let me go through his father's records. It was easy to get a copy of your birth certificate. That told me why Diana had been supporting you all those years."

Nick said, "It was your idea that Tony blackmail Diana, wasn't it?"

With a bizarre sense of pride, Fran lifted her chin. "Yes. It was an easy way for him to get back some of the money he lost in the market."

Imposing an iron control on herself, Laurel spoke with quiet emphasis. "And you decided to try your hand at extortion. You planted those items in Verna's column."

The woman straightened, her expression mocking. "I never planned to tell you how or where to deliver the money. I just wanted to watch you squirm until you read your name in Verna's column on Monday. And it will be there for everyone to see." An eerie smile curved her lips. "But I didn't kill Tony, and I can prove it."

"How?" Nick asked immediately.

"I was with Glen in L.A. that night, the entire night. If you want to know who murdered Tony, you might ask Reva."

Laurel and Nick looked at Reva as she picked up her tote bag and clutched it closely.

"That's nonsense," she said, her voice shaking. "If I had been there, Laurel would have seen my car."

Nick said, "You could have parked on the road above the beach house."

"You'd have a hard time proving that, Nick."

"Where's your gold lighter," he asked, "the one Tony gave you?"

"I lost it. What does that have to do with anything?"

"I think you left it at Tony's the night you killed him. It's still on the shelf in back of his bar. I'm pretty sure the police will find your fingerprints on it."

A terrible fear loomed on Reva's face as she fixed her eyes on each one of the three people staring at her. "That wouldn't prove a thing," she said in a husky voice. "I spent many nights at the beach house."

Lying, Nick told her, "Tony's neighbor saw an attractive blond rushing from his house after hearing Tony and a woman arguing. She said she could identify that woman and her voice. It was you, wasn't it, Reva?"

Reva blanched and inched her way closer to Laurel. In a trembling voice she said, "When I told Tony I was free to marry him, he laughed at me and said he never wanted to see me again. After all I had given up for him! But it was an accident, Laurel. I didn't mean to kill him. I swear it! He said that he had work to do and ordered me to leave. When he bent down and opened the cabinet in back of the bar, I—I hit him."

"With what?" Nick asked.

Reva stared at him with glassy eyes, then reached into her tote bag. "With this." She withdrew a gun. "I always carry it at night for protection."

Nick's eyes shot from the gun to Laurel, who was standing right next to Reva. *Damn it,* he cursed silently. He'd never expected either woman to come armed. Calmly he said, "Let me have the gun."

She glanced down at it, then stepped directly behind Laurel. "I don't think so."

Laurel froze when she felt the cold steel dig into her back. She saw Nick raise a hand, palm toward Reva.

"Don't do anything foolish," he said in an even voice. "You said that you didn't mean to kill Tony, that it was an accident. We all heard you and can testify to that."

"And who would believe me? No, Nick, I'm sorry. I'm not willing to take that chance." She took hold of Laurel's arm. "I'm sorry for this, too, Laurel, but you'll have to come with me."

Pulling her hostage, Reva walked sideways at first, then backward toward the French doors to the terrace. "I don't want to hurt Laurel, Nick, but I'm warning you. Don't *you* do anything foolish like phoning the police. I'll let her go as soon as I can."

Nick took cautious steps toward Reva, and she aimed the gun directly at him. "You'll let her go now," he said, "or you'll have to shoot me."

"Don't, Nick!" Laurel cried. "Reva won't hurt me. Just do as she says, please."

"I'd listen to her," Reva said. "After all, I don't have a lot to lose if you force me to shoot the three of you."

Nick glanced over at Fran, who stood rigidly, staring at the gun the woman held. Then he fixed his eyes on Reva. "The police might be convinced that Tony's death was an accident, but there's no way you'll get away with harming Laurel."

"Then don't try to stop me, and if I even think you've notified the police, you'll regret it."

"Take me instead of Laurel."

"I was fooled by one man, Nick. I'm not about to make the same mistake twice." She jerked Laurel's arm and pulled her through the French doors and out onto the terrace.

The second they were out of sight, Nick dashed through the house to the other side, hoping he could get to the parking area and Reva's car before she and Laurel reached it. When he got there, though, he saw only his car and Fran's and he realized that Reva must have parked out in front.

He ran around along the side of the house and screamed Laurel's name when he heard the sound of tires screeching on the driveway. He almost fell as he whirled around and tore back to the parking area.

WHILE SHE WAS DRIVING Reva's car, Laurel glanced over at the gun pointed directly at her. She saw that her friend's hand was shaking, but she couldn't imagine that Reva would actually shoot her—even though she had been terrified that her friend might have shot Nick, had he tried to get the gun. "Where are we going?" she asked in as steady a voice as she could muster.

"To my shop. I have some money in the safe there."

"Please, Reva, put the gun away. You don't need it. I'll drive you anywhere you want."

"I'm sorry, but I can't risk that now. Nick may decide to call the police, anyway. If he does, this gun is the only thing that will get you and me on a plane to L.A. From there, I'll take my chances."

"That's ridiculous! Why are you adding a kidnapping charge to what's happened already, and why risk other people's lives if you did accidentally kill Tony?"

Dejected, Reva moaned. "I really don't care about anything anymore. Sam was just about to give me another chance, but when this hits the press—and you can be sure Fran will see to that—Sam won't have anything to do with me."

"You don't know that for sure. If he loves you, he'll stand by you, no matter what."

"That sounds like a line from one of Diana's movies."

"Reva, there's a place for love in real life, too. Why don't you—"

"Enough, Laurel! Just drive."

NICK THANKED GOD that he wasn't in L.A. or San Diego, trying to follow Reva's car without his headlights on. Luckily Santa Barbara was a peaceful town at night, and he'd only passed two cars coming the other way so far. When Reva's car approached the downtown area, he thought that she might be heading for her boutique. Traffic picked up, and he switched on the headlights and followed at a safe distance.

He saw her car pull into the parking lot at the plaza; that confirmed his guess. Driving past the entrance, he pulled up alongside the curb and ran to the next walkway, hoping to find a back door to her shop.

REVA LOCKED the front door after she and Laurel entered the boutique. Quickly she turned off the burglar alarm and phoned the guard, telling him she'd be working in the shop for a while. With the gun still on Laurel, she ordered her into the office and kept one eye on her as she worked the combination lock on the safe.

She was just removing the money from the compartment when a muffled sound came from the rear of the store. Quickly she shoved the money into her tote bag and pressed the gun at Laurel's back. "You go first," she ordered, and pushed her toward the room adjacent to her office. "Open the door," Reva said quietly.

Laurel did, her stomach clenching as fearful images built in her mind. The storage room was dark, but from the corner of her eye, she thought she saw a shadowed movement near the refrigerator by the wall to her left. She wondered if Reva saw it, but decided she didn't when the woman urged her to the right.

With her heart pounding in her chest, Laurel took slow steps, her eyes adjusting to the semidarkness. Had it been her imagination, she wondered, or was someone hiding on the other side of the refrigerator? *Dear God,* she thought, *did Nick follow us? He could still be killed!*

At the back door to the shop, Reva reached for the light switch and flicked it on. She scanned the shelves of boxes in the storage room and glanced at the door that was slightly ajar.

Slamming it shut, she nudged Laurel forward to the center of the room. "You can come out now, Nick," she said in a threatening voice.

Laurel's heart sank when she saw him hobble out from behind the side of the refrigerator. *The damn trick knee,* she groaned silently.

He grinned at her sheepishly. "Sorry about this. Bad timing."

"You're going to be even sorrier," Reva warned, her voice and hand shaking.

Nick saw the terror in Reva's eyes and was afraid that the gun at Laurel's back would go off. "Reva!" he shouted, and lunged toward her.

The instant she aimed the gun at Nick, Laurel's hand crashed against Reva's wrist. An earsplitting burst of gunfire exploded throughout the room as a bullet ripped through the floor. Laurel thrust her body at Reva with every ounce of strength she had, knocking the gun from her hand.

Nick literally dove across the room and snatched up the gun before rolling over and landing on his side. With a firm grip on it—and his left leg straight out—he trained the gun on Reva. "Now," he said, catching his breath, "since you're such a good friend of Laurel's, there are two ways we can do this. You can phone the police right now and turn yourself in, or we phone them for you."

A sobbing Reva made the telephone call.

DETECTIVE RODRIGUEZ was waiting for them when the squad car took them to police headquarters. This time, though, when Laurel gave her statement, she included all the facts concerning Tony's extortion and Fran's involvement. In exchange for their help in solving the Koop case, Nick asked if Rodriguez would do his best to see that no charges were brought against Ron. Laurel breathed a sigh of relief when the detective said he would do what he could.

It was almost midnight when Laurel and Nick stood alone on the terrace, waiting for Diana and Ron to return from the country club. Laurel had held up exceedingly well during the trials of the evening, but now she didn't even try to hold back the tears. She started down toward the pool area, but stopped midway and covered her face with her hands.

Nick caught up with her and gently took her in his arms. "It's all over with now," he said softly, and kissed her hair as she rested against him. "No more threats, no more worries."

Wiping the tears from her eyes, she said, "I can't believe it. I really can't. Reva and Fran?" She looked up at him with reddened eyes. "What do you think will happen to them?"

"I don't know. I imagine there will be plea bargains and deals made, but whatever does happen, it was their own doing. Now, will you please start thinking about yourself for a change...and about us?"

Laurel ran her fingertips over her forehead. "I can't even think straight right now, Nick."

"Will you be able to tomorrow?"

"Tomorrow?" she repeated, and clasped her arms around herself. "I don't know. There are so many things to be done. I've got to make final checks on the travel arrangements to Hawaii and the reservations at the hotel."

Nick glanced up at the stars and nodded. "There are always so many things for you to take care of, aren't there?"

"It's my job. You know that."

"Your job leaves little room for me, doesn't it?"

"That's not true."

"Then let Diana and Ron figure out how to get to Hawaii. Come to San Diego and marry me."

A silence loomed between them as heavy as the mist that began to roll in from the Pacific. Laurel could feel her frustration building as she sought desperately for the right words, but nervous tension caused her to stammer. "I—I can't. I just can't...not now. Please, try to understand. Diana needs me."

"And you need her," he said in a flat voice. "I wish to hell I didn't understand." After raking his fingers through his hair, he eyed her squarely. "But there are some things I can't do, either, Laurel. For one, I can't go on beating my head against a brick wall, and that's what loving you has been like for me."

"Be reasonable," she pleaded. "The fact that Diana's had a daughter all these years will be big news. My father is bound to hear about it, and I don't know what he'll do. Diana doesn't think he'll just ignore it. I have to be at my mother's side if he contacts her or comes out here.''

"I have to admit that's a good reason, but I've gotten to know you pretty well. You'll come up with a better reason next week and the week after that." He started up the steps.

"Nick, where are you going?"

He looked back at her over his shoulder, and his eyes clung to hers. "To San Diego, where I belong."

In a choked voice, she asked, "I'll see you again, won't I?"

"Probably. We'll both have to give testimony if there are trials. Maybe we can do lunch one day. Say goodbye to Diana and Ron for me." After a lingering pause he said softly, "It was nice loving you."

"Nick!" she called, but he didn't stop.

THE MIDMORNING RAIN pelted the windows of the salon as Laurel gazed out blankly. Her head was still spinning from the phone conversation she had just had with Sylvia, Reva's mother, but even more troubling was the ache she felt in her heart and the loneliness that gripped her each time she thought of Nick.

"The rain's beginning to let up," Diana said. "Let's have some coffee in the solarium. Ron, would you buzz Elena?" While he did, she said to Laurel, "I don't know how you got through last night, and I still can't believe that Reva actually held a gun on you."

"Let's not talk about it anymore," Ron suggested. "Laurel's been through enough."

Forcing a plaintive smile, Laurel said, "Once we get to Hawaii, we'll all forget about this business."

Diana's face clouded, and she looked over at Ron, who offered her only a firm expression.

"Laurel," Diana said quietly, "I would still rather you didn't come to Hawaii with Ron and me."

Having thought that her mother had forgotten about that idea, Laurel was stunned to hear her propose it again. But this time she no longer had the strength to try to dissuade her. Listlessly she said, "If that's the way you want it, that's the way it will be."

"Don't be upset, darling, please."

Laurel smiled weakly. "I'm too exhausted to be upset. After these past weeks, there's very little that could bother me." She knew that was only half true.

"I'm glad to hear that," Ron said, "because there's something else we want you to know." Diana raised a hand, but he ignored the gesture. "When Diana and I return from Hawaii, we're going to be married. We want you to be happy for us."

Laurel had thought she was incapable of being shocked any further, not after the extortion business, Tony's death, the scene with Fran and Reva the previous night and Nick's walking out on her. But this— Mercifully her shock turned to a disquieting numbness. She looked down as Diana took hold of her hand.

"Darling, please say you are happy for us. It's so important to me that you honestly feel that way."

Happy? Laurel thought. A kaleidoscope of emotions whirled in her brain; she felt angry, bitter, confused and betrayed by the people who were most dear to her. She'd sacrificed so much for her mother, and this was the result! She pushed away a small voice that said, *Maybe you should have stopped sacrificing at some point....*

As though in a trance, she gazed into Diana's eyes. "Yes, Mother, of course I'm happy for you."

"Thank you, darling," Diana said, patting her daughter's hand. "But there's more news."

"More?" Laurel asked, and chuckled painfully.

"After we're married, Ron will accompany me on the cross-country promotion tour to promote *Winner Takes All*, and then I'm retiring. I've decided to sell the estate, and Ron and I plan to open up a fitness center somewhere far away from Hollywood."

Ron said, "We're thinking about one of the suburbs of Chicago."

Using all of her strength, Laurel smiled and pushed herself up from the chair. "That would be nice. Snow at Christmas and...uh...would you excuse me? I told Glen I'd phone him."

"Darling, have your coffee first."

"No, thank you. I don't feel like having coffee right now."

She propelled herself to the door of the salon and started up the stairs to go to her room. Suddenly the walls started to spin, and she grabbed hold of the bannister when she stumbled. Looking up, she saw that the ceiling was spinning, also. She closed her eyes and took a deep breath, fighting the vertigo.

When she reached the top of the stairs, she looked down and tried to focus her eyes. All seemed to be a fuzzy gray color; she fell back against the wall. For a while she rested, trying to remember where she was going and why. Then she thrust one foot before the other, dragging herself down the hall to her bedroom, where she collapsed on the quilted spread.

CHAPTER NINETEEN

ON MONDAY, Verna's column identified Diana Baxter and Laurel Davis as the mother and daughter that all Hollywood had been buzzing about. During the week, Laurel felt dazed as she and Diana were accosted daily—outside of the Bel Air apartment building and when entering the studio lot—by news people with their cameras and minicams.

Loyal to the end, Glen accompanied them, backing Laurel as she refused to answer any of the media's questions. However, she was more than surprised at the easy manner her mother assumed when she announced that Laurel was indeed her daughter. Each time Diana was asked who the father was, she merely flashed the famous Diana Baxter smile and said, "No comment."

Day by day, Laurel went through the motions that she thought were expected of her all the while thinking of Nick. Thankfully, she was able to smile when she and Glen said goodbye to her mother and Ron in front of the house in Santa Barbara.

Once Glen returned to L.A., however, a terrible fear and isolation overtook Laurel, and she began to tremble. She took off like a madwoman, running first toward the garage, then veering off toward the pond. When she almost ran into a palm tree at the water's edge, she braced her hands against it and let them slide down the trunk, then she sank down to the grass in tears.

With effort, she pushed herself up and leaned back against the palm tree. She blinked away her tears and tried to fight the overwhelming feeling that life was slipping by her. It was the same frightening feeling that she had experienced many times in the last ten years, but all it had taken to dispel it then was to acknowledge the most pressing responsibility she had facing her at the time.

Today it was so different. There was nothing at all she could do. Diana's career was a thing of the past now, and Laurel had to face the fact that Ron had replaced her as her mother's primary caretaker. Moreover, the dreaded phone call from her father hadn't come.

Laurel didn't know what she was going to do or even what she should do. She felt drained of energy, empty and alone. She had gotten so used to considering what was best for Diana that she had given little thought to what her own life would be like if ever she weren't needed. It had been so nice to feel needed by Diana after such a long period of feeling rejected.... But the end to her career as her mother's personal manager had come suddenly and with an impact that was devastating.

Foolishly she had let the happiness that Nick had offered her slip right through her fingers. Just the thought of him brought a renewal of the acute sense of loss she had felt ever since he had walked away from her. She wondered how much time would have to pass before the pain she felt in her heart was erased, and she could forget the prophetic words Nick had spoken: *Someday you may wake up and find yourself all alone.*

Upon losing him, she had realized how much she needed him. Upon losing Diana, she had realized that she herself was no longer needed; that Diana was well enough to want to take care of herself—and Ron—and that, quite possibly, she had hampered her mother's total recovery by holding on for too long. As she sat back against the palm tree, she thought of her last words to her mother before the taxi had pulled away: *"Be happy."*

"You, too, darling," Diana had said, never looking more radiant in Laurel's memory.

"Happy," she murmured, pushing herself up from the grass. She knew there was only one way she could ever be happy, and that was with Nick.

"Damn it!" she muttered, "when does my turn at happiness come?"

Perhaps never, she thought. *Not if you wait for it to knock at your door.*

Angry, she whirled around and looked back at the huge house. "Someone else will have to take care of you now. I'm going to take care of myself for a change!"

NICK'S FATHER LEANED BACK against the wall in his son's office, and he watched the younger man twirl the cold, black liquid in his coffee mug. "Why don't you stop sitting around and moping?" he suggested. "If it's Laurel you really want, go after her. I'll postpone my trip to Mexico with Mildred and take care of things here."

Nick peered up at him and shook his head. "Thanks, anyway, but the lady doesn't have time for me. Damn!" He banged his coffee mug on the desk. "Of all the P.I. agencies in California, she had to walk into this one."

Bob snatched a paper napkin from the box of donuts on top of a file cabinet and soaked up the coffee from Nick's desk. "Did you watch *Casablanca* again last night?" he asked dryly.

"Twice."

"Jeez, you're gonna wear out the tape."

Nick leaned back in his chair. "Where did you pick up a dumb expression like 'jeez'?"

His father tossed the napkin in the trash can at the side of the desk. "It beats cursing. Your mother always hated cursing. You know, I still miss that lady. She was one in a million."

Nick's eyebrows rose. "When do you find time to miss her? I can't even keep up with who you're currently dating."

"Stella wouldn't have wanted me to sit around pining and feeling sorry for myself like you are. And I don't mind telling you, you're not a credit to the Malone men. You give up too easily. If this Laurel Davis is half the woman you say she is, you oughta get off your duff and do something about it."

"Like what...kidnap her and drag her away from her mother?"

"If she loves you, that's probably what she's waiting for you to do."

Nick looked at his father with leery eyes. "You really think so?"

"Listen to the voice of experience. When it comes to the fairer sex, you gotta prove to them that you love them and can't live without them. It's something in their genes that requires that. That's where men are different. We tell women we love them and assume that's that, but the ladies want proof positive."

"Maybe I did give up too easily." Nick thought of his options, then frowned. "I don't know. Laurel doesn't need me anymore. The extortion case is closed, and so is the Tony Koop case. You saw her mother on the late news last night. The charges against her future husband have been dropped. I doubt if I'll even get an invitation to the wedding.''

Bob shook his head. "I'm glad your mother's not here to see what a quitter you turned out to be." He examined his son's face and realized that he wasn't making any headway. "Did I ever tell you how many times I asked your mother to marry me before she said she would?"

Nick looked up at him and shook his head.

"At least a dozen."

"You're kidding."

"Trust me on that. How many times have you asked Laurel?"

"Twice."

"Well, in my book, you've still got ten more times to ask her, if you really love her."

"I do," Nick mumbled.

His father slammed the desk with his fist. "Then do something about it!"

Nick looked up at him. "Have you had your blood pressure checked lately?"

Quizzically, Bob asked, "What's all this concern you have about me all of a sudden? Last night at dinner you were worried about my cholesterol."

With his chin resting on his palm, Nick said, "You're my father, aren't you? Why shouldn't I worry about you?"

Nick knew that some of Laurel's parental concern had worn off on him, and now he wondered if perhaps he hadn't been too hard on her for being so worried about her mother. "Damn," he muttered to himself. He hadn't seen Laurel in more than a week, and he hadn't been able to get a decent day's work done in all that time.

There was no way he was going to be able to live like this—without her.

"Ten more times," he muttered, then jumped up and rushed to the coatrack to get his jacket. "I'm going to Santa Barbara. Sure you don't mind my taking off again?"

"Mind? You're no good around here the way you are. Besides, what's it gonna cost you but a few hours' drive?"

When Nick's telephone rang, Bob said, "I'll get it." He picked it up. "Yes, Betty...oh?" His hazel eyes twinkled as he looked over at his son. "Send her in." He let the switch flick up. "You're gonna have to postpone your trip. You've got a client here to see you."

Nick tossed his jacket back on the rack. "Thought you said you'd handle everything, et cetera, et cetera."

"This case is right up your alley. I'll see you later."

As his father left the office, Nick started back to his desk. He was halfway there when he caught a whiff of a pleasant, familiar aroma. He turned and his eyes swept over the frosted glass on the door. He saw a woman's silhouette, but it wasn't just any woman's. He felt his heart begin to pound in his chest as he walked to the partially opened door and slowly pulled it back farther.

"Laurel," he murmured, drinking in the sight of her as she stood there in the same white linen outfit she'd worn the first day he'd laid eyes on her.

"Hello, Nick," she said in a silky voice. "Am I interrupting anything?"

"No, no. C'mon in and have a seat."

He closed the door behind her and followed her with his eyes, watching as she sat down in the chair in front of his desk and crossed her long, slender legs. He went to the desk and leaned back against the front edge. After swallowing hard, he asked, "What brings you to San Diego?" He saw her long lashes flicker a few times before she lifted them and raked her lovely eyes over him.

"I'm afraid I need your services once more."

His gaze unwavering, he said, "Just don't tell me that your employer is being blackmailed again."

"No," she said, and his heart skipped several beats when her lips formed a tantalizing smile. "I no longer have an employer."

"Retired?" he asked, trying to control the frantic feeling of joy that was rioting inside him.

"No, I decided I'd try to make it on my own as an artist. I understand that the landscapes in the San Diego area are rather...unusual. Something in the way the sun vivifies the natural colors, I'm told."

"Umm, yes. I've noticed that myself." Nick drank in her lovely features and felt the back of his neck heat up. "Just what kind of service is it you want me to perform?"

Laurel slowly smoothed her linen skirt over her knee. "I need a bodyguard," she said softly.

"I can certainly see why," he admitted, thinking she could probably see his heart beating against his dress shirt.

"Can you handle my case?"

He reached for the purse she was holding and placed it on his desk. "That depends."

"On what?"

He pulled her from the chair and slipped his hands around her waist. "On whether or not you can afford my fee."

"I came prepared to pay anything," she whispered in a silky voice, and eased her arms over his shoulders.

"Anything?"

"Anything."

With his lips close to her ear, he said quietly, "I only do Class A work. I don't like to rush things. Your case could take quite a while."

Running a finger over the cleft in his chin, she asked softly, "How long do you estimate?"

"A lifetime at least."

"I think I could manage that. In fact, I'm sure I can."

"Can you handle a house with a white picket fence, two children and a dog?"

"Yes," she murmured, tilting her head when she felt his lips move along the side of her throat.

"And a new name?"

"Such as?"

"Mrs. Nicolas Malone."

"You're hired," she whispered, and closed her eyes.

"You'd better believe I am," he said huskily, and tightened his hold on her. "Now, what's the first thing you want me to do as your bodyguard?"

"Just what you're doing, Nick. Hold me and love me forever."

Harlequin Superromance®

COMING NEXT MONTH

#362 WORD OF HONOR • Evelyn A. Crowe
As a child, Honor Marshall had witnessed her
mother's death in an air disaster. Years later, when
she found out it was murder, she vowed to seek
revenge. Special agent Travis Gentry agreed to help.
But his price was high.

#363 OUT OF THE BLUE • Elise Title
When a wounded Jonathan Madden showed up in
Courtney Blue's bookstore, it was like a scene from a
thriller—and Courtney had read plenty of those!
Jonathan was no mere professor, as he claimed to be.
But he was definitely hero material....

#364 WHEN I SEE YOUR FACE • Connie Bennett
Mystery writer Ryanne Kirkland couldn't allow
herself to think of a future with Hugh MacKenna,
the charismatic private investigator from Los
Angeles. Firstly she was blind, and secondly there
was a possibility she'd have to live her life
on the run. Hugh only wished he could make her
understand that his life was worthless
without her....

#365 SPRING THAW • Sally Bradford
When Adam Campbell returned to her after a
twenty-year absence, Cecilia Mahoney learned the
meaning of heaven and hell. Heaven was the bliss of
love regained, hell the torment of being unable to
find the only child Adam would ever have—the one
she'd given away.

Have You Ever Wondered If You Could Write A Harlequin Novel?

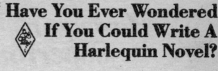

Here's great news—Harlequin is offering a series of cassette tapes to help you do just that. Written by Harlequin editors, these tapes give practical advice on how to make your characters—and your story—come alive. There's a tape for each contemporary romance series Harlequin publishes.

Mail order only

All sales final

Your favorite stories with a brand-new look!!

H A R L E Q U I N
American Romance®

Beginning next month, the four American Romance titles will feature a new, contemporary and sophisticated cover design. As always, each story will be a terrific romance with mature characters and a realistic plot that is uniquely North American in flavor and appeal.

Watch your bookshelves for a **bold** look!

ARNC-1